DEMANDS OF HONOR

STAR TREK ®

ERRAND OF FURY
BOOK 2
DEMANDS OF HONOR

KEVIN RYAN

BASED UPON *STAR TREK*
CREATED BY
GENE RODDENBERRY

POCKET BOOKS
New York   London   Toronto   Sydney

An *Original* Publication of POCKET BOOKS

 POCKET BOOKS, a division of Simon & Schuster, Inc.
1230 Avenue of the Americas, New York, NY 10020

This book is a work of fiction. Names, characters, places and incidents are products of the author's imagination or are used fictitiously. Any resemblance to actual events or locales or persons, living or dead, is entirely coincidental.

ISBN 978-1-4516-1346-9

This Pocket Books paperback edition February 2007

10 9 8 7 6 5 4 3 2 1

POCKET and colophon are registered trademarks of Simon & Schuster, Inc.

Manufactured in the United States of America

For information regarding special discounts for bulk purchases, please contact Simon & Schuster Special Sales at 1-800-456-6798 or business@simonandschuster.com.

To my mother, Elaine Ryan,
who always had books in the house.

DEMANDS OF HONOR

Prologue

CHRISTINE ALVAREZ ran to the back of the ship, entered the bathroom, and retched into the sink. Nothing came up, but that didn't surprise her; she doubted there was anything left inside her stomach. Nevertheless, she spent another ten minutes over the sink until her stomach settled down again.

When she stepped back out into the main cabin, she realized that gravity was back near Earth normal, at least as far as she could tell. Six weeks ago, when they were just one month into the trip, the artificial gravity had picked up a flutter. Every fifteen or twenty minutes, it was subject to random increases and decreases of about twenty-five percent up or down. It wasn't enough to be dangerous, but it was more than enough to play havoc with all of their stomachs.

Ironically, the "nearly full Earth gravity throughout every inch of the deck!" had been a selling point for the vessel, and a real point of pride for her father when he'd bought it. Of course, her family had never taken the ship on this long a journey, and the vessel had never logged this many light-years between maintenance. Heading back to the rear of the ship, she found Alan huddled over an open panel in the floor, while Cyndy stood nearby calling out instructions from her data padd.

"Any luck?"

She saw Alan's body tense and heard his sharp intake of breath. He was on edge, even more than the rest of them. He lifted his head and shoulders out of the panel and turned to her. "I can't reduce the power." Christine knew what that meant. The manual recommended reducing gravity to one-half g to correct imbalances, at least until the system could properly be serviced.

By now the five others had circled around to listen. "We're following the instructions, but we can't get the power to decrease. There seems to be a bug in the system."

There were immediate sighs from the others. "I'm sorry we can't all be as *comfortable* as we would like," Alan said. There it was: the rebuke. Alan had less and less patience lately. "But we all know why we are on this journey. We're almost there and we know why it's important. If this is the worst we face on this trip, then I'd say we're coming out ahead."

Christine felt a stab of shame. She was focused on a little space sickness when the stakes were so high, when billions of lives literally hung in the balance. Then the feeling was gone, replaced by another rumble in her stomach. For a moment, she thought she might have to run for the bathroom again, but it passed.

"Is there any chance the inertial system will fail?" Max asked. It was the biggest danger they faced. If something went wrong with the inertial dampening system when they were coming out of warp, or while they were decelerating from full impulse, the end would be quick for all of them.

"No," Tomas answered from behind her, and everyone turned to look at him. "The system has enough failsafes built in that it's virtually foolproof. And the variations are only affecting the artificial gravity. The dampening system is showing full power."

The crew seemed satisfied with that, and Christine felt herself relax. Tomas was their pilot, the best one in the organization and by far the most experienced in space. Of course, he was much farther out than he had ever been, and he didn't have nearly as much experience as her father's pilot—just as Alan had much less experience than her father's technicians. But there was no way to tell her father about this trip, let alone bring along his employees.

"Now, I want you to all come forward and see something," Tomas said.

Christine knew why he was summoning them and felt a twitch of excitement. They had waited a long time for this, and she had spent many hours huddled over the sink for this moment.

The six of them had to squeeze into the front of the ship, yet they all had a good view, thanks to the large transparent aluminum window that made up much of the nose of the vessel. When her father had bought the craft, she had thought that the large windows—like the Earth-normal gravity—were a needless extravagance. Since they were at warp, she could see stars appear to streak by, leaving colorful contrails. The view of space looked no different from the view they had seen since they'd left Earth orbit, but she knew the space itself was vastly different.

Now she saw the beauty that the stars held at warp speed. And yet there was something much more important here than the view.

"Just a few minutes," Tomas announced.

A moment later, an insistent alarm sounded from the intercom. Then an automated voice said, *"Warning, you are leaving Federation space. Warning, you are leaving Federation space. This is a message from Starfleet Command. Civilian vessels are prohibited from traveling past this point."* The message started to repeat, but Alan's hand shot out and hit a switch, silencing both the voice and the alarm.

"We regret that we won't be complying," Alan said, and the entire group of them laughed, Christine included.

"Can you give us a countdown?" Alan asked Tomas.

"Sure." Tomas waited for a long moment, then began, "Ten, nine, eight, seven, six, five . . ."

They all joined in now: "Four . . ."

"Three . . ."

"Two . . ."

"One."

Christine held her breath and Alan announced, "Ladies and gentlemen, we have just entered Klingon space."

A few seconds later, Christine realized she had forgotten to release her breath in her excitement. She did, and then took a deep gulp of air.

"Does it trouble you that we've broken about a dozen Federation laws just now?" Alan asked with a smile. Christine and the others laughed. "Good, because by the time we're finished, we are going to have broken a lot more rules." •

In that moment, Christine loved Alan more than ever. She felt the tensions and discomfort of the last two and a half months fall away, and she remembered why they were out here—and why she had fallen for Alan in the first place. She immediately regretted that they had had so little time alone together since this trip had begun. Shrugging inside, she realized it was another small sacrifice for their cause.

"Are you showing anyone on scanners?" Alan asked Tomas.

"Just a few commercial vessels at the extreme range of the sensors," Tomas replied. "I don't think we'll have any company for a while."

After a few minutes of looking out the window, the lights automatically dimmed. Christine realized how late it was getting. At the beginning of the trip they had maintained an extended party atmosphere and had slept at odd times, but they had soon realized that it was better for everyone's spirits and equilibrium if they maintained a more standard day/night schedule.

"If you want some sleep, I can keep the first watch," Alan offered. Christine felt a pang of disappointment. It was their turn to have the private stateroom. She didn't want to waste it, especially tonight.

"No, I'll stay here for a while," Tomas said, and Christine felt relieved.

Fortunately, the gravity fluctuations were minimal, and her stomach held as they got ready for bed and entered the stateroom. Once inside, Alan said, "You know, this is really just the—"

Christine stopped him with her lips. There would be plenty of time for talk later, and with Alan there was always plenty of talking. For now, she was determined to keep things simple.

A few hours later, a beeping woke her up. It took her a moment to clear her head. When she did, she realized that Tomas was on the intercom. *"Get out here everybody. That's the proximity alert."*

Christine rushed out of the room in her nightgown. A moment later, Alan pushed past her wearing only his shorts. Soon, Christine and the others were all looking out the front window of the ship at the moving star field. Nothing else was in sight.

"Where's the ship?" Alan asked, his voice maddeningly calm.

"I'm not sure." Tomas frantically hit controls on the panel in front of him. "Scanners aren't working right."

Christine and the others frantically scanned the space in front of the ship. She found herself wishing that her father had gone with a viewscreen instead of the window option. At least then they could change perspective and magnify as needed. She sat down in the copilot's seat and found the controls for one of the small viewers on the panel just below the window. She brought up a forward view on the screen, then found the perspective control. She scanned the area around the ship for a full minute before she found something.

"There." She pointed to the screen.

Magnifying the image, she saw a vessel of some kind. It looked large, but it was hard to tell for sure. The ship had two warp nacelles and a boxy forward section followed by a long series of more or less identical segments.

"It doesn't look like a warship," Tomas said.

"Probably a cargo ship," Alan said with authority.

Of course it was a cargo ship. The segmented rear of the ship must be the cargo containers, Christine realized. She felt a flood of relief. The point of this trip was to make contact, but she was sure that it would be better to make civilian contact first. There was a smaller likelihood of a misunderstanding that would lead to trouble— the kind of misunderstanding and trouble that defined Starfleet and Federation history.

"I'm trying to open a channel, but there is some kind of interference," Tomas said.

"Could they be jamming us?" Christine asked.

"It's a *civilian* ship," Alan said, another rebuke in his voice. "Remember, this is what we want. Up until now, virtually the entire relationship between the Klingons and the Federation has been defined by our military establishments. We're about to see the power of ordinary people *talking* to one another."

It occurred to Christine—and not for the first time— that at least half of the time that Alan spoke, it sounded as if he were making a speech. Usually, his words lifted her up, but with the ship outside and nervousness welling up within her, she was simply annoyed.

7

"I have something," Tomas said as he worked the controls for the transmitter/receiver.

A moment later they heard static coming through the intercom.

"Earther vessel, drop out of warp immediately or be destroyed," a gruff voice said.

Alan turned to the group and said, "Don't worry. Bluster is part of their culture. It's simply how they speak." Then he nodded to Tomas, who hit a button. Leaning down, Alan said, "Klingon vessel. This is the *S.S. Harmony*. We are a private, civilian ship with no weapons. We are no threat to you. I represent a small delegation from the Anti-Federation League. We are on a mission of peace to your homeworld to negotiate a resolution to the differences between our peoples. We have no quarrel with you or any other Klingon."

Finished, Alan turned and gave them all a confident smile. After a moment of silence, sounds of gruff laughter came over the intercom. *"Drop out of warp now or be destroyed, Earther 'peace' negotiators. You have one minute to comply."*

Christine felt the blood drain from her face and her stomach tighten. For the first time since she had known him, Alan was at a loss for words.

"I don't think they understand," Arleen said from behind them.

"Alan, make them understand!" Christine found herself nearly shouting.

That snapped Alan out of his trance. He leaned down again and said, "I said we are on a peace mission to your homeworld. We respect your culture and your ways, but we will not be deterred from our course. Perhaps we could talk further."

"You have forty-five seconds," the Klingon voice said.

"We are here to talk about peace!"

"You may talk . . . for about forty more seconds."

"Alan, what do we do?" Christine asked, trying to keep the panic out of her voice.

Alan looked stricken. "Tomas, do it. Bring us out of warp."

"I'll need some time to do the transition to sublight safely. This isn't a starship, you know," Tomas said, his hands shaking on the controls.

"How long?" Christine asked.

"At least thirty minutes," Tomas replied, an edge of fear in his voice.

Alan still looked stricken and didn't seem to know what to do. Christine pushed down her own rising panic and hit the transmit button. "We will comply, but we need thirty minutes to effect transition to normal space."

"You are lying, cowardly Earthers. Comply now. Your time is almost up."

"Damn you, you moron, we are a civilian ship, it will take some time!" Christine shouted.

"Christine, it won't do any good to antagonize them," Alan said.

"You're right, but until now we weren't in trouble," she shot back.

Her mental countdown told her they were almost out of time. The Klingon said, *"Our scan of your vessel suggests you may be telling the truth. Thus, we will assist you in your deceleration."*

9

"We don't need any assistance, we just need a few minutes," Christine said.

There was silence from the other side, but she could see the Klingon vessel on the viewer slowly change its orientation.

"What are they doing?" someone behind her asked.

Then a flash of energy came from the top of the Klingon ship, and Christine barely had time to register what was happening. *They're shooting at us,* she thought as the *Harmony* shook all around her. She closed her eyes and felt herself lurch forward, then backward . . .

And then everything went dark.

For a moment, Christine thought that was it—for the ship and for them. And then the emergency lights came on. A split second later the regular lights came back on and Christine had a single thought: *We're still here.*

She saw that the stars in the windows were still, telling her that they were now traveling at sublight speed.

"What happened?" she asked, taking a quick inventory of her five friends. Alan and anyone else who had been standing was now on the floor, but they were all moving and starting to get up.

"Alan, how is the ship?" Christine asked.

Alan was on his feet, working at a maintenance panel to her right. "Bad. They shot our engines. It was a low-power blast but the warp-field generator shut off immediately. Even if it's not badly damaged, we can't restart it, not out here."

"Impulse engine is online. We're at nine point eight lightspeed," Tomas offered.

"Earther peace negotiators, reduce your speed to space normal or you will be destroyed."

"Do it," Christine said to Tomas.

"Decelerating now, but it will take at least twelve hours to get down to space normal if the inertial dampeners hold," Tomas said.

That much Christine understood. She didn't know much about physics, but she understood that accelerating and decelerating from near lightspeed took tremendous power and it put the greatest stress on the inertial dampening system. A starship could do it nearly instantaneously, but the *Harmony* took the better part of a day to decelerate from lightspeed.

"Klingon vessel, we are complying, but we are a civilian ship. It will take us at least twelve hours to reach that speed, possibly more if you have damaged our systems," Christine said.

There was silence for a moment. *"Your ship is as worthless as you are. We will have to assist you again."*

"No!" Christine shouted into the panel.

Alan's hands were on her, lifting her out of the seat. "Go strap yourself in," he said, pointing her to one of the seats in the back. "All of you, strap yourselves in."

It wouldn't do much good if they lost inertial control. The ship would tear itself into small pieces and it would all be over before they knew it, but Christine strapped herself in anyway.

Alan took the copilot's seat and said, "Klingon vessel, shooting at us won't do any good. Our inertial control systems cannot handle a rapid deceleration. As I said, we are on a mission of peace to bring a better understanding between our two great peoples."

11

Kevin Ryan

"Earther, I do not think your people or your ship are very great, but perhaps you will prove me wrong," the Klingon said, laughing.

From her seat, Christine saw the Klingon ship change orientation again and move closer to them. It was hard to tell for sure given the magnification, but it looked as if the Klingons were coming alongside them. That gave her hope, since the weapon they had fired had come from the front of the ship.

Perhaps the Klingons had seen reason. She was vaguely aware of Alan's voice as he spoke to the Klingons. There was no response, and Alan's own words seemed to run together so that she could not decipher them anymore. Someone was sobbing nearby and her own heart was beating so loudly that it seemed to drown out other sounds.

What happened next seemed to happen in slow motion. There was a glow from the Klingon ship, then the glow seemed to reach out for them. The *Harmony* shuddered slightly but that was it. Perhaps the glow wasn't a weapon.

"It's a tractor beam," Tomas called out.

"Earthers, now we will assist your deceleration. If your ship holds together, you live. If not, you die."

"No!" Alan called out.

Christine simply held on. A commercial vessel would be built to much higher tolerances than a private ship like the *Harmony*. And cargo ships were built to last in the Federation. She doubted that it would be any different in the Klingon Empire. Whatever the Klingons intended, she was sure that it wouldn't be a twelve-hour deceleration.

Suddenly, it felt as if the ship were grabbed by a giant, unseen hand and tossed. She was thrown forward hard, but she realized with elation that she was still alive. Then the ship went dark and she was tossed backward . . . then forward . . .

The ship's inertial control system was trying to compensate for forces far beyond its designed limits. In the dark she saw sparks begin to fly all around them and felt a final sickening lurch accompanied by metal twisting and something large snapping. She heard voices screaming, and Christine thought one of those voices might have been hers.

And then the ship seemed to go still.

Christine was surprised that they were still alive as red emergency lights illuminated the cabin. She was aware of something wet on her face. When she reached up, she felt blood dripping along her cheeks. Well, that explained the pain in her head. Ignoring it for now, she unhooked herself and got to her feet.

There were moans nearby, but Christine ignored them. She knew that she had to do something important. She wasn't sure what it was, but she moved forward trusting that it would come to her. When she reached the control panel, she had to move Tomas, who was leaning against it. He was heavy, unconscious. *No, not just unconscious,* she thought, judging from the extreme angle of his head.

She glanced quickly to see Alan moaning in the copilot's seat. Then it came to her, what she had to do. Reaching down, she slapped the red button to transmit the distress call—one of the few procedures that her father had drilled into her. She spoke quickly, finding that her voice was remarkably clear under the circumstances. "This is the *S.S. Harmony.* We are in distress. Mayday. We have been attacked by a Klingon vessel in Klingon space. This is the *S.S. Harmony* to any Starfleet vessel. Help us." Christine hit another button to transmit their coordinates, then she took a breath. The message would repeat as long as the ship had power—which she didn't think would be long.

By now, Alan was moving his head, and Christine was satisfied that he was all right. Then someone behind her called out in pain. It was a woman's voice. Cyndy's or Arleen's. Christine got up and turned, trying to make sense of what she saw.

The rear of the ship was on fire, and sparks were flying from panels and open conduits. The sparks were actually giving off more light than the emergency lights now. As Christine took a step, she felt a giant hand reach out and slam her to the deck.

The fall knocked the wind out of her, and dazed, she tried to raise her head. Then, she felt herself almost floating off the floor for a moment before getting pulled back down. *Artificial gravity is going,* she realized.

After a few more fluctuations, she felt a familiar sensation in her stomach. A moment later, she started to retch. *Perfect,* she thought.

When the retching was over, Christine found that she had to struggle to breathe. *That explains the hissing sound,* she realized. The hull had been punctured, probably in a number of places. Christine put her head down on the deck; it wouldn't be long now.

She raised her head when she heard sound and saw movement above her. For a second, she thought that

Starfleet had heard their distress call. But she immediately realized that she wasn't looking at a Starfleet uniform.

A booted foot forced her onto her back. For the first time in her life, she saw a Klingon.

"This one is still alive," the Klingon growled.

Chapter One

Captain's Log Stardate 3197.2.
The Enterprise is headed for System 7348 at best speed, but it is still three days away. The crew is tense. Though the diplomats are even now making a final push, few doubt that war with the Klingon Empire is imminent. The question on the minds of the crew: will the first shots be fired at the *Enterprise* when we reach our destination? I know we will be facing a Klingon warship when we arrive. And despite the claims of the Klingon Empire, I am sure that whatever the Klingon vessel's purpose, it is not to make peaceful contact with the primitive genetic Klingons on that world. For now, we have no choice but to wait and see.

"CAPTAIN, I'M READING a distress signal," Lieutenant Uhura said.

Captain Kirk was immediately alert. He felt Doctor McCoy tense behind him as he turned to his communications officer and asked, "Who is it?"

Uhura shook her head. "It's very faint . . . I'm boosting power." She waited for a few seconds. "I have it. The message is from a civilian ship called the . . . *Harmony.*"

"Location?" Kirk said.

A flash of surprise registered on Uhura's face. "The message originates from 2.7 light-years *inside* Klingon space."

There was a collective intake of breath from the bridge crew, and even Spock raised an eyebrow. "What in hell is a civilian ship doing there?" McCoy said, giving voice to what everyone else was thinking.

"Mister Spock?" Kirk asked.

There was a momentary pause as Spock studied the viewer at the science station. Then the Vulcan looked up. "The *Harmony* is a privately owned passenger vessel. It left Earth orbit heading for an agricultural colony twenty-seven light-years from the point of origin of the distress call. The flight plan for the trip was filed by the Anti-Federation League."

"Someone made one hell of a detour," McCoy said.

"Could it really be them, Spock?" Kirk said.

The half-Vulcan nodded. "There is no record of the *Harmony* making orbit anywhere. And if the vessel traveled at nearly its top cruising speed, it could have reached Klingon space by now."

"Why would anyone do that?" McCoy said.

"The Anti-Federation League has been extremely critical of both Starfleet and the Federation throughout the current crisis with the Klingon Empire. They have launched a number of efforts via subspace communications to establish private peace talks with the Empire. The Empire has declined their offers to date."

"Then why would . . . ?" McCoy started to ask, his voice trailing off. It didn't seem to make sense, but Kirk already had the answer forming in his mind.

"They may have taken the initiative anyway," Kirk said. It fit the profile.

A few months earlier, the *Enterprise* had answered a distress call from an Anti-Federation League colony. They had come under attack from Orions, whom Kirk had good reason to believe were working with the Klingons to test Starfleet tactics and capabilities.

Sam Fuller had led the rescue. Fifty-nine colonists had been saved, with only one lost during the operation. The mission had been a success . . . a success that had cost the *Enterprise* too many of her crew. A number of others were injured, Sam Fuller among them. Sam had been lucky on that mission. His luck had run out just a few weeks later.

"How long would it take us at maximum warp to reach their position, Mister Spock?" Kirk said.

The Vulcan did not have to check his computer terminal for that data. "Twelve hours, fourteen minutes. However, I must point out that any delay in our arrival at System 7348 will only give the Klingons more time to establish their position there."

Kirk knew that. If war was truly inevitable, then any

advantage that he allowed the Klingons now might cost lives later. Simple logic, as Spock would say. Turning his head to Doctor McCoy, Kirk said, "Bones?"

"Jim, we don't even know if they are alive, or if they sent the message at all. This is more than likely a Klingon trick," McCoy said.

"Uhura, is the message genuine?" Kirk asked.

She nodded and went to work at her station analyzing the transmission. He knew it was an unfair question. There were a thousand ways to fake a message. And if the Klingon Empire wanted to trick them, they would have unlimited resources to put into making a perfect forgery.

Still, he could see Uhura's hands flying across her panel at near Vulcan speed. Kirk knew she was checking power readings and comparing them with the transmitter the records showed was on the *Harmony*. Then she would look for interference patterns that would show up if the ship was really under attack—signs of jamming as well as the effect on the transmission of shield or weapons energy.

Then Uhura would check the syntax and accent of the speaker, comparing it to what she could learn from the crew manifest of the ship. She would try to determine the identity of the person who made the transmission and see if their language and syntax was consistent with their planet and region of origin.

All of those factors could be faked by a sufficiently motivated and resourced group—such as the intelligence division of the Klingon Defense Force. Making a final call on the transmission would have been a large job for a small staff at Starfleet Command who had a few hours to concentrate on the problem. Of course, only a few minutes had passed when Uhura looked up.

"It's genuine," she said.

"How long ago was the message sent?" Kirk asked.

"Two days, twelve hours."

"And they are still more than twelve hours away," Spock pointed out. "Average survival time for prisoners of the Klingon Empire is substantially less than that."

"Sir," Uhura said, "the message was not specific, but I have reason to suspect that the *Harmony* was not under attack by a Klingon military vessel."

Kirk understood. That they survived long enough to send out a distress signal suggested as much.

"Please transfer whatever data you have to Mister Spock's station," Kirk said.

There was silence on the bridge as the crew waited for Kirk to make his decision. At the least, he knew he should be discussing the issue and its ramifications with his department heads. Too much was at stake to do otherwise. On the other hand, speed was the biggest imperative, in both a rescue mission and in their mission to System 7348.

"Jim, if you cross the border, the Klingons will consider that an act of war," McCoy said.

"Actually, Bones, Federation-Klingon accords allow for border crossing in emergency search-and-rescue situations," Kirk replied.

"However, in the current state of tension between the Federation and the Klingon Empire, the Klingons may interpret those accords . . . differently," Spock said.

"No doubt," Kirk said.

If you're in a tight spot and stuck for what to do, re-

member your oath. A security section chief named Michael Fuller had drilled that into Kirk when he was a newly minted officer on board the *U.S.S. Republic.* In the oath, all Starfleet officers swore *to protect and serve the Federation.* Well, the interests of the Federation were clear here. The *Enterprise* was needed at System 7348 to prevent the Klingons from causing any mischief.

The problem was that in the oath, Kirk had also sworn *to offer aid to any and all beings that request it.* Equally clear, and directly opposed to their duty at System 7348.

"Now, there will be times that your oath will seem to call for conflicting duties," Michael Fuller had said to them. "And some of you are wondering what you should do in those situations." Fuller had paused for a moment and looked at the group. "The answer is simple really. In those cases, it is your job to simply *know* what to do."

"Sir?" young Lieutenant Kirk had asked. "What if both duties seem equally pressing?"

"Like I said, as Starfleet officers it is your job to know what to do. There aren't enough regulations in the galaxy to guide you in every situation. We could spin out scenarios for the rest of the month and I guarantee that we wouldn't cover a fraction of the sticky situations you will each face in your careers. So all I can tell you is to trust your instincts and make the call. If you don't feel comfortable doing that, then there are any number of career opportunities for you in the merchant space fleet or the private sector." Then before any of the young officers could respond, he said, "Some of you think that's unfair, but it isn't unfair, it's Starfleet."

It didn't surprise Kirk that he knew what to do. Like

many complicated decisions, this one was surprisingly easy in the end.

"Mister DePaul, do you have a course laid in to the source of the distress call?" Kirk asked.

"Yes," the navigator replied. Kirk was pleased, not because DePaul had anticipated his decision, but because he had anticipated the *possibility* and acted accordingly.

"Mister Sulu, maximum warp to the *Harmony*'s last known position."

"Aye, sir," Sulu said as his hands moved over his console. "Course laid in . . . and accelerating to maximum warp."

The subtle change in vibration of the deck and the change in pitch of the hum of the ship's engines confirmed for Kirk that they were accelerating. A few seconds later, Sulu said, "Warp eight."

"Mister Spock, issue a yellow alert," Kirk said. "Lieutenant Uhura, put me on the ship's comm."

"Ready, sir," Uhura said immediately.

"This is the captain. We have received a distress call from a civilian vessel and have changed course to intercept. Our new course may take us across the Federation-Klingon border. I will keep you posted as the situation develops. Kirk out." Then Kirk said, "Uhura, have Security Chief Giotto meet me in the briefing room."

As Kirk got up, he noted that Mister Spock was already by his side.

"Captain, I need to get sickbay ready," McCoy said.

"Hang on, Bones," Kirk said, raising his hand. "Have M'Benga take care of that for now. I'm going to need you."

"Yes, sir," McCoy said, but Kirk could see that the doctor wasn't happy. If sickbay was going to be receiving casualties, he would want to see to all the preparations himself. Well, it couldn't be helped. Kirk needed McCoy's opinion for his next move. There was a conflict here, more than one actually, and Kirk wanted to hear what his two closest friends and advisers had to say about it.

"Gentlemen," he said, as he headed for the turbolift.

Chapter Two

I.K.S. D'K TAHG
KLINGON SPACE

KAREL HEARD THE COMMOTION before he saw it. He quickened his pace, but he did not run. As first officer of the ship, he had to maintain propriety. He entered the dining room and immediately understood what was going on. Since Councillor Duras had come on board the ship, there had been plenty of this sort of trouble.

The *D'k Tahg* had suffered significant losses to its crew in the recent skirmishes with the Starfleet vessels and some other incidents since then. When they'd returned to Qo'noS, they had not received regular Klingon Defense Force replacements. Instead, they had acquired a passenger: Duras, a member of the High Council, who had graciously offered his own troops as replacements.

Captain Koloth had been suspicious, but had had no choice but to accept. Councillor Duras was his superior. Koloth remained in charge of the ship, but Duras would be in charge of the mission to a planet in Federation space. Under normal circumstances, such an arrangement would be a disaster. A ship could only have one master. At some point, the needs of the mission and the needs of the vessel would differ and come into conflict. It was inevitable. In a normal situation, even honorable Klingons would have trouble sharing power. This was far from a normal situation.

And Karel had soon learned that the councillor was not an honorable Klingon. Almost immediately, he had tried to enlist Karel's aide in *overcoming Koloth's resistance.*

Of course, Duras had been clever and had said remarkably little directly, yet he had made his offer clear: if Karel cooperated and challenged Koloth's command, then he would have the assistance of Duras's men. It would be a simple trade, and for his efforts Karel would get command the of the *D'k Tahg.*

Karel, of course, had refused for many reasons, the simplest being that he had no doubt that Koloth was a better commander than he would be. Though he had always had his own ambitions, Karel had only been first officer for a short time. In fact, just a few months ago he was a junior weapons officer in the aft weapons room. He was not ready for command, and in the months since his promotion, his personal ambitions had changed considerably.

Within those months, his brother Kell had died. Now Karel had a debt that needed to be paid. An insult to his family's honor had to be avenged. Vengeance was more important than getting command of a ship.

Other factors were at work as well. Karel knew things about this mission that the rest of the crew, even Captain Koloth, did not. They had been told the *D'k Tahg* was making contact with a planet of primitive Klingons in a system in Federation space, which was true. However, in a personal, final message, Kell had told his brother of this planet. It was being mined by Orions working for someone placed highly in the empire.

The Orions were digging for dilithium, using deep-core mining techniques that would shortly have torn the planet apart and killed every Klingon who lived there. Incredibly, only the intervention of a Federation starship had saved the planet and defeated the Orions. Now, the empire was making a show of concern for the primitive Klingons, no doubt as part of their maneuvering before the war with the Federation.

After all, since it was in Federation space, the planet had strategic value in addition to the dilithium under its surface. Whatever game the empire was playing, it smacked of deceit and dishonor—the kind of dishonor that had swallowed his brother Kell.

Not all dishonor was so large, however. Much that he had seen in recent days was petty, like the disputes between the Duras's Klingons and the crew. These fights were numerous and over small issues. It was one thing for Klingons to test themselves against one another, but pointless bickering was something else entirely. Duras's crew complained about everything and were almost always the ones who started the conflicts.

And they almost always significantly outnumbered the

Klingons they were bothering—like now. Six of the councillor's guards had two of the *D'k Tahg*'s mess officers backed into a corner. Karel did not have to ask to know what the problem was. Duras had come on board with his own food stores. The food was much better than what Klingons on a warship usually saw.

The councillor had intended the food solely for himself and his Klingons, but Koloth would not hear of it. Without consulting Duras, he had ordered the food mixed with the ship's stores and rationed evenly between both the crew and Duras's guards.

Duras had been angry. In fact, *angry* had been an understatement, but Koloth had not cared. Surely, the captain had suspected that Duras wanted him out of the way and did not mind antagonizing the councillor. A Klingon such as Koloth was either fearless or a fool.

Karel had served with him long enough to know that Koloth was no fool.

"What is this?" Karel demanded, his voice booming.

"A simple dispute that is no business of yours," the leader of the contingent of Duras's men said, turning around to face Karel. The Klingon had murder in his eyes. *Over food?* Karel wondered, shaking his head. Karel knew him. His name was Rouk and he had previously made the mistake of crossing Gash.

The wound from that encounter was still visible on Rouk's forehead. Now it looked as if Rouk had gone looking for easier prey, and better odds for himself.

Gash had been under orders from Karel not to kill any of Duras's men unless it was absolutely necessary. The ship would be better off without most of them—and certainly without Rouk—but it was not worth the trouble it would cause with the councillor. Of course, Karel did not fear the trouble, but he recognized that a prolonged dispute with Duras would distract both him and Captain Koloth from guarding against whatever Duras was planning when they arrived at the planet.

And Karel's blood told him that the councillor was planning something. For that reason, Karel dismissed the notion of killing Rouk himself, as satisfying as that would have been.

"I said this is no business of yours," Rouk said, scowling at Karel. Obviously he still thought he had the advantage over the mess officers and Karel.

Karel did not flinch. "As first officer, *everything* that happens on this ship is my business."

"I have a legitimate dispute with these impudent *targs,*" Rouk said, gesturing to the two mess officers. Karel knew both Klingons and was pleased to see that they were not intimidated by the larger Rouk and other guards. The mess officers were smaller than Duras's men, and most of the *D'k Tahg*'s crew for that matter—which was, of course, why they were mess officers.

Kahless had taught that a warrior's body was just a shell. His true worth came from his blood and his heart. Karel smiled and said to Karn, the smaller of the two mess officers, "Are you willing to settle this dispute now?"

"Yes." Karn spat.

Karel watched Rouk's reaction to Karn's enthusiasm and saw a moment of doubt in the larger Klingon's eyes.

"Then the rest of us will give you room," Karel said to

29

Rouk. Then he gestured to the other mess officer and to Rouk's men, who looked to Rouk for a signal. The larger Klingon nodded, unable to do anything else. Clearly, he had not intended single combat, even with a much smaller foe, but he could not admit his cowardly intentions in the open.

Karel and the other mess officer took a position on the wall near Rouk's men. Karel decided he did not want them far from his sight—or his reach. When they were in place, Karel said, "*Bekk* Karn, do not kill him unless he forces you to." The mess officer looked disappointed, and Karel noted with satisfaction that Rouk was watching the exchange with more doubt now. He obviously understood that Karel and Karn knew something that he did not. Whatever he'd expected when he'd come into the mess looking for trouble, this was not it.

Karn did not give him long to consider the change in his fortune. With only a grunt of warning, the smaller Klingon launched a combination of strikes at Rouk that drove the Klingon backward into one of the tables. Rouk was able to deflect most of the blows, but Karel could see that at least one had connected solidly with the side of Rouk's face.

Finally, Rouk turned to one side and twisted away from the table behind him. He staggered back and steadied himself. Then, when Karn launched another attack, Rouk was better prepared, striking out with his own hands.

Karel immediately recognized Rouk's style of fighting as one of the most basic taught to military trainees. Against most enemies, it was quite effective, relying on power and intimidation. But Karn had become proficient in the Klingon fighting art of *Mok'bara*. In fact, he had been one of Karel's best students.

Rouk landed one solid blow on the side of Karn's head, but it only seemed to make the smaller Klingon angrier. Karn launched another attack that sent Rouk reeling backward over a table. Rouk's companions now looked not just confused, but shocked. They started to move toward their leader, but Karel grabbed one roughly and pulled him backward. Karel could see they wanted to enter the fight and had no doubt that they would do just that if he were not there. Of course, an honorable Klingon would never have allowed companions to help him in single combat.

But Rouk, like his leader, was not an honorable Klingon.

The large Klingon came up from behind the table with a small knife in his hand. It was not a proper blade, more of an assassin's weapon—a dishonorable tool for a coward's job. Rouk looked comfortable with it in his hand.

Though he was somewhat unsteady on his feet, the blade clearly gave him confidence. He lunged forward, leading with his blade. It was a clumsy attack and Karn was too skilled for it. He struck down on the blade hand even as he sidestepped the blow. Leaving one leg in Rouk's path, he shoved his adversary downward.

Rouk went down quickly, losing his hold on the knife. Even as he slid forward and crashed headfirst into the legs of another table, Karn dove forward, rolled, and came up holding Rouk's knife. Karel had to fight the urge to remind Karn not to kill Rouk, but he held his tongue. If he had to repeat a clear order to one of his warriors, that warrior had no place on the ship.

Karn kneeled over Rouk and reached down with one hand to turn the Klingon over so that he was faceup. Rouk was stunned, but not so much so that he did not see the knife and recognize the feeling when it was pressed to his throat.

Karel stepped forward and said, "Rouk, is this settled?"

Rouk looked in fear from Karel to Karn. He seemed surprised to still be alive.

"Is it?" Karel asked again.

"Ahhh . . . yes . . . it is settled," Rouk said, his voice uneven.

"Karn?" Karel asked.

Karn looked down on the Klingon under his blade and asked him, "Will you accept without complaint the same rations as every other Klingon on this ship?"

Rouk looked up as if he didn't understand. When he saw that Karn was serious, he nodded and replied, "Yes."

"Will you clean up the mess you have made in this dining room?" Karn asked.

Without hesitating, Rouk said, "Yes."

Karn leapt to his feet and answered the first officer, "Then I am satisfied." Looking back down to Rouk, he held up the knife and told him, "I will keep your child's toy. It may be of use in the kitchen."

Karel nodded to Karn and then turned to Rouk's Klingons and said, "You are dismissed." When they hesitated, he said, "Your companion does not need your help for his work."

The Klingons left the room. Karel waited a moment to make sure that Rouk would not do anything foolish, then left the dining room. Karel realized that the honor and hope of the Klingon Empire was in that cook. And Karn was not unusual on board the ship.

Since Koloth had taken command, Karel found that the spirit of the crew had greatly improved. Unlike many officers and leaders, Koloth did not find ways to pit his subordinates against each other. As a result, the crew kept their energy focused on their jobs and on defeating the empire's enemies. It was a good policy for training and maintaining good warriors, but more dangerous for Koloth himself.

So many commanders kept the crew at each other's throat because it kept them from challenging their authority. It was an effective way for a captain to stay alive, but it was terrible for operational efficiency.

On the *D'k Tahg,* the crew had flourished under Koloth. And Karel had to admit that as first officer he had had something to do with the improvement. Already, the ship's crew had beaten many long-held records in simulations and war games. It was an example of what Klingons could do if they focused their efforts and conducted themselves honorably, staying on the path of Kahless.

Like Karel, Koloth was a follower of Kahless the Unforgettable. And while most of the crew did not know that, they saw the results—warriors learned best by example. Yes, there was hope for the empire, hope for a future of glory and honor. Hope that it would recover from the kind of dishonor that had swallowed Kell.

However, for the empire to live out its promise, it first had to survive. And survival was by no means certain if it proceeded with war with the Federation. The same dishonorable leadership that had put Karel's brother on a dishonorable path had put the empire on the path to war.

At the moment, Karel realized that he would serve the empire best by getting some rest. He had finished another double shift and had much to do tomorrow to make sure the ship was ready when it reached its destination.

He checked in on the bridge and then headed back to his quarters. A message was waiting for him on the computer terminal.

Hitting a button on the console, he saw the title of the message and was immediately alert. "News from home," it read. Taking a quick glance at the rest of the message, he saw innocuous information about the weather and some agricultural reports. He did not even bother to read it. Instead he reached for a data tape he had put aside. Placing the tape into a slot in the console, he waited for the decryption program it held to do its work.

As Karel waited, he felt his blood nearly boiling. In a moment the information he had sought and paid dearly for would be his. He would know who had sent his brother on a mission of deceit and treachery—to live among humans, to hide his true face, and to strike them from behind.

A few moments later, the message changed. It now read, *The identity of the Klingon you seek is highly guarded. The Blade of the* Bat'leth *program has become a political orphan with most records of it purged. However, I have learned that the same Klingon was responsible for the mining operation on a planet in the Federation. Apparently, this was also a failure.*

That was it. No further information. Karel knew more than he had known before, but not much. He still did not know the identity of the bloodless Klingon who had stripped his brother of his true identity and put him in an impossible situation to start a battle with an honorable foe who should not have been an enemy.

It did not surprise Karel that the same Klingon was responsible for the reprehensible operation on the planet to which they were now headed. A Klingon who would sacrifice a whole planet of brothers would not hesitate to send a few Klingons to live among humans and die pursuing a mad plan.

Two failures . . .

The Klingon leadership might tolerate dishonorable acts to further the empire's power, but they would not tolerate failure—at least not for long. That meant that Karel might not have long to seek out his revenge. Until now, he had thought that the biggest obstacle he would face was the coming war with the Federation. If it began, his ability to take his revenge would be limited. For one, he might not survive long, and he would likely not see Qo'noS for some time. And he had no doubt that the Klingon he sought was walking the corridors of power there.

Now, he realized that he would have to hurry.

It would help to have Captain Koloth's advice on this issue. It would also help for Koloth to know the truth about their destination and the planet's recent history. However, there was no way to do that without telling Koloth everything. Everything about his brother, and everything about Karel's own mission of revenge.

The captain was honorable, but this was not his errand, not his fight. Koloth's help in restoring the honor of the House of Gorkon was too much for Karel to ask. And Karel's final vengeance might not be in the best interests of the ship. Even an honorable Klingon would differ with Karel in those circumstances.

No, whatever Karel did, he would have to do it alone.

Chapter Three

"UNACCEPTABLE," FOX SAID, standing and pounding the table. "That planet is not even on the list of disputed systems."

"Yes, but we agreed to talk without conditions," the Klingon ambassador said evenly.

"Then I need to amend our agreement and make it clear that I will not discuss absurd, trifling points that are not worth either of our time."

Ambassador Morg looked at Fox in silence for a moment and shrugged. "Very well."

Fox took no satisfaction in the minor victory. He knew the negotiations had ended days ago. Since then, there had been plenty of talk, but it had been just words. In the past, he had believed that as long as two sides were talking instead of fighting, there was hope. He still believed that was true. *Most of the time.*

But not this time. This was a dull charade where all parties knew the lie that stood between them but didn't speak it. So the farce continued. They argued forcefully about trade routes, economic exchanges, borders and boundaries, but it was sound and fury signifying nothing.

The only real thing to come out of these talks was the death of a talented and brave young man who had died in single combat with a Klingon diplomatic aide. Fronde's death had won the respect of the Klingon ambassador and allowed them to continue substantial talks.

Fox had believed they were making real progress; he still believed the Klingon ambassador had been sincere. However, making a brief visit back to Earth to report his progress, Fox had returned to the space station to find that the ambassador had been replaced.

The Klingon in front of him had insisted on starting over. The previous agreement was void, but he wanted to negotiate in good faith. In his many years in diplomatic service, Fox had been lied to by masters. This Klingon was no master. In fact, his heart didn't even seem to be in the task.

Admiral Solow had been right, as had his aide—the far too arrogant and far too young Lieutenant West. The Klingons were preparing for war and using the talks as a pretext to stall. Now, Fox was doing the same.

So each side argued, advocated its positions to buy time to kill each other more spectacularly when war came. Fox had seen many failures in his long career, but none as bitter as this one. And in no negotiation had the stakes ever been higher. Fronde might have been the first to die because of Fox's failings, but he would be far from the last. And that was only if the Federation won. Loss was too horrible to contemplate, yet it was a real possibility. And the specter of Federation defeat kept Fox at the table, trying to buy Starfleet time to make sure it didn't come to pass.

The Klingon demanded a change on procedure for negotiating trade disputes. "Completely unacceptable!" Fox shouted, on his feet again. The Klingons respected strength and anger, even in this mock, fraudulent situation. Fox found that he was happy to accommodate them.

Chapter Four

EARTH

LIEUTENANT WEST ENTERED Admiral Solow's office and stood for a moment in silence. The admiral studied his computer viewscreen and gave no indication that he had heard West enter, but the lieutenant had no doubt the admiral knew he was there, so he waited. After about two minutes, Solow got up, acknowledged West with a nod, and said, "Let's go."

Anyone who didn't know the admiral well would have thought he looked distracted, but West knew better. Solow was incredibly focused on the problems he was working out in his mind. He had no time for petty matters, and it had become his staff's job to take care of as many details as possible. The admiral needed his concentration. Hell, the entire Federation needed the admiral's concentration.

There was no conversation as they walked to the transporter pad. Small talk had completely disappeared. And besides, there was nothing to discuss. Both men had read the reports. And the reports had been clear. The meeting to come was a formality. In other circumstances, Admiral Solow would simply have sent West, or one of the other staff; the person they would be meeting with was possibly the only man in the galaxy that Solow would engage in a discussion that was mere formality.

"Energize," Solow ordered the transporter operator, and West felt the beam take him. He had traveled by transporter more times in the last two weeks than he had in his first twenty-three years. The novelty had disappeared.

West and Solow materialized on the Federation president's transporter pad on the fifteenth floor of the Palais de la Concorde. Waiting for them was the president's chief of staff, an Andorian named Shrel, who said, "Welcome," and led them down the hallway.

No other staff met them. Everyone else was too busy. Protocol had become less and less important, even in the president's office. There was no conversation. They were quickly ushered through the president's office doors, and West saw President Wescott sitting at his desk, looking over a communication intently. He looked up for a moment and nodded at them.

Wescott was alone in his large semicircular office and West knew why: the staff were all busy. Things were too hectic for any of them to make an appearance at this meeting. West had stepped into this office for the first time just two weeks ago. Then, he had been impressed by the panoramic views of Paris. Now, he felt nothing but impatience to get back to the work on his desk, the work that might still make a difference.

For the moment, though, the admiral needed him here. While every moment of the meeting would be recorded, regulations required a live witness. West would do this duty.

President Wescott stood and walked around his desk to greet them. He shook Solow's hand and then West's. "Admiral, Lieutenant," he said formally. The president looked older than he had in their last meeting. A few days seemed to have put years on his face.

"Admiral Solow, please make your report," the president said.

"Given recent events, reports from Starfleet intelligence, and the more recent report from Ambassador Fox, it is the opinion of Starfleet Command that war with the Klingon Empire is inevitable. Moreover, a de facto state of war currently exists. We believe that open hostilities will begin in short order, most likely with a Klingon strike on one or more Federation systems."

"What is our current state of readiness?" Wescott asked.

"With work on the *U.S.S. Constellation* finished, our starship refit program is complete. Additional ships have been recommissioned, including *Icarus* and J-class vessels."

Recommissioned is one way to put it, West thought. *Dragged out of mothballs would be another.* The *U.S.S. Yorkshire* had, literally, been a museum piece. The ship that had fought the Battle of Donatu V to a draw had for years been part of a traveling display touring the Federation. A few weeks ago, it had undergone a quick refit, and the admiral had signed an order declaring it ready for active duty.

Solow continued, "Seventy-eight percent of planetary defense upgrades are in place and the work is continuing. Key command and technical personnel have been reallocated with contingency protocols in effect."

That was a polite way of saying that Admiral Nogura and other people in key positions had been moved to secure locations throughout the Federation so that in the event of a Klingon invasion the command structure could be preserved in the event of a successful attack on Earth and Starfleet headquarters.

The president nodded. "With respect to hostilities with the Klingons, what is Starfleet's status?"

"Full readiness, Mister President," Solow said.

The president thanked the admiral. There was silence in the room for a moment before the president said, "Stop recording." The readiness report was now official and complete. Now all that was needed for a formal declaration of war was a war powers vote by the Federation Council, which would take place later in the week.

"Well, you were right, Lieutenant West. War was inevitable," Wescott said without any bitterness in his voice.

West had counseled that war was inevitable since before the incident at Starbase 42. He had railed against Ambassador Fox and had argued his position to the president himself. Now, he felt an irrational urge to apologize to President Wescott.

In the end, he said, "I was sorry to read Ambassador Fox's report."

"We all were," Wescott said. Fox had made it clear

that he believed the negotiations with the Klingon ambassador were a sham designed to buy the Klingons more time. West had believed he would never see the day that Fox would admit that the Klingons were not serious about seeking peace. But things had changed and Fox had lost a man in the negotiations.

"Can we win this, Herbert?" Wescott asked.

"We can, Mister President," Solow said.

"*Will* we?"

Solow gave the president a thin smile. "The simulations are inconclusive. Vulcan teams are working around the clock, but there are too many variables. And no war plan ever survives the first few minutes of actual battle, sir. I do think we have a chance, at least even odds."

"So only a fifty percent chance that everything we have built, everything we know, will be destroyed," Wescott said.

"I'm sorry I can't offer you better than that right now," Solow answered, genuine regret in his voice.

"I will not fire the first shot in this war," Wescott said, his eyes meeting West's for a moment, as if waiting for a challenge.

"I think that's wise, sir. My cultural research says that the Klingons will fight even harder if their government can claim that they have been attacked."

"Well, we wouldn't want to make them mad," Wescott said drily.

"Sir, I have a recommendation. I strongly suggest that you pull Ambassador Fox and his team out of the negotiations. When the Klingons finally abandon the pretense of talks, they will no doubt take the diplomatic team and try to extract information from them. If the team is captured, they will be *interrogated*." West felt a chill run down his spine as he said that word. He and Fox had had their differences, but he respected the man and wouldn't wish torture at the hands of a skilled Klingon interrogator on anyone.

"I made the offer through coded transmissions, but Fox and his people have volunteered to continue the charade as long as they can. Once we pull them out, the Klingons will know that we are ready to go to war. And we also need time."

It was a brave thing to do. Facing death was one thing, but facing a slow death at the hands of the Klingons was something else entirely. West was sorry that he had not gotten to know Fox better and that their few meetings had been so antagonistic.

"Thank you, gentlemen," President Wescott said.

"Thank you, Mister President," Solow said. The admiral and West turned and headed for the door.

West was anxious to get back to his work. He was finishing his report on Klingon cultural traditions and their approach to ground fighting. When he reached his office, a woman was waiting for him. She stepped forward and told him, "I'm Lieutenant Katherine Lei, reporting for duty, sir."

"Reporting?"

"Yes, sir."

"Reporting to me?"

"Yes, sir," she said evenly, though the firm smile disappeared from her lips. "The admiral assigned me to you."

"I see. The admiral, however, didn't mention you to me," West said.

"I can get my order confirmation,"

"Not necessary. I've been making a case for a staff and a full tactical xeno-studies department since I got here. It seems like you are the first step in that direction." West realized that Lei was young, no older than himself. He had never seen her before, but her name was familiar. And, he realized, she was attractive. Olive skin. Straight black hair. Hawaiian perhaps? Certainly somewhere in the Pacific.

"I just graduated. I've read your declassified reports. Some of your Klingon cultural analysis is really quite good," she said pleasantly.

"Some?" he asked with genuine surprise. He had quickly become the resident expert on Klingons and had literally written the book on Klingon culture and its relationship to tactics and strategy in warfare.

Suddenly, he remembered where he had seen Lei's name. "You wrote a thesis on the cult of Kahless."

"Yes. Have you read the paper?" she asked with genuine interest.

He nodded. "I found *some* of it quite good."

"Thank you," she said evenly. "Do you have any initial orders?"

"Come with me and tell me what you know about Klingon customs and norms with respect to ground fighting," West said, ushering her into his office.

Chapter Five

"MISTER SPOCK, what have you learned?" Kirk asked.

The Vulcan hit a button on the console in front of him. Immediately, the briefing-room viewscreen showed the image of a civilian space vessel. "The *Harmony* is a *Marquis*-class private vessel that can accommodate approximately eight passengers and crew."

Kirk knew the ship. "It's a yacht."

"Aye. Fast enough for a private vessel, but it doesn't even have proper navigational deflectors, let alone defensive shielding," Scott said, shaking his head.

Spock shook his head. "The craft is designed primarily for short trips through charted systems along known spaceways."

47

"I presume, then, that it doesn't have any weapons?" McCoy asked.

Scott shook his head. "Not this model. The main energizer would never support them."

"And due to their ideological bent, it is unlikely that the Anti-Federation League would perform the dramatic upgrades necessary to allow for weapons of any kind," Spock said.

"So they marched into Klingon space on a pleasure craft?" McCoy said.

"Apparently," Spock said.

"Anyone with any experience in space would know that the Klingons would see the arrival of an unarmed ship as an insult at best," Scotty said.

His statement hung in the air for a moment until Security Chief Giotto broke the silence. "Captain, the crew of the *Harmony* chose to enter Klingon space. They were aware of the risks."

Kirk nodded; he knew how the lieutenant commander felt. "However, we are under an obligation to provide assistance in this case. Though they are members of the Anti-Federation League, they are still Federation citizens."

"Captain, with all due respect, we also have an obligation to get to System 7348 before the Klingon battle cruiser arrives. If we don't, the Klingons will have time to fortify their position," Giotto said.

Kirk saw the serious concern in the chief's face and understood it. He also knew that more than one of his department heads and the other assembled staff were thinking the same thing. "The issue we have here is do we take a significant risk to save the lives of people who should have known better, or do we attend to a larger duty to protect the Federation from a bigger and graver threat: Klingon incursion. Now, we do know that right now civilians are in custody of Klingons and no doubt have a very short time to live." Kirk waited a moment for that to sink in. "They are in real and immediate danger, but we might be tempted to ignore the situation to concentrate on the problem posed by the Klingon warship approaching System 7348 because of what they may and likely *will* do when they get there. Certainly, no one would blame us for continuing to the system because of the grave threat that ship poses. However, I will not trade the lives of civilians for what might happen, or even what probably will happen. We will not compromise who we are even if it means risking our larger survival."

There was a flash of understanding on Doctor McCoy's face, and a raised eyebrow on Spock's, which amounted to the same thing. Once, when Kirk was young, he had seen a man named Kodos execute four thousand colonists on Tarsus IV because of a food shortage. At the time, the decision had had a cold logic: the colony's food supply had almost completely been wiped out, and the entire settlement could not survive until resupply ships came. Kodos had expressed regret and then done what he said was necessary to preserve as many lives as possible.

The decision was indeed logical. However, it was not only an immensely immoral decision but a fatally flawed one. Through a series of events that no one could have foreseen, the supply ships had come early, and Kodos became one of the most hated names in the galaxy.

Kodos the Executioner had traded the lives of the

people under his protection to serve a larger purpose. Kirk would not do the same.

"I thank you all for your input, but my decision is final," the captain said.

"Understood," Giotto said. The chief's people would carry out any rescue mission and would be in the most danger, but now that the decision was made, Kirk was sure that Giotto was already reviewing rescue scenarios in his head.

"Lieutenant Parrish," Kirk said. "Recommendations on the rescue mission."

Lieutenant Leslie Parrish was one of the few surviving crew members from the incidents on Systems 1324 and 7348. She was also one of only two survivors from her squad of the Klingon assault on Starbase 42, where the Klingons had taken too many good people, including Sam Fuller. She had about as much experience at fighting Klingons in close quarters as anyone alive in Starfleet today.

"I would send in one full squad, hit the Klingons hard and quick. Because of their cultural prejudices against 'Earthers,' they don't expect much from us. As a result, they have a hard time adjusting to setbacks. Chances are we can get in and out before they can mount an effective response."

Kirk shifted his gaze to Giotto. "I agree, sir," Giotto said.

"I would like to volunteer my squad for the job, Captain," Parrish said. "Besides my own experience with Klingons, we also have Michael Fuller on our team."

She was right. As a survivor of the Battle of Donatu V, Fuller had even more experience with Klingons than

Parrish did herself. Of course, there were complications with Fuller, and with Parrish herself for that matter. However, the place to have those discussions was not in an open meeting.

"Thank you, Lieutenant, I will take that offer under advisement. Lieutenant Uhura, continue to monitor all communications from the Klingons. Mister Spock, please let me know when long-range scanners have a lock on the merchant Klingon vessel now holding the prisoners. I want to know as much about that ship as possible. Then Kirk scanned the room, looking for any questions or concerns, but there were none, just people anxious to get back to their jobs now that the ship was getting closer to Klingon space.

"Mister Spock, Doctor McCoy, and Lieutenant Commander Giotto, stay with me. Everyone else is dismissed," Kirk said, and the group filed out of the briefing room. Kirk was not surprised to see that Lieutenant Parrish remained behind.

"Captain, may I have a word?" she asked.

Kirk knew this was coming. "Of course."

"Sir, have you considered my request? My squad—"

The captain raised his hand and said, "Is the best choice for the rescue mission." Parrish nodded, but Kirk continued, "But you will not be leading them."

"Sir?"

"Lieutenant, we have had this discussion before. You are pregnant and I will not send you into a dangerous situation. You have remained on duty only to train your squad."

"But, sir, there is no squad leader on board with more experience in close fighting with Klingons. I understand

51

your concerns about my condition, but these circumstances are *extraordinary.*"

"They are, Lieutenant, and it *is* true that no current squad leader has more experience than you in this area. That is why I am relieving you of command of your squad and promoting Mister Fuller to section chief. He will command the squad and the mission."

Parrish looked sick. "Sir, my squad—"

"I'm sorry, Lieutenant. You have done an excellent job training them, but you cannot go."

Parrish's face was set, but Kirk could see a swirl of emotion beneath it. After a moment, she said, "If Fuller is squad leader, that will leave an opening in the squad. I recommend Ensign Jawer to replace him."

It made sense. Jawer was also a survivor of the three encounters with the Klingons.

Kirk nodded. "I will have Lieutenant Commander Giotto make it official. Thank you, Lieutenant." Then, before she could turn to go, he said, "I'm sorry, Leslie."

But her face was a mask. She simply nodded and left the briefing room.

Leslie Parrish walked slowly through the halls of the *Enterprise*. She had been relieved of her squad and was no longer an active-duty officer in Starfleet. True, since her pregnancy her duties had been limited to running training exercises, but since the *Enterprise* hadn't been in any hostile situations since then, it had been easy to fool herself into believing that nothing had changed. Now she saw that things were really different. Hell, *everything* had changed.

Because of Jon and the child she now carried inside her. Their child. His child. A half-Klingon child.

Doctor McCoy had been clear. A human/Klingon pregnancy was difficult at best. There would be complications and it would be dangerous for her. And then there was the question of the kind of life the child would have in the Federation after the inevitable war with the Klingons.

And she would have to give up not just this mission, or the next one, but her career in Starfleet, the only job she had ever wanted. Her first squad leader, Sam Fuller, had called security the "highest calling in Starfleet." She had seen what security people could do. It was important work. And she knew she had something to offer. She had proven that much to herself in the last few months where she had seen people around her die for their beliefs—people like Sam Fuller, even people like Jon. Whatever his biology, he had been as much a part of the crew as anyone else.

Those people had stood for something, and they had all died for something. Nevertheless, in a short time, the Klingons would try to smash it all: Starfleet, the Federation, and everything they represented. If she stayed on the *Enterprise*, she could make a difference in that fight, but she couldn't stay if she had the baby. The best she could do would be to watch from the sidelines and wait—two things she had never been good at.

It made sense; it was perfectly logical. The fact was, she could do more good in Starfleet security than out of it. And yet . . .

That would be the end of Jon. If she didn't have this baby, there would be no physical proof that he had ever existed. He would be a name on a Starfleet report, and a memory in the minds of the few people that served with him.

Did he even have a family? Did anyone who really knew him even know what he was doing? He had given up his face and his identity to infiltrate Starfleet. He had done it to serve the Klingon Empire, but in the end he had given up that allegiance to fight against Klingons with Starfleet—with her.

It was an amazing story, most of which had died with him on Starbase 42. What would be left if she didn't have his child? What would be left of him in this galaxy, and what would be left of what they had shared together in the brief weeks they had known one another?

Leslie Parrish had faced impossible odds on more than one mission on board the *Enterprise*. She had faced death and helped the people around her succeed when every rule in the book said they should fail. And never in all that time had she felt so overwhelmed by a decision.

Kirk stood up when Giotto and Fuller entered the briefing room. "Mister Fuller," he said, pointing to a seat. As much as any officer Kirk had ever known, Fuller was born to lead. And for nearly all of his quarter-century Starfleet career, Fuller had been a security squad leader, politely declining all offers of promotion.

Kirk had served with Fuller as a young officer and understood the decision. Michael had done a hell of a lot of good as a section chief, as had his son Sam before his death. Something about the bond within the security squads was unique in the service, a bond that was related to the shared dangers they faced and the high casualty rate in their ranks.

"Mister Fuller, have you seen the briefing materials on the situation with the *S.S. Harmony*?" Kirk asked.

"Yes, and I understand we are effecting a rescue. I volunteer, of course, but I assume there is more to this than a request for volunteers." Fuller had lost none of his sharpness in the years since Kirk had served with him. And he was no less direct. "Do you still have concerns about my ability to carry out my duties with respect to Klingons, Captain?"

Klingons had killed Fuller's son, and Michael had reenlisted in Starfleet because of the coming conflict with the Klingon Empire. Of course, Kirk still had concerns, but he was also sure that Fuller was the best person for this job.

"The reason you are here, Michael, is that I am giving you a field promotion, effective immediately, and putting you in command of the rescue operation."

"Captain?" Fuller asked respectfully.

"We both know that you are the most qualified person on board for this sort of operation, and you belong running a security squad," Kirk said.

"I made a choice to reenter the service as a line security officer. I'm not seeking promotion—"

Kirk waved him off. "The team needs a leader and you are the best person. And, because of Leslie Parrish's pregnancy, I am short a section chief. It may not be what you want, but it's what the mission and the ship requires."

The captain could see that Fuller wanted to say more but kept it to himself. He wouldn't put his personal wishes ahead of a mission. "Understood, Captain," Fuller said finally.

Kevin Ryan

"As section chief, you are now cleared to see the service records of your squad members," Lieutenant Commander Giotto said.

"I have already seen them."

Of course, as a frequently called-upon consultant to Starfleet, Fuller had kept his security clearance. "Good, then you can assemble your squad and begin preparations immediately. Your replacement in the squad will be Ensign Jawer," Giotto said.

Something moved on Fuller's face, and Kirk realized what it was: Jawer had served under Fuller's son Sam on his last few missions. After a moment, Fuller said, "I've seen his record. We're lucky to have him." Kirk could see that Fuller was anxious to go. "If that's all, Captain?"

"Yes, dismissed," Kirk said.

Fuller was out of his seat and headed for the door. Before he reached it, Kirk said, "Congratulations, Mister Fuller."

Fuller turned and gave him a thin smile. "Thank you, sir."

Chapter Six

ORION-BUILT MINING FACILITY
SYSTEM 7348
FEDERATION SPACE

ENTERING THE FACILITY, Gorath felt the power of the mine built by the green-skins. The power they held had nearly torn the entire world apart, though now it represented the future for his people. Also, the mine sat on the planet's true power—crystals buried deep under the ground. The value of those rocks that had brought the green-skins here in the service of their masters, whom Captain Kirk of the humans called Klingons.

These Klingons were of Gorath's people's own blood, yet they had sent the Orions to take the crystals and in the process destroy this branch of the family tree. It was madness done to power the Klingon ships that traveled between the stars. These ships would make war on the humans and their allies. Gorath had fought with Kirk and his people. They were good and noble warriors who had helped Gorath and his fighters destroy the green-skins.

Gorath was shamed that people of his blood would take such a course, but he could not change the past. He could, however, ensure that his planet's crystals were never used against Kirk's people.

He found his son, Adon, showing a small group of his people how to operate one of the control stations that ran the machine that powered the facility. The humans called it the *warp reactor* in their language. Gorath had made an effort to understand the outsiders' technology as well as their language.

The computers the green-skins had left behind were programmed to communicate in Orion, Klingon, and the human language. Gorath had as many of his people as possible learn Human. Someday, they would come back, or the green-skins would, or the Klingons, or some other people. Gorath was determined to keep that day as far in the future as he could, but when it came, he and his people would be ready. They would have the means to defend themselves, and they would have crystals of value to trade.

Before that day came, there was much to do. Already they had repaired the damage done to the facility in the last battle with the green-skins. All of the nine clans had sent people to help, as they had all sent people to fight the Orions—well, *almost all of the clans* had fought. Gurn's clan had been the only one who had not joined the combat. Gurn and his warriors had arrived a full day after the battle was won and their world saved.

Of course, they had had to travel the farthest, so

Gurn's claim that they had come as soon as they could might have been true—the only problem was that Gorath had seen the lie in Gurn's eye. Gurn's people were not all sniveling cowards, and Gorath had seen that a people could be better than their leaders, but not often and not by much.

A good leader could make his people stronger, better, and achieve more than they knew. Watching his son instruct the others, Gorath knew that they would have that sort of leader in the future.

For now, of course, Gorath was the leader of the largest clan, and the clan on whose land the green-skins had built their mine. So he had ended up in charge of the facility. For now, that meant mostly scheduling time for people in each clan to learn the green-skins' equipment.

There had been some disputes in the beginning, as different clanspeople jockeyed for more time, particularly with the Orion weapons. Not surprisingly, most of the disputes had involved people of Gurn's clan, and Gorath had suspected Gurn's hand in some of the other disputes. Gorath had settled all matters immediately, remembering that *an open wound festers quickly.* No one, not even Gurn, had dared to question his judgment openly.

Gorath was considered a great hero among most of the clans because he had led the first raids on the green-skins that had captured many of their weapons. He had also led the final battle that had destroyed their enemy. Gorath knew that most clan leaders would have done no less, but he found that the respect the other clans showed him was actually useful in keeping the groups from setting against one another. And they had to remain united for the day that they joined the rest of the galaxy outside their world.

"Father," Adon said when he saw Gorath. Then Adon lifted a hand to show that he would be a moment and leaned down to resume the instructions he was giving to the man sitting at the computer terminal.

Adon had taken to the human language quickest of all of their people. He was also best at talking to the computers and had an almost instinctive understanding of the machines. In all areas, he was ahead of his father. Well, not all. In the races they had devised with the Orion flying-weapon platforms, Gorath could still beat his son, barely. In time that too would change, but that would not be for a summer or two, at least.

Finished with his pupil, Adon said, "We are almost done for the day."

"The warp reactor?" Gorath said.

"We are still running at only a fraction of its power. Enough to move air and water and power the smaller equipment."

"Have you tried *increasing the power?*" Gorath asked.

"Not yet. I want to make sure that it will not blow us all up first."

"Wise."

"We still have much to learn about how these machines work," Adon said, waving his hand around the reactor room.

"There is no one better for that job, my son, than you." Gorath's compliment was sincere.

Adon gave him an embarrassed shrug. "The computer does most of the work, and it explains whatever I need to know."

Gorath shook his head. "You have done more here in a short time than I could have done in a dozen summers." Gorath took his son's shoulder. This caused blood to rush to Adon's face. He might have been smarter than his father, but he was still a boy of fifteen summers and was quick to embarrassment.

"I am ready to go with you," Adon said, changing the subject.

"No. It will be just endless talk from Gurn. A father would never wish that on his son."

Adon smiled. "I don't mind . . ."

Gorath waved him off. "Why don't you stay here and explore the computer simulations?"

Adon immediately raised his head. He and some of his friends enjoyed playing with simulations on the green-skins' computers. Gorath himself had no patience for them, but the offer of a whole evening playing those games was too much for Adon to refuse.

"He does talk an awful lot, Father," Adon said, smiling.

"I will see you when I return. Then I will relay it all in painful detail."

His son laughed as Gorath turned to go. He left the complex and headed to the meeting pit outside his village. In the past, councils were held in the clan pit of the village holding the meeting. However, since the green-skins had gone, the people needed more meetings between the clan leaders. Well, whether they needed them or not, they had held many more councils than ever before.

Gurn had suggested a new meeting area outside of any individual clan's village. He said it was to ensure that all clans were treated equally and given equal respect. The real reason, of course, was that after the Orions left, all councils had been held in Gorath's village because of its proximity to the mine.

Gorath had accepted the idea of a new meeting pit because to resist was to give credence to Gurn's suggestion that perhaps too much power and influence was landing in a single clan: namely Gorath's. Gurn's was the loudest voice making that charge and, for a time, the only one. However, since the green-skins, all of the clans were worried about the future, and internal squabbling—petty as it was—was preferable to confronting the real dangers they had all faced and might face again.

There had been many changes since the Orions had come and gone. The green-skins had brought change with their deadly machines. And while Gorath might curse the green-skins—and he often did—he would be a fool to deny that the world was very different today because of them. Now, for his son and for all of his people he would have to make sure that the changes did not destroy them, as the green-skins nearly did.

To that end, Gorath would endure worse than one of Gurn's tedious and needless councils. Of course, Gorath had seen something he did not like in Gurn's eyes in the last meeting. He could not put it into words, but he did not doubt the call of his blood. That look was the reason he did not want Adon to come along. Though Gurn was probably too much of a coward to challenge him directly, physically or otherwise, Gorath didn't trust the man and he instinctively wanted to keep Adon away from those who wore false faces.

The walk to the new council pit would take him some time, and he found that he enjoyed the trip by himself. Walking the woods of his people, he remembered the time before the green-skins had come, the simpler time of his youth. In his blood, he knew that he and his people would never see those times again, but it did not hurt to visit in his memory from time to time.

Normally, he would have his second accompany him to council meetings, but Felan had died fighting the Orions. Originally, Gorath had not replaced him immediately because Adon was almost old enough to assume the position. Gorath had decided to wait until his son was ready, but now he doubted the decision. He realized that the clan council had grown small and petty just when the threats against them had grown great. He had no desire to expose his son to that world, not until it was absolutely necessary.

In any case, there was always hope that the clan leaders would come to their senses. *Not with Gurn constantly whispering in their ears,* he thought. It was true and Gorath realized that he had let the problem go on too long. Something had to be done about Gurn. Gorath had resisted because there hadn't been any real conflict between the clans since the time before his great-grandfather's memory, and perhaps even longer than that.

His people were hunters and never shirked individually from a fight or struggle—as they had not shirked from battle with the green-skins. But there was no need for the clans to fight among themselves. Each had all they needed and more from the rich land. Up until the Orions came, there had been nothing worth fighting over.

Now, there was the mine and the Orion machines. But Gorath felt that there was more to it than that. Other forces were at work here, his blood was certain of it. He realized he had been too preoccupied by the effort to get the mine repaired and operating, and to begin teaching more of his people how to use Orion weapons and equipment, even as he was learning himself.

And he had allowed himself to be distracted by the endless bickering of clan disputes. That would change tonight. Gorath wasn't sure what he would do, but he trusted his blood to guide him. At heart, Gurn was a coward and it wouldn't take much to intimidate him. That would be a start. That the warp reactor was working to provide the machines with even more power was good news. Perhaps that would impress the council. They could now focus on building their future.

When Gorath arrived at the council pit, he saw that each clan leader was there with his second, except for Gurn, who had four of his people with him. Gorath shook his head. He had spent a dozen summers as clan leader and had never seen another leader come to a council with anyone other than his second.

"Honored Gorath, we are pleased to welcome you," Gurn said expansively. Immediately all heads turned to Gorath, who nodded.

Besides making himself a central part of every council discussion, Gurn had taken to using ridiculously formal speech. Gorath had to fight the impulse to say something rude and merely nodded.

"We can begin now. All of you have sent messages laying out what you would like to discuss tonight. Well, almost all of you," Gurn said, shooting Gorath a look.

Besides electing himself to run the meetings, Gurn had decided that all clan leaders had to send him a list of subjects they wanted to discuss in each council. In the

)ast, clan leaders would simply get up and speak, or not, ıs they felt the need. Now, there was so much discussion ınd so many new issues that Gurn's rule almost made iense. However, Gorath still refused to follow it as a natter of principle.

"First, we have a request from—"

Gorath stood up and interrupted him, taking pleasure n the scowl from Gurn that it earned him. "Before we)egin, I have an announcement, some good news for all)f the clans."

All heads turned to Gorath and Gurn stepped forward. 'Well, we are happy to change the order of our discussion 'or 'good news.' Please speak." Gurn waved expansively.

Ignoring the fool, Gorath stepped to the center of the)it. "I am pleased to announce that the mine's warp re- ıctor has been successfully tested and is now operating. t is not yet at full power, but we have enough power to echarge all of the vehicles and weapons for further raining. We can also begin using some of the heavier nining equipment."

Cheers went up among the clan leaders and their sec-)nds. Gorath now looked at Gurn and enjoyed the man's)ewildered expression. After only a moment, Gurn re- :overed and said, "That is excellent news. But why did /ou not call your fellow clan leaders so we could all :njoy the glory of the moment?"

The clan leaders looked to Gurn. Most of them nod- led, and Gorath could hear grumbling. He acted imme- liately. "There was a danger. I chose to face it myself." Γhat brought murmurs of approval, but even that posi- ive change worried Gorath. The leaders had never been io fickle before.

"We applaud your courage, but we had agreed to vote on all serious matters. We must speak with one voice on the dangers that threaten us all," Gurn said. Then he gave another generous wave. "What is done is done. And we are here to talk about the future. If there is no more good news, then we can continue with tonight's most important subject. We have learned that the world on which we live is part of a larger place, a galaxy of worlds. Though we are a strong and brave people, this collection of worlds measures strength by the power in a people's machines, not by the strength of their hearts or their blood. Everything we know has changed. When the green-skins came, they brought devices that could have torn everything we knew to dust. We cannot continue to live in the old world, following our old ways." Gurn shot Gorath a look at that last part.

"For our great people to survive, to thrive, and to take our place in the galaxy, we will need machines as great as we are. Gorath and his people have gotten more power to the mine, but how long will it last? We have only begun to understand the Orion equipment. Even Gorath admits that there was a great danger simply starting the reactor. And if we somehow escape disaster from the machines, what do we have? A few paltry weapons left by the green-skins? Some rocks from under the ground that we cannot use or trade without help? What do these things mean when there are ships that travel between the stars, ships that can bring destruction to all of us?"

Gurn paused, looking over the crowd. They were all waiting attentively for what would come next. Whatever it was, Gorath was sure that he would not like it. Gurn did not keep them waiting long.

"We need a new kind of strength for the new world in which we live. We cannot afford to stand alone with so many dangers awaiting us." He pointed up to the sky. "There are people of our blood who have offered us friendship. They have offered us great machines which we can use to defend ourselves from green-skins or anyone else who would do us harm. These people, these Klingons, have built a great empire, an alliance of many worlds. No one in the galaxy dares stand against them."

Gorath couldn't wait. He stood up and shouted, "These Klingons sent the green-skins here to destroy us!"

Gurn lifted his head and looked down on Gorath, the way a parent looks down on a foolish child. "You will have a chance to speak, please wait until then." Turning back to the others, he continued, "That is what the humans have told us. We cannot measure their truth. And the humans also want these crystals. The Klingons merely want to talk to us, to make us an offer of assistance. To tell us more of their empire, so we can decide for ourselves if we wish to join. They will be here in less than three days. We can choose to welcome them, or to turn them away."

Gorath felt the blood rush to his face. That was it. Gurn had already spoken to the Klingon leaders. He must have taken one of the talking machines from the mine. If the Klingons were coming in three days, Gorath was not sure whatever they decided in the council pit would make any difference.

Gurn gave an absurd short bow to the clan leaders and took his seat. Gorath did not wait, he stepped to the center of the pit. "The Klingons sent the green-skins here to destroy us. The human captain, Kirk, told us this and

I believe him because the humans came and helped us stop the Orion monsters. Those of us who fought with the humans," Gorath said, shooting a look at Gurn, "know them to be people of honor. They shed their own blood to defend us; they left their own dead on our fields of battle. And it is true that they also want this dilithium, but remember, they could have taken it from us if they wanted to. Instead, they respected our wishes for them to go. They also offered us assistance, protection, and machines, but I sent them back to their ship because we are not ready to enter their galaxy. We have much to learn, much to understand about their devices and their ways.

"When we have learned enough, we will emerge on *our* terms. Gurn says that we need machines and a new kind of strength to defend ourselves. I say this is not true. We destroyed the Orions with the strength of our blood. We will decipher the puzzles of their machines with our minds and hands. And then we shall enter the galaxy as masters, servants to no one but our own blood and will. Gurn says the Klingons will be here in three days. I say we turn them away. The humans left our world when we asked them to. If the Klingons have honorable intentions, they will do the same. If not, I say we fight them with the last drop of our blood and the last bit of our strength. I have hunted with all of you, fought green-skins with most of you. Stand with me now and no enemy can stand against us."

Gorath finished and scanned the crowd. He had won some of the hearts around him, but some of the faces were impossible to read. He had no illusion that this would be easy. What Gurn was offering was tempting—

immediate safety without effort, incredible machines for worthless rocks. The path Gorath was offering would take many summers, require much of his people, and was full of uncertainty. But as his father had taught him, *If you lie down with flen, you wake up with mites.*

"We shall vote. Those who would welcome our brothers in blood, stand with me. Those who would turn them away, stand with Gorath," said Gurn. The clan leaders hesitated, considering the two men. Slowly, they made their way to the pit. Besides Gorath and Gurn, there were seven clan leaders. All Gorath needed now was four, yet he could see that not all were decided.

One leader joined Gurn, one joined Gorath. Another for each side. Then another. One remained: Balen, who considered both men for a moment . . .

And then stepped to Gorath's side.

That was it. This battle was won, at least for now. Gorath would have expected Gurn to fume, but he merely nodded and said, "Let no one challenge the will of this council."

Afterward, they had the customary meal, but there was little talk. At the end, Gurn approached Gorath and said, "I congratulate you. You remain a leader to us all."

Gorath merely nodded and turned to go. He had no desire to trade dishonest words with a snake. He wanted to get back to his village, to see his brother and his son and tell them about what had happened here tonight. It was more than just talk, and Gorath was sure that the matter was not finished. At the least, in three days they would need to be ready for battle. When the battle with the green-skins had come, Adon had been too young to fight. But since then, he had passed his fifteenth summer. This was a battle that he would join. Gorath had to make sure that he was ready.

On his walk back, Gorath found that he was more troubled than when he knew the Orion machines might kill them all. Then he had been worried about his people's survival. Now, he thought that they might lose something even more valuable than their lives. Even the trees and the night wind could not quiet his mind.

He heard noises around him, but did not think much of them until he saw the five people holding torches ahead of him. He didn't have to see their faces to know that they were Gurn and his people. Gorath was immediately alert, his hunter's instincts automatically at work. He cursed himself for allowing Gurn to surprise him. The *flen* had something planned, and Gorath realized that he had misjudged the coward. He had never thought Gurn would take any direct action against him.

"What do you want, Gurn?" Gorath shouted before he was even close enough to see the men's faces.

"Gorath," Gurn replied, his voice showing uncertainty. He was wondering, no doubt, how Gorath knew who he was in the dark. Good. His men would be nervous too. That would work to Gorath's advantage.

"We need to talk further," Gurn said, coming close enough so that Gorath could finally see his face, and the faces of his four men. Gorath was pleased to see that they *were* nervous. Good. He intended to give them more to worry about, if necessary.

"Is it really talk you are here for, Gurn?" Gorath said, making the question a taunt.

"Ah, yes, I have grave concerns about the course of action you have set for us," Gurn said, gaining confidence as he spoke. Immediately, Gorath saw that Gurn would need to speak for a few minutes to gather his courage before this began.

Well, he would not engage in such a dance. Gorath took two steps toward the group and was pleased to see them all take a step back. "Are you here to kill me, Gurn? You *five?*" Drawing his *mek'leth,* Gorath swung it in front of himself a few times for emphasis. "I did not expect to hunt tonight, but a man does not always choose his fate."

Gurn took another step back. "You have put us all in danger," he muttered.

"No, you have lain down with *flen.* You are upset that I would not lie down as well. Now, either stand aside or you will see how much danger *you* are in."

Gurn held his ground and said formally, "A judgment has been rendered against you."

"By the council?"

"By me," Gurn said.

"Are you prepared to carry out the judgment yourself?" Gorath said as the other four men drew their weapons.

"The stakes are too high here to trust our future to single combat, as much as I would enjoy it." Gurn made a hand signal and the four men began to spread out.

"Let me ask you, are the stakes *ever* low enough for you to do your own fighting?" Gorath said, taking another step forward. He judged that if he got a little closer to Gurn, he could reach the man before Gurn's people could stop him.

"Your skills as a hunter and a fighter are legendary among our people. For that, if for nothing else, you have earned my respect. But the future belongs to those who see beyond the next hunt, and those who use greater weapons than simple blades," Gurn said.

"One at a time, or shall I end your cowardly lives together?" Gorath said, making eye contact with each of Gurn's men. They were nervous. They didn't have the false courage of bullies with an advantage.

"Destroy him together. Take no chances," Gurn said.

A red haze descended over Gorath's vision. The time for talk was ended. He knew he had little time in which to act. The four men in front of him were cowards, and he had no doubt that he could best each of them individually, but he knew he would not get that courtesy from this lot.

Now he had one goal: get to Gurn before the others could get to him. His ancestors had a simple axiom: *When outnumbered, attack.* Gorath didn't hesitate. He attacked.

Racing forward, he let out a fierce battle cry and slashed at the man on his right. The guard was too surprised to offer a serious defense, and Gorath felt his blade make contact with the man's neck. He didn't wait to see what happened to him and kept moving forward. He only had one desire now: kill Gurn. And do it before he further poisoned their people.

Gorath was peripherally aware of someone slashing at him from behind. A blade raked down across his left shoulder, cutting him deeply. Gorath ignored the wound, leaping the last steps to Gurn, who held his own sword feebly in front of him. Slicing downward, Gorath knocked the *mek'leth* out of the coward's hand and lifted his own blade again to bring it down one more time to end Gurn's pitiful life.

As he swung his sword, he was aware of movement behind him. Someone was rushing him. The prudent move would be to turn and defend himself. Of course, the odds were still four to one, and Gorath might not get another chance at Gurn. He ignored the man behind him and completed his attack on the traitorous clan leader.

As the blade came down, Gorath was pleased to see the terror in Gurn's eyes. However, an instant before he made contact, someone knocked into him from behind. Apparently, in a surprising burst of courage, one of Gurn's thugs had simply thrown themselves at Gorath to protect his clan leader.

Still, Gorath tried to complete the blow, bringing his blade down with all his strength as he felt himself thrown forward. Though strong, his aim was off and Gorath could see the blade make only glancing contact with Gurn's face and shoulder.

Then he was rolling on the ground, with someone still clutching him from behind. He rolled on his left shoulder, which screamed in pain, but it allowed him to keep hold of his *mek'leth*. As he sprang back to his feet, he slashed back with his weapon, trusting his hunter's instincts to guide the blade. They did not fail him. He turned to see the man clutching his stomach. It was a deep wound and would likely be fatal. Most important, however, the man was out of the fight for now.

The other two guards were eyeing him warily and keeping a respectful distance. Gurn was clutching his face, which wore an expression of pain and disbelief.

When Gorath spoke, he directed himself to the guards. "End this foolishness. This is not a man you can follow. We are a proud people. We defeated the green-skins, we can defeat the work of a coward in our midst. Do not let him poison you against your own kind." Gorath saw the beginnings of shame in the men's eyes. That was something. If they could be shamed, they might again know something of honor.

"Now you wish to talk?" Gurn said.

"Not to you, coward," Gorath said.

"Either way, talk will not save you today. There are three of us," Gurn said, holding up his *mek'leth.*

"And a moment ago there were five."

"But you are injured," Gurn said.

Gorath gave a glance to his left arm. The blow had struck him in the back, but he could see blood running freely down to his hand and then the ground. He tried to lift his left hand and found that it would not easily obey his commands.

Gurn was giving him an unpleasant smile.

"I need only one hand to finish you," Gorath said.

After a quick hand gesture from Gurn, the two guards approached him slowly from either side. Gorath realized that they were lost. Whatever Gurn had offered them was worth more to them then their honor.

Gurn raised his own blade and said, "Strike him at the same time." That was it. Gorath knew he needed to act quickly. He could still get to Gurn before they stopped him, and killing Gurn meant everything now. Gorath's people were depending on him—his son was depending on him. He felt a growing sadness that he would not see Adon again, would not see him grow to a man. Ultimately, Gorath had to push away his son's image. He could not be distracted now.

He prepared for a final leap to Gurn, planning his

move. However, when he began, he found his body slow, sluggish. *I'm losing too much blood,* he realized. Still he made the effort and moved forward with all the speed he could muster.

It was almost enough.

He sensed the blows coming and struck out with his *mek'leth,* the blade that had been his father's and his grandfather's. The sword had felled many beasts and a number of green-skins. It was well made and true. In skilled hands it was a powerful weapon. Through it, Gorath felt the power of his ancestors, and yet he did something he had never done before on a hunt, or in battle . . .

Gorath missed. His body, slowed by loss of blood, had failed him.

The blade touched only the air in front of Gurn's face, and then Gorath felt the blows come—one to his right arm, one to his left side. Immediately, he dropped the blade. Yet he kept to his feet. It was a last surprise for Gurn, and Gorath enjoyed seeing it on the coward's face.

Gurn was speaking but Gorath did not bother to decipher the words. Everything slowed. Watching dispassionately, Gorath saw Gurn pull his blade back and strike out with its point. Gorath felt the blow as pressure on the right side of his chest. He looked down and saw that Gurn's blade was actually quite deep inside his body.

Turning his head up, he looked at Gurn's face and saw that the coward was still afraid of him, even as he was tasting victory. With a small measure of satisfaction, Gorath found himself falling. There may have been more blows, but Gorath was beyond feeling then. It was dark and it took great effort for him to continue breathing.

Gorath's failure taunted him. He had failed his people. He had failed his son. His son. Adon's image rose in his mind and comforted him. If there was hope for his people, it lay in his boy. He was still young and Gorath had much he still wished to teach him. Yet, in many ways he was wiser than his father. He would grow to be a better man than Gorath himself.

His son . . .

The final darkness came and Gorath took Adon's face with him on his journey.

Chapter Seven

I.K.S. D'K TAHG
KLINGON SPACE

"First officer Karel, come to the exercise area imme-diately," Captain Koloth's voice boomed through the in-tercom.

Immediately, Karel put his food down and got up from the table.

In the past, a summons from a commander had always led to a reprimand or worse for Karel. Too often, senior officers tried to lead through fear. Well, as first officer, Karel had changed that on this ship. Warriors worked harder and performed better when they were not con-stantly worried about how a commanding officer might punish them for a small mistake or minor offense. Of course, Karel dealt harshly with serious infractions. To do less would invite sloppy performance and, more important, hurt the battle readiness of the ship.

Fortunately, Captain Koloth shared Karel's views on treatment of the crew. Of course, that was not surprising given the fact that, like Karel, Koloth was also a follower of Kahless the Unforgettable. With warriors like Koloth at the helm of its warships, there was hope for the empire, Karel thought. Of course, first, the empire would have to survive the next few months and the inevitable conflict with the Federation. That survival was by no means certain, but Klingons like Koloth would give it at least a fighting chance of not only continuing, but continuing with its honor intact.

Karel entered the training area and was surprised to see it empty, except for Koloth, who was standing in the center of the room. This time of day there should have been at least twenty Klingons perfecting their skills and testing themselves against one another. Something was going on and Karel was immediately alert.

He noted that Koloth was wearing his uniform, not the white *Mok'bara* clothing both he and Karel wore when they trained together. Finally, he saw that his commander was not pleased. Karel stepped toward him, glancing down to see if Koloth was holding a weapon. He was not, but an accomplished warrior did not need a weapon to kill, and Koloth was an accomplished warrior.

"Captain," Karel said, looking into his commander's eyes. He saw murder there.

With lightning speed, Koloth's hand shot out, the back of it making contact with Karel's face. It was a single blow, not hard enough to injure him. Koloth did not attempt another one.

Still, the insult was there and Karel would have to answer it. "Strike me again and I will kill you," he said, keeping his voice even.

"Why wait for my blow? That is your intention, to kill me. Though it is early for you to make a challenge. You have been first officer for mere weeks," Koloth said.

This didn't make any sense, yet he saw the deadly purpose in Koloth's eyes. "I intend no challenge at the moment, honorable or otherwise," Karel said.

The captain studied Karel, looking at his eyes. Koloth seemed surprised by what he saw there: the truth.

"Then it seems we have a different problem. You have been a good first officer and I owe my life, in part, to you, but I will answer treachery as strongly as a challenge."

"Treachery? Captain, I do not know what is going on here," Karel said, not even trying to hide his confusion.

Koloth studied him. "One week ago there was a malfunction in the surveillance system in the computer room when you were alone inside it. Logs outside the room show High Councillor Duras coming and going, yet there is no record of what passed between you. What happened in that room, First Officer Karel?"

"Duras offered to help me make a challenge against you, in return for cooperation with whatever he has planned when we arrive at System 7348." Karel paused for a moment. "I declined his offer."

Karel realized he had erred by not telling Koloth about the encounter. But of course, he could not have had that discussion with his captain. There would be no way to hide from Koloth's sharp eyes that Karel knew

79

more about System 7348 than he could tell his commander. He knew that the Orion mine there had been funded by someone in the High Council.

Koloth saw the conflict on Karel's face. "Why did you not tell me immediately that this had happened?"

Deceit is a twisted path, Karel thought, recalling Kahless's words. Before Karel could respond, Koloth asked, "Does it have to do with the encoded message you received today? Don't bother to answer, your face responds for you. Now, will you tell *me* what is going on?"

Or will we fight until one of us is dead? Karel thought. It was an important question, and for a moment Karel was not sure which path to take. Koloth was an honorable commander who was justifiably concerned about the secrets his first officer was keeping from him.

On the other hand, if Karel told Koloth the truth, his quest for revenge for his brother's death as well as his effort to restore whatever honor he could to the empire could end right here. Though Koloth was a follower of Kahless's path to honor, Karel could not expect him to agree with or join him on his mission.

Two followers of Kahless, two practitioners of the *Mok'bara* fighting art. Karel had no doubt they were nearly evenly matched. It would be an interesting battle . . .

"First Officer Karel, I have a ship to run—or whichever one of us survives this encounter has a ship to run."

In the end, Karel found his decision was simple. "Captain, there are a number of things I wish to tell you."

Koloth seemed surprised by Karel's decision and perhaps pleased. "No wish for a command of your own today?"

"Not today," Karel answered honestly.

"Why?" Koloth asked with interest.

"Because though I may be able to best you in combat, your experience makes you the best possible captain of this ship. And at the moment, the empire needs good, honorable warriors."

That touched something in Koloth. "Yes, we face dark times. And not all dangers are from without. What do you wish to tell me?"

Karel told his captain about the infiltrator program that had sent his brother on a dishonorable mission. He told Koloth about his brother's decisions to stand with the humans and his final, honorable path to *Sto-Vo-Kor.* When that portion of the tale was told, he watched Koloth carefully for a reaction and found nothing but calm interest on his captain's face. Deciding that he had come this far, he told the rest of the tale and described the empire's involvement in the dilithium mine on System 7348, and its later effort to destroy the mine and the planet. Finally, he described the contents of the message he had received earlier informing him that the same member of the High Council was responsible for both the infiltrator program and the near destruction of an entire world full of people of their own blood.

When the tale was told, Koloth simply nodded. "What do you intend to do about all of this?"

"I intend to kill the bloodless coward responsible for my brother's death."

"Even if he is a member of the High Council?"

"I will follow my path to vengeance wherever it leads. My brother's spirit demands it."

Koloth gave Karel a grim smile. "I see that you have

ambitions beyond even command of your own ship."

"Both the honor and future of the empire require action."

"True. We have all seen deceit and dishonor at work in Kahless's empire. There is much work to be done to set it right. I will do what I can to help you in your personal battle, but your allegiance to this ship must remain strong. We will be at System 7348 shortly, and I suspect that Duras is leading us into a slime devil's nest. I will need your full attention on this mission."

"I will do my duty to you and this ship, Captain."

Koloth nodded. "Then, we will see about saving the empire."

Jawer, he said, "Before I tell you what I know about this mission, I would like to welcome Ensign Jawer to the squad. He has served this ship with distinction, earning him a number of decorations and citations for both bravery and creative thinking." Turning to Jawer, Fuller said, "We're lucky to have you, Ensign."

Jawer immediately blushed at the attention. *Damn but they are young,* Fuller thought.

"Now, you all know me from training, and you may know something about my career in Starfleet before I reenlisted. I was a section chief for more than twenty years. I'm telling you that now because I know there can sometimes be resentment in a squad when one member is promoted quickly and assumes command of the team. If any of you have concerns, let's get them out in the open." Fuller paused, waiting for a response from the people in front of him.

"Sir," Ensign Parmet said. "We all know who you are, and I think I can speak for everyone when I say that we are lucky to have you as our commanding officer." There were nods from most of the others, especially from Jawer.

One face, however, remained skeptical, and Ensign McCalmon stepped forward. "Yes, we all know who you are. No one has any doubts about your experience or your leadership skills—the fact is that you were in Starfleet longer than any of us has been alive. However, *I* am concerned about your age. Again, *you were in Starfleet longer than we have been alive.* I am also concerned about the fact that up until a few weeks ago, you had been out of the service for more than two years. Whatever the mission is, it's obviously dangerous. I, for one, would like to know that you are up to it." Her tone was even, with the slightest challenge in it. Fuller knew that Ensign McCalmon was from the Guana province of Earth. She had received high marks in virtually all areas of her training.

Parmet and Jawer seemed mortified. "Sir—" Parmet began, but Fuller silenced him with a wave.

"It's a fair question. And we have to settle any issues quickly because we will be leaving in a few hours. By way of an answer, I will release my recertification and fitness scores to you. Will that satisfy you, Ensign?"

She gave him a thin smile. "Well, I haven't seen the scores yet."

"Fair enough. In the meantime, I can't tell you much about our mission, but I can tell you this much right now: it's a rescue operation of Federation citizens held prisoner in Klingon space."

There was a collective gasp from the group. "We're really going into Klingon space?"

"Yes, a small group of civilians are being held captive by Klingon cargo haulers. Our job is to go in and get them out."

"Is that all, sir?" McCalmon asked wryly.

"That's all for today," Fuller replied. He could see the questions on their faces and held up his hand. "And that's all I can tell you for now, but I wanted you to know that much to prepare yourselves mentally for what we're going to have to do. We'll be leaving soon, but we're still working out the particulars of the mission."

The group nodded and seemed satisfied with his explanation, which was something. It was even true, to a point. They *were* leaving in a few hours and there *were* still details to work out. The problem was that *all* the details still had to be worked out. They didn't even have the beginning of a plan to accomplish the mission.

Fuller had an idea, but he didn't think the captain was going to like it. No, correction, he knew that Captain Kirk was going to hate it.

"I'm going to meet with the captain and Commander Giotto now. I will see you all in the mission briefing in thirty minutes. Dismissed," Fuller said, and the squad headed for the door. As they left, he watched their faces. They were nervous. Hell, they would be fools if they weren't—but they were looking at him with confidence, especially Parmet and Jawer. But instead of buoying Fuller, those looks cut at him.

They would be depending on him to get them through, but the odds on this sort of mission were damned high. The chances were excellent that they wouldn't all make it back, even if they succeeded in their primary objective.

Of course, first things first. Right now, he had a plan to sell to the captain.

When the captain entered the briefing room with Spock, McCoy, Giotto, and Scott, Fuller was already there. They sat quickly, and Kirk turned to Giotto and said, "Does security have a proposal?"

"Yes, sir. It's Mister Fuller's. I'll let him explain it," Giotto said, gesturing to Fuller, who immediately stood.

"The first and most important suggestion is that my team take care of this situation, without having the *Enterprise* cross the Klingon-Federation border."

"What?" the doctor said, expressing the surprise that registered on all the faces but Spock's.

"For a number of reasons, including the very serious

possibility that this may be a trap designed to catch the *Enterprise* or another starship on the Klingon side of the border." Fuller waited for a moment for that to sink in. Of course, everyone at the table knew that the Klingons had set a trap twenty-five years ago at Donatu V. They had destroyed Fuller's ship, and only through courage, ingenuity, and a series of devised miracles was Fuller even standing in this room.

"It is a real possibility," Giotto said.

"You're proposing to complete this mission with a shuttle?" Kirk said. The idea made the captain uneasy. The book said that the smart thing to do would be to use the *Enterprise*'s overwhelming firepower to disable the cargo ship and then board with a small team. The team would still face significant dangers on the Klingon ship, but that course would at least ensure that they reached the target.

"It does increase the risk to our squad, but seriously minimizes the risk to the ship," Fuller said.

"Tell me what you have in mind, Michael," the captain said, knowing that he would not like the answer.

"I propose we outfit a shuttle with external phaser banks." Fuller saw nods from the men there. Shuttles didn't normally carry weapons, but phasers were a relatively simple retrofit.

"Will shuttle-based phasers be enough to disable the Klingon freighter?" Kirk said.

"Hard to say for sure." Then Fuller leaned down near Spock's station and hit a button. Immediately the image of a Klingon merchant vessel appeared on the briefing-room viewscreen. "We don't know the exact model of the ship we will be facing, but this is one of the most common types known to operate in that sector of space. Generally speaking, Klingon haulers are much more heavily armed and shielded than analogous Federation vessels."

"You could get out there and find that your phasers won't penetrate their shields," Scott said.

"True, but that's why I propose affixing a single external photon torpedo to the shuttle and use that to get past their shields. The phasers will take care of the rest. Then we can board and rescue the hostages," Fuller said.

"You can't be serious," McCoy said.

"I am, Doctor. This not only will protect the *Enterprise*, but it will help us maintain a greater safety margin for the hostages. If it's a trap, the Klingons will be waiting for a starship. And the moment the *Enterprise* steps over the border, it would light up every sensor and relay in the sector. However, a shuttle may be able to get in undetected. Even if it isn't a trap, the cargo ship would see the *Enterprise* coming at a much greater distance, giving them time to kill off the hostages. A shuttle can take them by surprise and then keep them too occupied to act against the hostages."

Fuller watched Kirk, deep in thought.

"Jim . . . ," the doctor began.

"It is a logical way to minimize risk to this ship and the hostages," Spock said.

"What about the security team?" McCoy asked.

"The risk to them will be greater, with too many variables to calculate odds with any accuracy," Spock said.

"These are human beings we'd be sending out there, not variables," McCoy nearly shouted.

Kirk silenced the discussion with a raised hand. He

understood the doctor's concerns; the problem was that there was no way to conduct a rescue operation like this one without significant risks. "Is it technically possible? Mister Scott? Can you outfit a shuttle with phasers and a torpedo quickly?"

"Aye, the phasers are simple enough. They will be relatively low power, but the shuttle will be able to maintain them nearly indefinitely," Scott said. "The trick is the torpedo. I can rig a containment field tied into shuttle power, but you won't have a launch mechanism."

"A simple release is all I need," Fuller said.

"Aye." Scott nodded.

"In English please," McCoy said.

The chief engineer said, "We can rig a torpedo to the shuttle with a manual-release mechanism. In space, they point the shuttle at the target, release the torpedo, and pull away. The problem is that they will have to get very close to do it and will only have one shot."

"We only need one. The Klingons wouldn't likely grant us a second chance anyway," Fuller said.

"The other problem is that the containment field will not last for very long. It will also be a drain on the shuttle. You'll have enough power to reach the cargo ship and perhaps a twenty-minute safety margin. If there's a delay, you'll have to release the torpedo or risk having the field fail." Scott didn't have to explain further. Kirk knew that if the containment field that separated the matter and anti-matter in an armed torpedo failed, the torpedo would immediately detonate. If that happened with the torpedo still attached to the shuttle, a cleanup crew would be able to fit the remaining pieces of the vessel inside a small cup.

"Or, if the shuttle is hit by weapons fire and there is a

sudden interruption in the shuttle's power, it would lose containment," Spock added.

Before McCoy could voice another complaint, Kirk turned to Giotto and said, "Commander?"

"I'm also uncomfortable with the risk to the team, but it does give the *Enterprise* and the hostages the best chance. It's not a good option, it's just the best one we have."

Kirk decided quickly. "How much time do you need to outfit the shuttle?"

"To give you a reasonable safety margin? More time than we have. However, I can have her ready to launch in ninety minutes," Scott said, already getting to his feet.

"Dismissed, Mister Scott," Kirk said, also rising. "Mister Spock, how long until the *Enterprise* is in position?"

"Thirty minutes," his first officer answered.

"Mister Fuller, do you have a qualified command pilot on your squad?" Kirk said.

"Yes, sir."

"Get your people ready then," Kirk said, and Fuller was out the door.

The captain was sure he was doing the right thing. He had taken an oath to protect Federation citizens, and he would not sacrifice them to protect the Federation from a theoretical danger, no matter how inevitable it seemed. However, until now, he had expected to take at least part of the risk of the operation himself—to the extent that the entire ship would help effect the rescue. Now, however, he would be sending seven people on a small vessel—a vessel designed for short trips in space and hops down to a planet from orbit—and sending them into enemy territory to take on a larger and better-armed ship.

His instinct was to lead the rescue himself, but given

the larger threat the Federation still faced from the empire, he could not justify that action. What Fuller had proposed was logical, the best possible plan under the circumstances, and Michael Fuller was arguably the best man in Starfleet to lead the team.

Nevertheless, Kirk found that none of those truths gave him the slightest bit of comfort.

Fuller assembled his squad in the shuttlebay where Scott and his team were already working on the shuttle. He quickly briefed his people on the mission. There were a few surprised gasps of breath, but he finished without interruption.

"Let me get this straight," McCalmon said. "We're going to invade the Klingon Empire in a *shuttlecraft?*"

Fuller gave her a thin smile. "Technically, yes, but our objective is not a full-scale invasion, just a simple rescue."

"Perhaps we can conduct a full-scale invasion when the rescue is finished, no?" Ensign Quatrocchi said with a full smile. Quatrocchi was from Italy and spoke English with a moderate accent.

"We are not currently authorized to extend the parameters of our mission, but I will take that suggestion up with the captain," Fuller said, returning the ensign's smile. "We had a saying years ago. Shuttles are good for exactly two things: going slow and getting lost. Today, we are going to try to add a third capability to that list. I won't kid you, there is a strong element of risk here. If anyone doesn't feel comfortable with the mission, now is the time to speak up." He turned his attention to McCalmon. "Ensign, I trust you have had time to review my recertification records."

"Yes, and, as you know, you would be near the top of *this* year's graduating class. I'm comfortable with you, and I'm satisfied with the risk. However, I *do* have a problem with the people we're going out to rescue."

Parmet looked stricken and ready to say something, but Fuller raised his hand to silence the young man. Fuller didn't expect or want blind obedience—at least not until the mission started. If there were questions, better to get them out in the open now.

"You've been reading up on the Anti-Federation League, then?" Fuller said.

"Yes, and I had some experience with them in San Francisco during one of their anti-Starfleet demonstrations." Some of the others nodded, and Fuller could see that she was just saying what everyone was thinking. "They hate the Federation and everything it stands for. However, to be fair, they seem to hate Starfleet even more. And, according to the mission data we've seen, they are in Klingon space in violation of a number of laws and regulations. And their self-styled peace mission is foolish at best, and treasonous at worst. If I'm reading this situation correctly, we'll be risking our lives to save people who hate our guts."

"You obviously have strong feelings about these people. Do you think that would compromise your ability to fulfill your duties?" Fuller asked.

"Not at all, sir, but I simply wanted to make it clear that I think our friends in the Klingon's hands . . . well, I don't like them, sir," McCalmon said.

From the nods in the rest of the squad, Fuller could see that the others agreed with her.

"Noted, Ensign. We have to respect the infinite diversity we encounter, but we are under no obligation to like everyone we meet. Consider this an opportunity to reach out to people who may just need to get to know Starfleet better."

"With all due respect, sir, I think the minds in the Anti-Federation League are pretty well made up with regard to Starfleet."

"You're probably right, but I did say that we would be facing some pretty tough odds here," Fuller replied.

That done, they went over the mission again. When Fuller was finished, Jawer asked, "Sir, will you be flying the shuttle?"

Fuller shook his head. "No, we have a more highly rated command pilot in the squad. Ensign Quatrocchi, you just volunteered."

The tall ensign nodded. "Yes, sir."

"You are rated on this model shuttle, but understand that additions to the external configuration will change the mass distribution. I want you to log some time on a simulator—as soon as Lieutenant Sulu finishes working one up for you."

"Yes, sir."

"Until then, you can all join me in the armory. We're going to pick up training phasers and get to work," Fuller said.

Chapter Nine

**ORION-BUILT MINING FACILITY
SYSTEM 7348
FEDERATION SPACE**

ADON HAD JUST FINISHED with a simulation when he heard a noise outside the computer center. The smile died on his face and he was immediately on his feet. A moment later, one of the clan came running in. It was his uncle, his father's younger brother. The man's face was twisted by . . . what? Fear? Grief?

"There's been an . . . ," his uncle said, faltering when his eyes found Adon's. "It's your father."

Moving before the words had fully registered, Adon asked, "Where?" as he headed for the door.

"They will reach the village in a few moments."

Adon raced through the halls, with his people trailing behind him. He picked up a few details on the way:

94

there had been an accident, his father had been hurt.

What kind of accident could Father have had at a clan meeting? a voice in his head asked.

An attack, he replied to himself. That is what Uncle was going to say. His father had been attacked, probably by an animal. There were predators on their world, but they rarely ventured close to the villages—having learned long ago that they would more likely find death than a meal in Adon's people.

But there is no more dangerous predator than Father, Adon thought.

Something was wrong. *Father must be badly hurt,* he thought. Adon ran faster for the village. Even if he was hurt, Father was strong. And the green-skins had left more than weapons and mining machines. There was equipment for treating injury and illness. Father would recover.

Unless he's already . . . , the voice in his head began, but Adon silenced it before it could finish. Finally, he reached the outer residences and raced on to the center of the village where a small crowd was gathering. He recognized one of Gurn's people there, which made him shudder. Before he could even make an inquiry, he saw movement ahead. Someone was coming. No, not someone—*two* someones—and they were carrying a third person.

Father . . . , he thought, and raced for them.

As he arrived, Gurn and one of his clan placed Adon's father on the ground. They did it slowly, almost reverentially. Something was wrong with that. If father was hurt, he needed attention. They needed to move quickly. He might need the green-skins' machines.

"Father," Adon gasped out loud as he got down on his knees.

The wounds were terrible. There were bites on his hands and chest, as well as one on his throat.

"Help me get him to the mine," Adon said desperately as he pulled on his father's arm. There was something wrong. Father felt too heavy, and the others weren't moving. He felt a hand on his shoulder and turned to see Gurn looking down at him.

"He is dead. I am sorry, young Adon." For an irrational moment, Adon wanted to kill the clan leader for speaking such a deplorable lie about his father. Gorath couldn't be dead. The clan needed him, especially now . . .

. . . and Adon needed him.

Adon felt his control start to crumble, but he forced himself to his feet and looked at Gurn. The man was wearing a crude bandage on his face. Looking around, Adon saw the clan leader's other men had also been injured.

"What happened?" he asked sharply.

"After the clan meeting, we heard a struggle and ran to see your father battling three *quoth*. He fought bravely and we tried to help him. Together, we fought off the beasts, but it was too late for your father." Gurn put his hand on Adon's shoulder. "I am sorry, son."

Reflexively, Adon shook off the hand and looked up at Gurn suspiciously. His blood was calling out a warning. Then he saw something, a line of blood under the bandage on Gurn's face. *A straight line of blood*—from a straight wound, the kind made by a blade not a bite.

His eyes automatically searched out his father's

mek'leth, which was lying on his chest. Kneeling down, Adon saw blood there. Of course there was no way to tell if the blood was from the beasts.

Or was there?

Yet the sight of his father's bloody and torn body soon pushed all other thoughts aside, and Adon felt his control disappear. Sobs racked his body as he clutched his father.

Adon finally agreed to allow his father's body to be moved from the clearing. Along with Uncle and three of his father's closest companions, Adon carried his father to their home. Two of Adon's own companions joined them there.

He fought down his grief and worked with his uncle to prepare his father's body. Cleaning his father, he saw that the wounds were terrible. Yet, dressed in his departing robes, Gorath looked as if he might simply be asleep. That thought brought a fresh well of grief that threatened Adon's scant control. In truth, he was simply a boy who desperately needed his father to tell him what to do. He needed his father to get up from the table and tell him that it had all been a terrible mistake. Then he needed his father to set this great wrong to right.

Yet his father was still as he lay on the table in the center of their home. Uncle and those who were closest to Adon and Gorath performed the departing ritual. When it was done, his uncle put a hand on Adon's shoulder as they sat. Adon was tempted to fall into his uncle's embrace and wait through the night with them.

When one of their people died, those closest to the family had the duty of keeping vigil to see the departed off during the first night. The next day, there would be visitors to receive and then a burial. Of course, that was under normal circumstances, and what had happened here was far from normal.

And the danger that had claimed his father was far from passed and might well swallow the entire clan, if not their entire world. If Adon had his father's strength, he would be on his feet immediately setting the wrong right and getting his revenge.

He said a quick prayer to the man that had been his father and clan leader. No great wisdom came to him, but he found that he was able to stand—on what could only have been strength borrowed from his father. He looked at Gorath's still form and realized that the great man was gone. He might not have his father's strength, but he would have to make do with what he had.

The others looked at him expectantly, as if they had seen something on his face. Finally Uncle said, "What is it, Adon?"

"My father has been murdered." Adon was surprised at the calm in his voice. He chalked that up to a parting gift from Gorath.

"The *quoth* are beasts," Uncle said.

"It was not beasts that murdered Gorath." Then Adon told the others what he had seen and what he now suspected.

"Gurn is capable of this, I am certain," Uncle said finally. "But to move against him the way things are now, we need to be sure."

"The green-skins' machines can tell us if the blood on my father's sword is a beast's or a man's," Adon said. "I will go alone to the mine and find the truth."

"You will go nowhere alone," Uncle said as the six men around him rose.

"It will not go unnoticed. There will be talk if we all leave during the ritual," Adon said.

"There has been much worse than talk here today, and there will be much worse yet," Uncle said.

The men went quickly to their homes and retrieved their own *mek'leths,* and returned to Adon.

"We served your father. We will serve you," Uncle said seriously.

There were nods of assent from the other men. It was absurd, of course. Gorath was a great man. Adon was simply his son and the one who happened to be left alive. Yet, the others were looking at him as if they were seeing some of his father in him. Well, Adon knew the truth, but he simply nodded his thanks.

"Adon!" a voice called out as a figure came running across the center of the village. It was Bethe who came to a stop in front of them, eyeing them seriously. She took particular interest in the swords they wore. "What are you doing?"

"For the moment, nothing," Adon said.

Bethe raised her eyebrows at that but said only, "Gurn has called an emergency meeting of the clan leaders."

"Not of *all* the clan leaders," Uncle said. Technically, of course, Adon was the new clan leader, but that was simply too much to comprehend.

"He said he did not want to bother you in your time of grief," Bethe said.

"Well, these are dangerous times. I will have to go to this emergency meeting," Adon said, keeping his voice as even as he could.

"Adon, what are you really doing? What is really going on here?" Bethe wasn't the only one who had noticed Adon and his group outside. Villagers were peeking out from their homes. They all knew something was happening.

"Tell everyone to wait until I get back. I will explain then," Adon said.

Bethe nodded and seemed to accept that, for which Adon was grateful. If they were lucky, Adon and his small circle would take care of Gurn and his men quickly and quietly. Then, when the crisis had passed, he could reveal all.

Heading for the meeting place, Adon felt his blood burning. Before the night was over, he would know the truth and he would have his revenge. But before they were halfway there, Adon heard someone approaching from behind. It was Bethe. When she was close enough, she said, "The villagers await your return and your news. You must know, they will follow the son of Gorath wherever his path leads."

Looking down, Adon saw that Bethe was wearing a *mek'leth* of her own. He shook his head. "What are you doing?"

"I am following the son of Gorath wherever—"

He shook his head. "Return to the village."

"No," she said evenly.

"I thought you would follow me," Adon said, frustration in his voice.

"I serve your interests, not your will," Bethe said pleasantly.

"There is a difference?"

"Of course."

"A small one I think." Adon looked at the path ahead and realized that he had no time to argue with Bethe. In fact, he had a much larger battle to fight. And while he would have preferred to have her out of danger, he did need the help. He shrugged and continued toward the clan meeting place.

His blood began to call out a warning, and Adon walked faster, then trotted, then ran. The group burst into the meeting pit to see the surprised faces of clan leaders and their seconds. Most surprised was Gurn, who had a dozen men around him—all of them, Adon noted, armed with Orion pistols and swords.

"Young Adon, what are you doing here?" Gurn's voice was even, almost pleasant, and it took every bit of strength Adon possessed not to race forward and strike down his father's murderer. The guards would not allow it. It was not fear for himself that stopped him, but fear that he would fail. Adon vowed that he would have his revenge, even if it could not be at this moment.

"Why are you calling a meeting of the clans?" Adon asked, ignoring Gurn's question. Then Adon noticed that at four points surrounding the pit green-skin flying craft were hovering in the air. Father had taught Adon to pilot those craft, which were flying platforms with room for a single standing pilot with a large cannon mounted in the front. Gorath and Uncle had taken some of the craft from the Orions and used them in the battle to save the planet.

Now, four of Gurn's clan were standing on the vehicles that watched the skies, pointing out toward the surrounding woods. Adon noted with distaste that the pilots were wearing the Orion armored suits and helmets that covered their faces completely.

"You wear pistols and bring those green-skin weapons to our meeting place?" Adon did not bother to try to hide the challenge in his voice.

"I have just told the great leaders of our people that we are in grave danger. I would have summoned you, but I knew you were standing vigil with your father," Gurn said, his voice and face losing none of their false pleasantness.

"I serve my father's clan, and if there is a grave danger, I will help deal with it," Adon said.

"Very well. Before your father died, we were discussing an offer by the Klingons to talk with them and seek their further help and protection."

"You would talk to the ones who tried to destroy us and the world beneath our feet?" Adon said.

"You are young and will learn that things are not always as they first appear. The Klingons have provided us with new information to prove that the humans are the ones who sent the green-skins here," Gurn said. Before Adon could protest, Gurn continued, "Before your father died, we voted to turn the Klingons away, which we were content to do with Gorath's wisdom and strength to guide us. However, with Gorath dead, we must look to new places for security. So we will meet with the Klingons tomorrow and hear what they have to say."

"No, my father has made his wishes clear," Adon said.

"And he was very persuasive earlier, but things have changed and the clan leaders now speak with one voice."

"Interesting that they all speak with *your* voice, Gurn."

To that open challenge, Gurn only smiled. "Go home, young Adon. You have lost your father tonight and we have all lost a great friend and a great leader. If you would take your father's place at our council, you will have to accept the will of the majority—as your father did."

Adon cursed himself. He had come for revenge and found that, for Gurn, murdering Gorath was just the beginning. He was bringing back the people who'd tried to leave their world a dead pile of rocks—all for a few worthless crystals.

And for this confrontation, Adon had brought only a few clansmen with swords. He should have seen the danger and brought the green-skin pistols his father kept in the house. Then he could have killed Gurn before anyone could stop him. It was a mistake his father would not have made. Of course, Adon reminded himself, he was not his father. And now their whole people would pay for his error.

Still, there was hope. He could still redeem himself and put a stop to this madness. First he would have to get to the mine and use the green-skins' equipment to show his clan that it was Gurn's blood on his father's *mek'leth*. Then he could convince the other clans of Gurn's treachery. Yet he would have to work fast. The Klingons were coming tomorrow and he knew in his blood that all of the clans would have to be united to face them.

In disgust, Adon turned to his people and said, "Come, we have much to do." Gurn said something as they left, but Adon was past hearing it. Soon they were racing to the mine. There, he knew, was the means to reveal the truth about Gurn as well as the means to defend their people.

When they arrived at the mine entrance, Adon was

surprised to see that the small group of his clansmen who were supposed to be keeping watch inside the mine were outside. "What is it?" he called out.

"Gurn's people came and . . . forced us out," one of the women said. She had a wound on her forehead. In fact, most of them had minor wounds. She shrugged apologetically. "We fought, but they had pistols. They have told us that we will not be allowed back inside until it is safe. They spoke about a coming crisis."

"There is, but it is one of Gurn's own making. I believe Gurn killed my father to bring the Klingons here."

"What do you want of us?" the woman asked.

"For now, just stand with me. Let's see if Gurn's men have the courage to stand against Gorath's will." Adon led the now larger group to the mine's heavy doors. A dozen of Gurn's clansmen were standing by, all of them wearing swords and about half of them carrying pistols.

"Stand aside for the son of Gorath," Adon said.

"No," one of the guards said. Their leader, Adon guessed.

"The mine belongs to all of our people. It was my father's will, it was the will of the council."

"Gurn has given us orders. We must take charge for now," the guard said.

"Nevertheless, stand aside."

"We respected your father, his courage and his strength. But now he is dead and Gurn will lead all of our people. We do not wish to harm the son of Gorath, but we will kill you if we must."

For a moment Adon considered fighting. He knew his people would fight beside him. The battle would be short and bloody—and would no doubt end in their defeat. He cursed himself for failing once again. He should have come to the mine first, before Gurn could secure it. He had already suspected Gurn was a murderer. He should have seen this move coming as his father would have.

Turning, he led his clanspeople back toward the village. There was still a way to defeat Gurn's cowardly treachery. His father had faced worse odds against the green-skins and had prevailed.

And while he was not the man that his father was, he would have to become one, and quickly, or all of their people would likely perish.

Chapter Ten

**CARGO VESSEL *B'ARDAQ*
KLINGON SPACE**

CHRISTINE WOKE UP with a start, having no idea how long she had slept. The Klingons had kept them in low light with no distinction between night and day. As soon as she woke, she got to her feet. The deck was cool and leeched away her body heat when she slept on the floor. She was still wearing the short nightgown she had thrown on before they had been attacked by the Klingons. All four of them were dressed for bed, not imprisonment in a small, cold cell on a Klingon ship.

Four of them.

There had been six. There should have been six, but Tomas had died in the attack. It was a miracle that they all hadn't been killed. The ship had nearly been torn apart. She was no technician, but she had immediately seen that her father's prize would never fly again.

Still, incredibly, there had been five of them left alive, but Max had been injured. Christine had seen that one of his shinbones had broken and was protruding from his torn skin. He was also moaning and holding his stomach.

He did not moan for long.

One of the Klingons had kicked him to turn him over, examined him for a moment, then plunged a three-bladed knife into his chest. Christine's screams had earned her a hard blow to the face that cut the screaming short.

Other than murdering Max, the Klingons had not mistreated them. At least, the Klingons hadn't hurt them any more. Christine and the others had been beamed aboard this ship and quickly ushered into this room, a room just large enough that they could all lie down at the same time, if they did it carefully.

A few moments after Christine got to her feet, Alan woke, followed by Arleen and Cyndy. They tended to sleep and wake at the same time—their proximity made it virtually impossible to do anything else.

Looking down, Christine saw that the worms in the four bowls had stopped moving. Each day—at least Christine assumed it was each day—the Klingons brought them four bowls of worms. The word they used for it sounded like *gak*. But none of them had been able to eat the squirming meal. The next day, the worms would be dead and the Klingons would take them away and replace them with a fresh bowl.

Their captors also brought them glasses full of liquid that was warm and looked like blood. It tasted strong and bitter, but Christine and the others drank it, deciding not to think about what it might be. It must have been giving her some nourishment. Still, the two days without food were taking their toll. The ache in her stomach was constant now. And she felt physically weak and light-headed.

"Anyone want mine? I'm not hungry." Arleen was the only one still able to make jokes. However, no one either laughed or smiled.

Finally, Christine said, "Alan, we have to do something."

"Do something?" he asked.

"We need real food. We need to talk to someone about . . . about what is going to happen to us, about what they are planning."

"I don't think they mean any harm with the food. I think it's what they eat themselves," Alan said, shrugging.

"Yes, but *we* can't eat it. And while they might not mean harm with the food, they certainly meant harm when they murdered Max, so I, for one, would like to know what their plans are for the rest of us." Christine heard the frustration in her voice. Remarkably, it was the first emotion she had shown since the scream-stopping slap.

"I don't know if you've noticed, but they only speak Klingon and they seem to have no interest in talking to us," Alan said.

"We have to do something!"

Alan looked at Christine blankly. He had worn that

same expression since things had gone so horribly wrong. She realized now what the expression was: defeat.

Under her gaze, Alan shrugged. "Okay, maybe it's time we talk to the concierge about the service." For a moment there was a flash of his old bravado. Christine found that it simply annoyed her now.

Walking two steps to the door, Alan lifted his fist, and with more strength than Christine felt she had, he pounded on the door several times. He waited a few seconds, then did it again. Before he could do it a third time, the door opened and one of their captors stepped in and shouted something in his language.

"We don't understand you because you killed the only one of us that spoke Klingon," Alan said. "But I need to speak to someone in charge immediately. You can bring a translator if you have to, but we need to start communicating right now!"

The Klingon looked at him with surprise, then disappeared into the hallway. A few moments later the door opened again, and another Klingon, the one who had killed Max, stepped into the room.

"What do you want?" the Klingon barked out.

"So, you *do* speak English," Alan said.

"Obviously," the Klingon said.

"Why haven't you talked to us?" Alan asked.

"I have nothing to say to Earthers. You are fortunate that I suffer your continued existence on my ship."

"Well, we have things to say to you. I think there has been a misunderstanding here."

"There has been no misunderstanding. You were in Klingon space and we apprehended you."

"But we were on a peace mission. We *are* on a peace

mission. We've come to talk to your leaders," Alan said.

"You insult me by speaking of *peace*," the Klingon said, making the word a curse.

"I don't think you know who we are. We are no friends of the Federation, we're on your side—"

"I know *exactly* who you are. You belong to a group called the Anti-Federation League, traitors to your own people. I have learned much about your cowardly and treacherous people. But you, you stand against those of your own blood. I thought there was nothing lower than Starfleet. I see that I was wrong." The Klingon spat on the floor and turned to go.

Christine felt dizzy. Things were even worse now. "Wait, what is going to happen to us?"

The Klingon turned and looked at her. "You are being given to a Klingon military vessel for interrogation."

"There's no need to interrogate us. We came here because we *want* to talk!" Alan said.

"We shall see."

"I demand to talk to a representative of your government immediately," Alan said.

"You will talk to the Klingon Defense Force interrogators. Perhaps if you impress them and survive the interrogation, they will consider your request." The Klingon laughed and turned for the door.

What happened next surprised Christine more than anything else since the beginning of this trip. Alan lunged forward and grabbed the Klingon by the shoulder. "I demand you release—"

Almost faster than Christine's eye could follow, the Klingon turned and grabbed Alan by the forearm and gave it a sharp downward tug. Christine heard the bones snap and saw Alan's look of stunned surprise. Before Alan could even cry out, the Klingon grabbed his other arm and did the same thing.

Alan screamed and slumped back into Arleen's and Cyndy's arms. The Klingon sneered, "I have been charged with delivering you alive. That means that you will eat the food we give you or you will suffer the consequences." Then he disappeared out the door, which closed behind him.

Christine immediately turned to Alan, who was slumped against the wall, his arms hanging limply in front of him. Even in the dim light, she could see that they were both broken, seriously, at the forearm.

"Alan . . . ," she said as she approached him. His face was set in pain and he moaned as she reached out to touch him. As gently as she could, she took him by the shoulders. "Slide down so you can sit."

It took a moment for what she had said to register with him. Finally, he nodded, and the other three of them helped him into a sitting position. Alan slipped the last few inches and screamed when he hit the ground. Through gritted teeth, he managed to get his arms into position on his lap.

They will have to be set, Christine thought, but that would have to wait. There was something they needed to do first, before the Klingon came back. Clearly, the Klingons wouldn't hesitate to hurt them badly. They needed their strength.

So we can last longer when they torture us? a voice in her mind asked. She silenced the voice through force of will. All she could worry about was the here and now, which was plenty, as far as she was concerned.

"We have to eat, now," she said, surprised at the strength in her voice.

"I can't, not that," Cyndy said.

"We have no choice. I'll go first." Christine grabbed a small handful of the squirming mass in the bowl and, without thinking, forced it into her mouth. She didn't chew and swallowed quickly, surprised when she didn't retch. Well, she was hungry. The next handful went down even easier, the next easier still.

Chapter Eleven

U.S.S. ENTERPRISE
FEDERATION-KLINGON BORDER

CAPTAIN KIRK STEPPED ONTO the deck of the shuttlebay, and immediately Fuller and the squad stood at attention. Kirk crossed the distance and took in the group of men and women he was sending out into the unknown. Correction, he was sending them into dangers he knew and understood all too well. They were all young, except for Fuller, of course.

Kirk had sent Fuller's son to defend Starbase 42 and Sam had not come back. Would Sam's father come back? The odds were at least fair that he would not. However, on the surface, the mission was logical—Spock had certainly thought so.

Every member of Starfleet took an oath to protect and defend the citizens of the Federation. That oath now

113

Kevin Ryan

required that they attempt a rescue. And a small team had the best chance of getting to the hostages before the Klingons could kill them. Yes, it was well reasoned and perfectly logical. Nevertheless, some of the seven people in front of Kirk would likely die in what might be a completely vain attempt to rescue people who were already dead.

Logic was enough for Spock, but Kirk found it a cold comfort now. And it would be of no comfort to the families of any of these men and women who were lost. The captain, of course, allowed none of what he was thinking or feeling to show on his face. Instead, he simply nodded to Giotto, who said, "Squad is ready for inspection, Captain."

Kirk made eye contact with each member of the squad. He and Fuller went back years. Jawer had served on the ship for months, but the others he had met only briefly. "Mister Fuller, are you and your people ready?" Kirk said.

"Yes, sir. As soon as you give the word, Captain."

"The word is given, Michael," Kirk said, shaking Fuller's hand. Stepping back, Kirk addressed the whole squad. "This ship, Starfleet, and the Federation owe you all our thanks." Kirk would have liked to say more and he suspected the squad might benefit from more of a pep talk, but he knew time was short. "I will leave you in Mister Fuller's capable hands. Good luck." Then he headed with Giotto to the shuttlebay lift that would take them to the observation booth.

With the captain gone, Fuller turned to the squad and ordered, "Suits, now." He picked up his own silver EVA suit from the container and slipped into it. Like most experienced security officers, he didn't much care for working in the suits. Though relatively lightweight, they still restricted one's movements and slowed reactions during missions where small fractions of a second could mean the difference between life and death.

However, on this mission, the suits were a necessity. And there was no point in delaying putting them on. The seven of them could suit up inside the shuttle, in flight, but it would be awkward in the confined space. They would wait, however, to put on the helmets until the last possible moment.

When everyone was set, he said, "Check your weapons. Make sure each is set to heavy stun only." Then he reached down to test the two phasers that he wore on each side of his suit. He was a firm believer that too much firepower was not enough. For a ground assault, he preferred phaser rifles, but the rifles would limit their mobility in the confines of a ship. The Mark II phaser pistols they carried were more than powerful enough. If set too high, they could breach the hull of the ship they would board, possibly ending the mission for all of them.

Each member of the squad checked in, and Fuller gave the shuttle a final visual inspection. The shuttle was boxy, a far cry from the sleek, long-legged beauty of the starship that housed it. Chief Engineer Scott's additions, which had been welded onto the roof of the craft, made it look downright ungainly.

Yet those additions might be what allowed them to return to the ship. The oblong torpedo would have to work if they were ever going to get inside the Klingon freighter. The addition of the class 1 probe—which sat

Kevin Ryan

beside the torpedo—had been Scott's idea, and it had been a good one. It was rare enough to encounter an engineer who was able to give you exactly what you needed. To find an engineer who gave you things you hadn't even thought to ask for was remarkable indeed.

"Sir, should we board now?" a voice asked from behind him. Fuller turned and saw Lieutenant Eileen Caruso standing three meters from him. He nearly smiled with pleasure before he remembered that Caruso had died a full twenty-five years before at the Battle of Donatu V. It was impossible. Fuller blinked and Caruso disappeared, replaced by Ensign McCalmon—who, with her dark skin, didn't look anything like Caruso had when the lieutenant was alive. Caruso had died young, but she had lived long enough to save Fuller's life on board a dying ship.

"Yes, Ensign. Everyone on board," he said. As he waited for the others, he berated himself. After he'd got James Kirk's message about Sam's death, he had seen his son in crowds for weeks. Caruso was a new trick of his subconscious. Would he start to see them all now. Andrews? Woods? Captain Shannon?

He couldn't afford to lose his grip now. His squad was depending on him. He had to complete this mission because Sam was also depending on him. His son was calling out for justice. Fuller knew that justice would not be served by confronting the Klingons on board the cargo ship, but he had to survive the encounter so that it could be served later. He had no doubt that the time would come, and quickly, when he would face a bigger force than a handful of Klingon civilians.

He had to reassert control. As he stepped into the shuttle, Fuller found himself thinking about Ben Finney.

116

They had served together years ago, along with a young officer named James T. Kirk. They had seen a few things in those days. Some of those things still visited Fuller in his dreams.

Finney had, on the other hand, left an essential part of himself on one of those missions—though no one had realized it then. In fact, Finney had seemed fine until years later when he had lost his own battle for control and had tried to frame Kirk for murder. Fuller found himself wondering if Finney had started seeing people from the old days before the final break came.

Taking the copilot seat, Fuller began running the pre-flight check and pushed all of the thoughts out of his mind. He was surprised at how easy it was. For now, the mission was everything. The young lives in this shuttle were depending on him.

Scott was looking over the shuttledeck officer's shoulder when Kirk and Giotto entered. Immediately, the small room was overcrowded. Nevertheless, none of them would be anywhere else at this moment.

Except for the shuttle, the shuttlebay was clear. Mister Kyle stepped out onto the empty deck carrying a long pole. "We have to arm the torpedo manually," Scott said.

Kirk understood. Rigging an arming mechanism in the shuttle wouldn't make sense for a single torpedo. Kyle touched the torpedo with the device, hit a switch on the staff, then backed away. As soon as he was clear, the shuttlebay officer hit a button on the control panel and a light came on telling them that the bay was de-pressurizing. Though it took less than a minute, for Kirk the process seemed agonizingly slow.

Finally, the light turned to green, and immediately the bay doors began to open. Kirk leaned down and hit the button on the intercom and said, "Good luck, Mister Fuller."

"Yes, sir. Thank you, sir. Fuller out."

The shuttlecraft lifted slowly off the deck and headed out into space.

Bring them back, Michael, Kirk thought. *Bring them all back.*

Parrish watched the shuttle launch from the viewer in the security office. She had thought about seeing the squad off, but had decided against it. They needed to focus on their mission and adjust to their new leader. Saying good-bye might have helped Parrish, but it would not have been good for the squad.

I should be in there with them, Parrish thought. She should be leading the squad. Even though Fuller was more than qualified, leading this mission should have been her responsibility. And because she wasn't there, Jawer had gone. Jawer, who had survived missions where most of the people around him had died. He was the last survivor, besides Parrish, of her first squad—the one led by Sam Fuller.

If Jawer died, would it be Parrish's fault? It would be easy to lose herself in such speculation, but the captain's words kept coming back to her. "Risk is our business," he had said on more than one occasion. And in the discussion about this mission he was adamant that the Federation "will not compromise who we are even if it means risking our larger survival."

Jon had not sacrificed who he was—a brave and honorable man—even when it meant betraying his mission for the Klingon Empire and his own people. As a security officer, it had been her job to protect people. That position was essential to who *she* was. If she decided not to have this baby, she could continue the service—a service that was needed now more than ever.

But to do that she would be sacrificing whatever was left of Jon in this galaxy, and whatever was left of what they had shared, which was also part of who she was. It was then that she realized that there was one more life that she could protect.

After endless days and nights of agonizing over what to do, Parrish found that her decision was quite simple in the end. It wouldn't just change a few things, it would change everything. The doctor had already told her that there would be complications and a danger to her. Well, she had faced danger before.

Parrish got up and headed for sickbay.

Chapter Twelve

I.K.S. D'K TAHG
FEDERATION-KLINGON BORDER

WHILE KAREL HEADED TO the bridge, he had to resist the impulse to run. Given the current situation with the Federation, he knew that each summons by his commander might mean the start of serious trouble for the ship. What that danger might mean for the empire was another matter—one he had had to put aside to concentrate on the most immediate dangers. And topping that list was Councillor Duras and whatever he was planning for System 7348.

Just a few weeks ago, Orions working for someone on the Klingon High Council had tried to destroy that world. Now, they were headed there to . . . what? The official story was that they were going to start talks with the biological Klingons on the second planet to enter the empire. Even if that was true, it was the smallest part of the reason.

The obvious answer was the dilithium, which the empire badly needed for its war effort. But it was impossible to be sure of anything with Duras, who had shown himself to be both treacherous and dishonorable. Would he sacrifice the Klingons on the surface to get what he wanted to fuel his dishonorable war? Certainly. What of the *D'k Tahg* and its crew?

That Duras had yet to fully reveal his plans told Karel that whatever danger he posed to the ship might come from any direction. Karel had faced difficult battle before, fights that had taken the lives of most of the warriors around him. He neither hesitated nor flinched from danger he could see and could fight. But this, this was intolerable. It worried him like no honest battle had ever done.

After Karel had told Koloth the truth about what he had learned of his brother's fate and what it meant for the empire, Karel had felt a brief period of relief. He knew now that he had a partner in his fight. However, he also knew that they might soon be fighting a member of the High Council as well as the Federation.

Entering the bridge, he saw Koloth in his seat. The captain looked well, but Karel knew that this mission was taking a toll on him. Koloth now left the bridge only for brief periods to eat and sleep.

What they were about to do would worry any commander entering a battle, and Karel had no doubt they were, in fact, entering a battle. But what sort of battle? And against whom?

Koloth acknowledged him with a nod. "Councillor

Duras will be arriving shortly. He has an announcement for us." The captain's tone was flat, but no one on the bridge had to wonder for a second about how their commander felt about this mission.

Karel checked with the navigator and said, "Ten minutes until we cross the Federation border, Captain."

Koloth acknowledged that with a nod, and a moment later Duras entered the bridge with three of his armed guards. Unlike their former captain, Koloth did not keep personal guards on the bridge. He depended on the loyalty of his crew and his own ability to answer honest challenges. Thus, the sight of Duras's guards was yet another reminder of all that was foolish and dishonorable about the empire today.

"Councillor, we are about to enter Federation space," Koloth informed him.

"Excellent," Duras replied.

"This ship and crew are entering enemy territory, Councillor. I would like to tell them what to expect," Koloth said.

Duras seemed to be weighing his next words carefully. "Communications Officer. Put me on ship-wide intercom."

It was, of course, a breach for Duras to give orders to Koloth's warriors on his bridge, but that was no doubt what the councillor intended. When the communications officer signaled he was ready, Duras puffed himself up and began. "Honored warriors of the Klingon Empire, we are about to cross the border into the territory of the cowardly and treacherous Federation. We go to claim a world full of those who share our Klingon blood. We also will likely fire the first shots in the final battle with the Earthers. I am pleased to tell you that meeting us at our destination will be the Federation starship *U.S.S. Enterprise*, which recently took the lives of many of this crew in their pitiful effort to defend one of their starbases. When the time is right, you will all be able to seek your revenge. In the tradition of Klingons throughout the ages, we shall serve our vengeance very cold to the Earthers."

There were rumbles on the bridge and Karel had no doubt there were cheers throughout the ship. The crew had all lost comrades in the battle of Starbase 42. Karel, of course, had lost his own brother, who had been serving on the *Enterprise*.

In the fight against the Earthers, Karel had seen the humans fight bravely. And, most important, they had won the day.

"This is a battle that was begun twenty-five years ago at Donatu Five, where the treacherous Earthers denied us our rightful victory, placing a great stain on the honor of the Klingon Empire. We shall reclaim that honor and take our final victory over the Federation now."

This time, Karel could actually hear the cries of Klingons throughout the battle cruiser. Whatever else Duras was planning, he was offering the crew something they wanted badly: blood.

There was silence on the bridge for a long moment. Finally, it was broken by the navigator, who announced, "We are entering Federation space now."

Immediately, there were grunts of approval from the bridge crew. Karel glanced at the captain and saw his

Chapter Thirteen

SHUTTLECRAFT *GALILEO*
KLINGON SPACE

THE FLIGHT PATH was remarkably complex, but Ensign Quatrocchi executed it flawlessly. Like the Federation, the Klingons had an intricate web of sensors watching the border. They were designed to detect large, powerful vessels like starships. Thus, under normal circumstances, the shuttle should have been able to slip over the border fairly easily without raising an alarm. Certainly larger merchant and smuggling vessels had been able to do it for many years.

The problem was that the current political climate was far from normal. Fuller knew there was a reasonable possibility that this whole situation was a trap to lure a starship into Klingon space. The Klingons had used a similar tactic at the Battle of Donatu V, when

Fuller's first vessel, the *Endeavour,* had been ambushed by three Klingon cruisers.

Now, the destruction of the *Enterprise* or any of the eleven other ships in her class would give the Klingons an early tactical advantage. And it would allow the Klingons to claim that the Federation had provoked the war by violating their space.

Of course there was a better than even chance that the distress call was genuine and the situation was just as it seemed. The problem was that if it was a trap, Fuller would have little time to make that judgment and get his team out of there.

Fuller checked the sensors again. For a ship its size, the shuttle had remarkably robust sensors, which were given a temporary boost by the class 1 probe Mister Scott and his team had attached to the craft.

There it was, an energy spike, and it matched the range for Klingon merchant vessels. There were no other readings anywhere within two square light-years, certainly nothing like a Klingon warship's warp signature. Of course, there were ways to mask those kinds of readings, so absolute certainty was a practical impossibility here. Then again, certainty—absolute or otherwise—had never been much of a part of his career in security.

"I have them on sensors. It's a Klingon cargo ship with no sign of other vessels in the area," Fuller said. One hundred percent certainty may have been a practical impossibility, but his squad needed *him* to be infallible. Once again, he was reminded why he did not want to serve as a section chief again: what his people needed and deserved and what he could deliver were light-years apart.

Dozens of names were on a wall at Starfleet Command because Fuller had been all too fallible. For the most part they had been young officers, and they had all been good people.

People like Sam, a voice in his head supplied. Fuller had to quiet that voice by sheer force of will. He couldn't be distracted now. Otherwise there would be seven more names on that wall by the end of the day.

"We're ready, sir," Parmet said.

Fuller turned and looked at the squad, who were all looking back at him with earnest, trusting faces. They believed in him, believed in the myth of his record—not seeing or actively ignoring the many failures that had cost the lives of people just like them.

Like Sam.

Fuller shook off his doubt. Their faith, however misplaced, would help the mission now. Nodding, Fuller instructed, "Put your helmets on." Five of the squad complied immediately. Quatrocchi and Fuller would have to wait. As pilot and copilot, they couldn't afford the limited visibility and restricted movement until the Klingon ship's weapons and shields were down.

"Ten minutes to Klingon weapons range," Fuller said. *Even longer until we reach the range of our weapons,* Fuller thought, but didn't say. Though it was true that the Klingon weapons had greater range and power, the security team still had a few tricks up their sleeves.

At the halfway mark, Fuller hit a sequence on the console and said, "Launching probe now." They heard a click on the hull and the probe appeared in front of them, racing toward its position.

A moment later, a light came on in front of him. The

Klingons had seen them and were hailing the shuttle. He would have preferred for his conversation with them to wait, but he had no choice. Fuller activated the probe. Immediately, it started jamming the Klingon ship's communications and sensors. Now, they would have trouble tracking the shuttle and would not be able to raise an alarm.

The shuttle would also be out of communication with the *Enterprise*, but they were observing communication silence anyway. Of course, the jamming also affected the shuttle sensors, but Fuller was just able to get a visual on the Klingon ship. Pointing to the viewer in front of them, Fuller said, "There."

"I see it," Quatrocchi said.

"Full speed. Interception course."

"Aye, sir."

What happened next would happen quickly, Fuller knew. He studied the small image of the Klingon ship. It fit the basic profile of a Klingon cargo vessel. There was still no sign of any Klingon warships, and Fuller had to put thoughts of a trap aside. They were committed now, and the Klingon vessel would give them enough trouble. If there was a Klingon military vessel in range, this mission would be over for them in a few minutes anyway.

Four minutes to go. Three. The Klingon ship loomed larger, revealing more detail. Fuller was able to identify the class of ship, and the computer told him the most important details. "The vessel has forward and rear disruptor cannons. The shield emitters are in the approximate center of the command and propulsion segment. I need you to get me a shot on the shields first."

"Yes, chief," Quatrocchi said.

Then, to Fuller's surprise, the Klingon vessel began to move, but not toward the shuttle, which it was no doubt having trouble pinpointing.

"Stay with him," Fuller said.

The shuttle matched the movement and Fuller saw what the Klingon vessel was doing. "They're looking for the probe. Get us in there."

Quatrocchi pushed the speed and Fuller could hear the shuttle engines straining. It couldn't maintain the speed for long, but it wouldn't have to. The battle would be over long before the engines burned out.

On the viewer, the cargo ship executed a turn and its cannons came alive, spewing green energy at the space in front of the Klingon ship. Fuller could not make out the probe at this distance, but, apparently, neither could the Klingons because they kept up a steady stream of fire that looked almost random.

Fuller understood. "They're trying to hit the probe, but they can't get a lock or even a visual, so they're firing at multiple coordinates in the probe's general area." It wasn't a bad approach—the only one the Klingons had. Of course, it would take a good bit of luck for them to hit the probe before the shuttle engaged them.

Before that thought had fully formed in his mind, there was a flash of an explosion and Fuller realized that the first bit of luck of the day had just gone to the Klingons. His sensors came online. "The probe's gone."

No one spoke, but they all understood. The Klingons would be able to transmit their situation to any nearby ships. Even another merchant ship could tip the balance in the Klingons' favor here.

Fuller didn't hesitate. He hit the transmit button on

the console. "Klingon vessel. This is the Federation shuttle *Galileo*," putting emphasis on the word *shuttle*. "We demand you hand over the Federation citizens you are now holding. Drop your shields and power down your weapons or prepare to be destroyed."

There was silence on the other end of the line for a long moment. Then there was loud, hearty Klingon laughter.

"Federation shuttle. You are in no position to demand anything. I encourage you to keep your shields up and, by all means, use your weapons. We will destroy you anyway."

The Klingons cut the line.

"Um, sir?" came a voice from behind him. It was Parmet. Fuller couldn't mistake the concern in his voice.

Fuller kept his eyes on the window in front of him. They were now close enough to the Klingon ship to see it unmagnified. "The challenge will keep them from asking any other ships for help. It will be a matter of pride for them to deal with us themselves," Fuller said. "Mister Quatrocchi, change of plan. Meet them head-on at full speed. No maneuvers. Just give me a straight shot."

Quatrocchi acknowledged and Fuller ran a quick diagnostic on the photon torpedo. It was functioning and its containment field was showing a solid hour of power.

A disruptor beam flashed by the shuttle, close but not close enough to touch their shields. The second shot hit them a glancing blow, and warning lights lit up the panel in front of him. Fuller ignored them and returned fire with phasers. They would be ineffective against the Klingon ship's shields—particularly at this range—but they might distract the Klingons for a few moments.

Another disruptor blast exploded in front of them, and Fuller didn't have to check his instruments to know that it had made a direct hit on their forward shields. They would be lucky if the shields were still holding at even 50 percent. Another shot might finish them, or even if it didn't, it might disrupt the torpedo's containment field.

Fuller returned fire but resisted releasing the torpedo. If he fired it too soon, the Klingons might have enough time to target it and detonate it in space. There was another blast, a direct hit that shredded their forward shields, which, at this moment, were the only ones that mattered.

Time was up and Fuller didn't hesitate. He released the torpedo, putting it on a straight path for the Klingon cargo ship. Photon torpedoes were guided weapons and could track their targets. However, at this range it would only be able to adjust course a few hundredths of a degree before it hit the Klingons or overshot them.

"Evasive maneuvers," Fuller called out, and he felt the shuttle lurch to one side as Quatrocchi pushed the ship to its limits. There was a green flash and Fuller realized they had been hit again. Yet the shuttle was still in one piece, so the aft shields must have held.

Switching his eyes to the viewer, Fuller saw the torpedo speeding toward the Klingon ship. The Klingons fired wildly at it, but it would have taken pretty extraordinary luck to hit something moving that fast, even at close range. This time, luck wasn't with the Klingons, and the torpedo exploded in a brilliant flash of light against the front of the cargo ship.

Fuller's sensors were fried so he couldn't tell if the

Klingon shields were down. He would have to assume they were. A visual inspection told him that the forward disruptor cannons were twisted metal. It also told him exactly where the ship's transmission dish was located—near the front of the command area. Fuller aimed at it and with one shot the dish disintegrated. Now the Klingons would not be able to make a report even if they wanted to.

"Bring us to their rear," Fuller said, and the shuttle immediately swung around. To Fuller's surprise the Klingon ship started to turn as well, no doubt trying to bring the rear guns to bear on the shuttle. Quatrocchi matched the movement, keeping the shuttle skimming the length of the cargo ship and keeping them out of the deadly weapon's field of fire.

The trip was short, and at the last moment Quatrocchi lifted the shuttle ten degrees to give Fuller a clear shot. It would briefly put them in the sights of the Klingons' one remaining weapon, but it was necessary.

Fuller targeted the guns and fired. Luck was with them again and the guns exploded. "All their weapons are down," Fuller announced, and he could feel the relieved sighs of his people.

Quickly, he reached for his helmet and put it on as Quatrocchi did the same. "The easy part is over. Now let's go in and get the hostages."

Doctor McCoy leaned down and said to Kirk, "Jim, when was the last time you slept?"

"Slept?" Kirk asked.

"Yes, when did you last sleep?"

For a moment Kirk wasn't sure. Certainly, not since they had received the distress call. Before that . . .

"See, Captain, that is the point. If you have to think that long about it, it's been too long since you've done it."

"Bones," Kirk started to protest, but McCoy cut him off.

"Jim, it will be hours before we hear from the shuttle. Until then, there's nothing you can do for them. But when we do hear, they will need you to be in reasonably good condition."

Kirk almost protested out of habit, but stopped himself for two reasons. One, because it wouldn't do any good. And two, because McCoy was right. There was nothing he could do for Michael and the others on the bridge. As he stood up, he said, "Mister Spock, let me know the second the shuttle appears on long-range sensors."

"Of course, Captain." Spock had been up for at least as long as Kirk himself, but Vulcans could go without sleep for days or longer without any significant cost to their performance.

"And, Captain, you should stop by the dining room on your way," McCoy said.

Kirk nodded, realizing that the doctor was right again. He stopped into the dining room and picked up a chicken sandwich and a cup of coffee. He would have his meal in his quarters, where he could monitor the situation while he ate.

Sitting at his computer terminal, Kirk realized that he had been hungry. He ate mechanically and quickly, but he was glad he had eaten—he could not afford to get light-headed or be thinking about food later.

That done, his thoughts kept going back to Sam Fuller and his father. Michael Fuller had been the best person to lead the rescue. Kirk's decision to send him was right and perfectly logical, as Mister Spock would say. However, it might also well mean that Kirk had sent two friends, father and son, to their deaths just months apart.

The condolence message to Michael Fuller reporting his son's death was among the most difficult of Kirk's career. To whom would Kirk send the father's condolence message? He knew that Michael had never married Sam's mother. Was there anyone left to receive the transmission? Anyone whom Kirk had not put on a path to death?

The intercom beeped once and Mister Spock's voice came on. *"I'm sorry to disturb you, Captain, but long-range sensors indicate that the Klingon cruiser* D'k Tahg *has entered system 7348."*

"Thank you, Mister Spock." The captain realized that despite his doctor's orders, he would not be getting any sleep for some time.

Chapter Fourteen

THE CLAN WAS LOOKING to Adon, waiting for word. Surely, the son of Gorath would know what to do. Surely, he would have their path mapped out. Adon was sorry to disappoint them. At the moment, he had his grief and his anger, but little else to offer them. And time for action was growing short, he could feel it. Night was falling.

There was *one* thing he could do. One thing that tradition demanded and his father deserved. When Uncle approached, Adon said, "We need to bury my father immediately."

Uncle nodded and the clan went about their task. They didn't rush the ritual, not exactly, but they moved with purpose as if they all understood that something would be required of them, and soon. Adon silently asked his father for guidance again and again. He wished for only the smallest part of his father's wisdom.

No answers came, at least not that could be heard over the roar of his grief, anger, and his desire to take the life of his father's murderer. When the ritual was finished and night had fallen, Uncle and Bethe were at his side. He felt their eyes and thoughts on him. They were waiting.

Like the others.

Still, his anger roared in his blood and in his chest. And then he had it, not an answer, but a beginning. He found that he had something to say to his clan after all: "My people, I am not my father. I cannot tell you now that I know a path to victory. I have only the burning of my blood and a single task that I must perform." He could see them waiting for his next words, looking to him as their leader despite what he had just said. "Tonight, in the darkness, I will descend to the mine through its shaft and take the crystals we pulled from the ground with our strength."

"The crystals are rocks to us, valuable only to those from the stars. The risk would be great. What purpose would that serve?" Uncle said.

"Revenge," Adon said. "At least the first and smallest part of it. My blood burns now to end Gurn's treacherous, pitiful life, but that battle would be over before it would begin. They have many weapons, and the power of the green-skins' mine. And they have their new alliance with the Klingons, who tried once to destroy us. I take the crystals because Gurn wants them, because his Klingon masters want them. I take them because we won them with the courage and blood of our people under the leadership of Gorath of our clan."

There it was: purpose. He could feel it. If it wasn't his father's spirit speaking to him, it was close enough for Adon. Finally, he had a task that satisfied part of the calling of his blood and seemed to satisfy the clan. Once again, they were looking to him as their leader. On this small matter at least, he hoped he would not disappoint them.

"I go now and I go alone," Adon said, heading immediately for his flying machine, Uncle and Bethe still by his side.

"I will go with you," Bethe said.

"No, I must go alone."

"You have a plan then?"

Adon hesitated for a moment before he said, "Of course."

"How are you going to carry all of the crystals by yourself?"

This time his hesitation was longer. Bethe kept her eyes on him the entire time. "Your plan?"

"I am still working on some of the details."

"Whatever the plan is, it will benefit from another pilot. You may be the best we have, but, after you, there is no one better than I."

"No, my father is the best pilot we have," Adon said reflexively, but he knew when he was beaten. "But it is true that you are the best after me. I welcome your assistance."

"You accept good counsel, like your father," Uncle said, looking at him with that maddening approval. He had just been outmaneuvered by one of his childhood playmates, and Uncle seemed to think that it was another sign that he was a worthy leader. Adon shrugged and climbed onto the flying machine that had been his father's as Bethe climbed onto the one Adon himself had used when he and his father had raced.

Adon switched on the talking device. "Low power. Keep the weapons off." It would keep the machine's noise to a minimum.

"Of course," Bethe said.

"Follow me." He took the vehicle into the air. He stayed close to the ground, below the level of the trees. The mine had cameras pointed in all directions—the green-skins had guarded their work carefully. In the dark, the craft would be harder to see, particularly if they kept to the cover of the trees for as long as possible. The same cameras could also see in the dark, but Adon doubted that Gurn and his people even knew about that, let alone how to use the monitoring equipment.

The trip took longer at that altitude because the constant maneuvering around trees meant they had to keep their speed low. Still, Adon pushed his own craft to the limit of safety, and Bethe matched his movements. She was perhaps the only other member of their clan left who could do that.

They had to travel to the rear of the mine, then follow the rim of the great pit the green-skins had dug into their world. It was wide and so deep that if a person fell into it, he would have plenty of time to consider his fate before he reached the bottom.

Adon reached the rear of the mine complex and motioned to Bethe. She nodded and they started their descent. There were cameras in the shaft, but Adon doubted that Gurn would have thought to have them manned. The computer could have watched the cameras, but Gurn would have had to think to ask it to do so.

Still, there was a chance they would be seen. If that happened, Adon was prepared to fight. In fact, he would welcome the opportunity to satisfy the burning of his blood.

They descended for several minutes and Adon watched as they passed level after level of the mine. There were few lights and no people that Adon could see—and more important, no alarms.

Finally, they reached the level they needed and Adon saw an ore hauler. That changed things. He had considered simply tossing the crystals into the great pit and letting them be smashed, but they had been hard won and he was reluctant to let them go. The ore hauler was essentially a large platform with waist-high sides. It was large enough for several people and still had a cargo area big enough for twenty containers.

A new plan formed in his mind, this one complete with details. He motioned to Bethe, who nodded and landed her craft on ground as he landed his directly onto the ore hauler. He hit a switch on his controls, and a metallic clang told him the flying machine was magnetically locked into place on the hauler.

That done, he stepped off the hauler and drew his weapon. Bethe had hers out as well as they surveyed the inside of the mine. There was no movement and only the red lights that ran at night were on. It was silent except for the dim hum of the equipment.

"There is no one here," Bethe whispered as they moved forward. The storage area was nearby and open. There had been no reason to lock the crystals away before, and not surprisingly, Gurn had lacked the imagination to take any additional precautions. The twelve containers were there, and a quick inspection told Adon they were full. By attaching Orion lifting plates, Adon and Bethe were able to load the containers on the hauler quickly and lock them in place.

He was about to go when another idea came to him. It would take some time, but he thought it worth it. In a few minutes, they managed to place empty cargo containers where the ones they were taking had been. Then they headed for their craft.

"Can you manage the hauler?" Bethe asked, her voice even.

"I will try, thank you," Adon said. Of course, he had piloted them before. Compared to the flying machines—which were agile predators—the haulers were slow and lumbering beasts. However, to be fair, they were designed primarily to go up and down carrying heavy loads. Adon would be asking a bit more of this one today, but not much.

The machine powered up quickly, but far from silently. If Gurn was listening, the alarm would come any second now. If that happened, Adon would have to climb onto the flying machine and abandon the hauler.

But again, no alarm came. By silent agreement, Adon took the hauler into the shaft and starting ascending as Bethe kept pace beside him, glancing over at him nervously from time to time. The trip took longer than the one down, and Adon kept waiting for an alarm or for Gurn's people to appear on flying machines, but no one came. Finally, they were out of the shaft.

There was no way to take the hauler through the trees, so Adon kept it just above them. That made the journey back quicker but more dangerous. Again he waited for pursuit, but they reached the village without incident. He realized what a fool Gurn was as he landed the craft. That this man had killed a man as great as his father seemed impossible.

Stepping down to meet his uncle, Adon realized that he had struck the first blow against Gurn and his plans. There was a small measure of satisfaction in that. Well, he meant to take even greater satisfaction and take it soon.

Bethe was quickly by his side and Adon realized that she had been there since news of his father's death.

"You have Gurn's rocks?" Uncle said, a smile on his lips.

"Yes, apparently Gurn and his people were all sleeping," Adon said.

"What now, Adon?" Uncle asked.

Adon was surprised to see that he had an answer to that question.

"Sublight speed, Captain. We have entered the system," the pilot announced.

"Science Officer, any sign of the *Enterprise*?" Koloth asked.

"No, Captain."

Karel was surprised. How could the Federation ignore an incursion into their space by a Klingon warship? What possible emergency could be more serious than that?

"Excellent," Councillor Duras said. "The humans must fear to face us, even now."

Few Klingons would disagree with that assessment of humans, but Karel knew it was false. From Koloth's face, Karel could see that Captain Koloth felt the same way.

Duras stepped forward and said, "Full impulse to the second planet."

To his credit, the pilot ignored the councillor and looked at Koloth, who smiled and gave the order. "*Three-quarter* impulse to the second planet."

There were smiles and satisfied grunts among the bridge crew as the ship made its way. Challenging the councillor was dangerous, but Duras had already conspired to kill Koloth, so there was little point for him to try to curry Duras's favor—which was not the captain's style anyway.

The conflict between the two men would come out into the open before much longer. Soon enough, Duras would start down his treacherous course. It was a course that Duras had known Koloth would not follow, which was why the councillor had offered Karel the ship.

"Captain, have the transporter room on standby to transport me and twenty of my warriors to the surface," Duras requested.

Koloth nodded. "I will send First Officer Karel and twenty additional warriors."

"I need no assistance," Duras said.

"Of course not, but my crew would benefit from observing you win a victory for the empire."

There was complete silence on the bridge as Duras looked at Koloth. If looks could kill, Koloth would be on the other side of the River of Blood.

"As you know, I am content to leave you in command of this ship as long as you understand that I am in command of this mission," Duras said.

"No one disputes your authority," Koloth said, but Karel could hear a *yet* in his captain's tone. "But I need my people to assess any possible danger to this ship."

Duras gave Koloth an unpleasant smile. "Send your team, but I will accept no interference on the surface."

Koloth nodded and turned to Karel. "First Officer Karel, select your crew and prepare for transport."

Karel headed for the door, mentally compiling a list of the Klingons he wanted by his side. He needed good warriors. However, he also had to make sure that enough of the best fighters remained on board. While Duras was on the surface, Koloth and the ship would still be in danger from the large number of Duras's soldiers.

For now, Karel and Koloth would be fighting a battle against shadows. In this arena, Duras would have the advantage. But sooner or later, the fight would have to come into the open and Karel vowed to be ready.

Chapter Fifteen

SHUTTLECRAFT *GALILEO*
KLINGON SPACE

Fuller knew they had to move quickly or the Klingons would likely kill their captives before the team arrived, unless they could keep the Klingons too busy to do it. He quickly scanned the squad, who all had their helmets on now. "Everyone sealed in?" The squad confirmed, and Fuller hit the button to decompress the shuttle. In seconds, there would be a complete vacuum inside, creating an atmosphere no more hospitable than open space.

Fuller clicked on his built-in communicator. "This configuration has two levels in the command and propulsion section with four air locks total, two on each side of the ship with one on each level. There is also a small air lock in the rear at the end of the access shaft."

The shaft was a tunnel that ran above the cargo containers, connecting them and giving the crew access to each.

"Parmet and Quatrocchi, you're with me on the port side. Jawer and McCalmon, you take the starboard air locks. Baxter and Jameson, you take the rear air lock," Fuller said. The rear air lock was the least likely to be defended and would be the easiest to get into. However, once inside, they would be nearly sitting ducks with a long straight path in front of them and little or no cover.

A red light came on, telling them that the shuttle was clear of air, and Fuller opened the hatch. He stared out into the vacuum of space and had to push aside the twenty-five-year-old memories of his friends and crewmates blasted out into that abyss by Klingons who had boarded their ship.

"Good luck," Fuller said to Baxter and Jameson, who launched themselves, one at a time, into space. The hull of the Klingon ship was maybe eight meters away. The trip took seconds and they hit the ship fairly gently, grasping it with their magnetic boots.

"We're on," Baxter's voice was heard though the comm system in their helmets.

"Get in position and wait for my signal," Fuller told them. Quatrocchi immediately piloted them to the command segment of the ship and brought the shuttle to a stop. Fuller could feel the seconds ticking by. He didn't want the Klingons to have time to get into suits and meet them in space. Their plan would work best if the squad faced the Klingons on board the ship.

Jawer and McCalmon were the first out. Then, Parmet and Quatrocchi. Fuller was last, using his arms to push off the shuttle door and aiming feetfirst at the top of the hull. For a moment, he was flying in space, then his feet clicked onto the ship. Using only hand signals, he sent Jawer and McCalmon on their way. Then he and his team headed for the aft air locks.

"Get us ready on the upper air lock," Fuller said to his people. "I'll take the lower lock." Walking in magnetic boots was awkward, and Fuller hadn't done it in over five years, but his balance came back immediately and he was thankful for small favors—knowing that they might soon be in short supply.

He reached the air-lock door and took out the charge he wore around his waist. He put the charge over the door's locking mechanism. Then he took a quick look through the heavy door's small window. He could see the air-lock chamber itself and the inner door behind it, but no Klingons.

That wasn't a surprise. They were most likely standing to the side of each inner air-lock door waiting for the boarding party. Well, they would get it soon enough, and perhaps a surprise or two as well.

Fuller immediately went to join Parmet and Quatrocchi. He saw the device they had placed over the forward door's locking mechanism. A moment later, the two other teams reported in.

Fuller acknowledged and hit a button on the small keypad he wore on his wrist. Though he couldn't hear the explosions, he could feel them through his boots, and he could see the flash at about thirty meters to the rear of the ship.

He knew that alarms would be sounding all over the ship, and the Klingons would be rushing to the damaged air locks to face them. Without hesitating, Fuller hit another button on the keypad and activated the second type of device they had brought.

The magnetic disk lit up and Fuller knew it had come to life. This one, of course, didn't explode. It simply flashed for a few moments, and then the outer air-lock door slid open. Fuller and his team slipped inside, gravity immediately taking them as they stepped over the threshold. As soon as they were inside, Fuller closed the door and hit the control to repressurize the air lock.

It took precious seconds, giving Fuller plenty of time to worry about whether the Klingons had been sufficiently distracted by the explosions or if any warriors would be waiting for them just outside the inner door. A light came on and Fuller knew they had atmosphere. Without waiting a moment, he hit the button to open the inner door, and it obediently slid open.

No one was there.

Still, they could be lying in wait on the wall on either side. Fuller prepared to lean slowly out of the air lock when there was a blur of motion next to him and Parmet stepped out into the ship, both phasers raised.

Fuller cursed under his breath and followed the young man. Looking around quickly, he was relieved to see that the hallway was empty. "Ensign Parmet?"

"Sorry, sir. I jumped the gun," Parmet said over the comlink.

"Stay close to me and do this one by the book." Quickly, Fuller took off his helmet and tossed it aside as the others did the same. They needed their eyes and ears for this one. They were in a large room piled with equipment, one of two on this level. It opened to a corridor that ran down the center of the ship, and Fuller headed for it.

As he stepped into the corridor, he saw a Klingon appear in front of him. Before the danger had even fully registered in his mind, his hand fired the phaser on its own. The Klingon went down immediately, falling at the heavy stun setting. Immediately, another Klingon appeared and fired at them from farther down the hall.

Fuller returned fire as the other two men with him did the same. A Klingon head peeked out. Then another one emerged from the room across from the one they had entered. Quatrocchi hit him with one shot, but the fire intensified from down the corridor. Fuller and Parmet hugged one wall, while Quatrocchi lay against the other.

The continued fire was putting smoke in the air, and Fuller knew they couldn't keep this up for long. Eventually, the Klingons would get lucky, and they outnumbered the security squad by at least two to one. He didn't know how the other teams were faring, and there was no time to find out.

"Fall back," he said. If the layout he had studied was correct, the corridor they were in now terminated in the ship's control room in the very front of the ship. If they were lucky, the control room had been abandoned by the crew, who were eager to fight off the boarders. His challenge to the Klingons would have made them angry enough to get sloppy.

A few seconds later, they were backed up against the control-room door. The Klingons were firing at them from the other end of the corridor and were getting braver, moving toward them. There was no time to waste, they needed the cover of the control room.

Fuller hit the control that opened the door and leapt

inside before he looked, depending on the element of surprise to help him if anyone was there.

He saw the Klingon in the pilot's chair a millisecond before the alien saw him. Fuller raised and aimed his phaser just as the Klingon did the same. It was going to be close, very close.

Even as Fuller fired, he realized that the Klingon was moving just slightly faster. But a fraction of a second before Fuller fired, he saw another beam lance out from next to him. The Klingon fired. Then another phaser fired. The four weapons in the small room discharged nearly simultaneously, and Fuller actually saw the disruptor bolt that nearly took his head off, missing him by inches.

A moment later the Klingon slumped to the floor, after taking a phaser beam to the chest. The shot had come from Fuller's right: Quatrocchi.

"Thank you, Ensign," Fuller said.

"My pleasure, sir."

Immediately, the three men turned and took positions on either side of the door, Fuller and Parmet on one side, Quatrocchi on the other. From their semiconcealed positions, the three men started firing down the corridor at figures that dashed from side to side, firing back.

A bolt tore into the deck in front of the door, and Fuller realized that the Klingons had not set their weapons on stun, or anywhere near it. The bolts were not enough to dematerialize a person, but they would do heavy damage to any body they touched. The disruptor bolts posed another danger. A wild shot could easily hit the forward window of the ship. At that power, a hit on the window would mean an immediate hull breach and a fast decompression of the control room.

The Klingons moved forward, getting more aggressive as they neared their enemy. The fire was nearly endless, and more than one shot hit the control panels behind Fuller's team. Another shot tore into the body of the Klingon that Quatrocchi had stunned, and Fuller could see that the damage was immediately fatal.

It was a game of inches now and the Klingons had the advantage. Well, if Fuller, Parmet, and Quatrocchi could hold out a little longer, there was hope that the other teams could accomplish something.

A moment later, Fuller heard shouting that sounded distinctly human, and instantly the fire on their position stopped. Yet he could hear the sound of disruptor fire continuing and could see flashes of green through the smoke. No, not just green. Blue. The blue of phaser fire.

Someone had come up behind the Klingons and was hitting them pretty hard. The sound was nearly deafening, with human shouts met with Klingon war cries. Then, the sound of disruptors quieted and there were only a few phaser blasts. And then silence.

After a few seconds a female voice called out, "Fuller?" It was McCalmon.

"Here," he said. "Is Jawer with you?"

"Yes, sir," Jawer's voice said.

A few moments later, Jawer and McCalmon appeared out of the smoke. "We thought you might need some help up here," she said.

"We did, thank you," Fuller replied. Then he could hear a series of weapons blasts and then more silence.

"Baxter? Jameson?" Fuller called out, and both men appeared in the corridor as if answering his summons.

"I think we got them all," Jawer said.

"We counted ten in the corridor," McCalmon said.

"We took down one by the air lock and one in here," Fuller said, gesturing to the dead Klingon in the pilot's seat.

"And there were four near our air lock. They had us pinned down for a while," Baxter said.

That was fourteen, about right for a ship of this class.

"Let's not take any chances. We go door-to-door and check every inch of the ship. I don't want any surprises. Baxter, you and Jameson collect the Klingon bodies and put them all in one of the rooms by the air locks. If you even suspect one might be waking up, stun him twice."

The two men acknowledged and were off.

"There was no one in the cargo area. And I don't think there could be anyone hiding in the containers. They had pretty heavy-duty security seals on them," Jawer said.

"Probably because they're carrying precious cargo or military equipment," Fuller said. "Or both." From what little Fuller knew of the Klingon merchant cargo business, it was often marked by disputes over cargo inventories and value. Whatever the cultural reasons, it made trade between the Federation and the empire (when that was still possible) thorny at best.

They checked the upper level first and did it quickly. It carried stores for the crew, extra equipment, and the small engineering section. All of the rooms and compartments were empty. They headed down a ladder and quickly reached the lower level, which usually included a cargo ship's crew quarters, galley, and recreational facilities. It was also where the hostages would likely be kept, if they were still alive.

Fuller split his people into two groups. He, Parmet,

and Quatrocchi checked the port side, while McCalmon and Jawer checked the starboard. They were nearing the very rear of the ship and Fuller was worrying that there might be no hostages on board when Jawer said. "Sir, I have a locked door here."

A dozen steps later, Fuller found Jawer and McCalmon standing in front of an ordinary door. Jawer had pulled open a control panel and was obviously trying to open the door. Fuller pulled him away with a tug, aimed his phaser, and fired.

The control panel disintegrated and the door slid open immediately. Fuller half-expected to be facing down the business end of a Klingon disruptor. Instead, he saw four people lying on the floor of the tiny room, one man and three women. At first, he thought they were dead, but a woman raised her head to look at them and the others stirred.

He recognized the people, at least the expressions on their faces. They had the look of people who had spent too long inches from death and far from hope . . . survivors. They looked haunted and dazed. They were also dirty, and each had slowly healing cuts and bruises. Their clothing, what little they wore, was torn and barely holding together.

"I am Michael Fuller of Starfleet. We're here to take you home."

Three of the people looked at him dumbly, while the woman who had first lifted her head started to cry. He heard a few throats catch next to him. Jawer was looking on, pain on his face. McCalmon had tears in her eyes when she stepped forward and said, "Do any of you need medical attention?"

The crying woman started to get up and gestured to the man next to her. Crude splints were on each forearm, and Fuller could see that the bones were broken and had been badly set, if they had been set at all. Fuller helped up the woman, whom he immediately thought of as the one in charge.

"Can any of you walk?" he asked.

"I can," the woman said.

The other two women grunted something and started to stand with help. The man simply nodded. It took two people to get him on his feet, but he was able to stand.

"Jawer, see if you can get their transporter online. Parmet, go back to the shuttle and get us four more suits, just in case," Fuller said, and the two men sprinted off to their tasks.

Fuller, McCalmon, and Quatrocchi started leading the people to the ladder. The first step was to get them to the upper deck. The man with the broken arms was having trouble walking. McCalmon had only the standard medical training, but since she carried the medical kit, she was their medic. "I can give you something for the pain," she said, and the man nodded. A moment later, she had a hypo spray out and administered it.

The man straightened immediately.

"My name is Christine," the woman said, seeming to gain strength. "This is Alan, and this is Cyndy and Arleen."

Fuller introduced himself again as well as the others. Just as he reached the ladder, Fuller's communicator beeped. It was Jawer. *"Transporter is fried, sir. I'm sorry."*

"Fine, meet us in the control room. Fuller out."

"No transporter?" Christine asked. "Are we going to be stuck here?"

"No, we have a shuttle, but we're going to have to get you into space suits to get you there," Fuller told her.

Christine looked worried. Fuller smiled and said, "This is what we do. We'll have you out of here in no time. There's a starship standing by."

That seemed to satisfy her. Of course, the transfer would take some doing, particularly for the injured man. These were civilians with no zero-g or vacuum survival training. For a moment, Fuller considered sedating them, but decided against it. He couldn't risk strong drugs on their clearly weakened bodies.

Getting them up the ladder was difficult. Again, especially for the man. On the upper deck, Jawer was waiting. "Parmet's waiting with the suits," he said.

Fuller sent Quatrocchi and McCalmon ahead with the survivors with orders to get them to the shuttle. When they were gone, he said to Jawer, "I need you to completely disable the warp and impulse drives, as well as any long-range transmission capability."

Jawer nodded. "The warp drive's already done. The shuttle phasers took care of that. I can finish the impulse drive for good quickly."

"Good. Then I want you to check the ship's computer. Find out what they're carrying."

Jawer nodded and went right to work. Fuller headed to Baxter and Jameson, who were guarding an open door. Looking inside, Fuller saw that the Klingons were lying on the floor, unconscious—though one of them was starting to stir.

"They've been quiet," Baxter said.

With that, the Klingon who had been moving shot to his feet. He stood up and faced them. "Earther! You dare to attack us? I will destroy you, you cowardly scum—"

Fuller's phaser was immediately in his hand, and a blue beam knocked the Klingon back to the ground. He was immediately silent. Then Fuller hit the control to lock the door.

"Watch them until we're ready to leave," Fuller said, and headed to the port air lock.

Parmet and Quatrocchi were helping Christine and another woman into a suit. Beyond them, he could see two of his team inside the air lock itself as the outer door opened. They helped one of the other survivors outside and to the shuttle door. A moment later, they had her inside and were returning to the air lock.

Two more left, Fuller realized. They were moving quickly.

His communicator beeped and Jawer said, *"Sir, you had better come see the cargo."*

Less than a minute later, Fuller was looking down an open hatch at a stasis chamber full of worms. "The computer called it *gagh,*" Jawer said. "There's also something called bloodwine, and *rokeg* blood pie."

Fuller knew what that meant. "Turn the stasis fields off."

"I can do it, sir, but it's just food."

"Out here and in these quantities, the only ones who would see this food are Klingon warriors. This is food from home, given to soldiers to keep their morale high. See that it's no use to them when they find it."

"Easiest to just disengage the cargo containers entirely. That will cut the power," Jawer said.

"Good, we need to lighten the ship before we go."

A few moments later, Parmet reported that the last survivor was on board. Fuller ordered everyone but Jawer and Baxter back to the shuttle. He left Baxter guarding the door and took Jawer to the control room.

They had to push aside the dead Klingon to get to the controls, but Jawer was able to quickly release the cargo containers. "That's it. They have battery power and life support, but no ability to move or communicate."

The last step was an improvised time lock on the door holding the Klingon crew, who had seemed to have woken up and were shouting and banging on the walls. Jawer had modified one of the electronic lock breakers they had used to enter the ship and placed it on the door.

"Give them, say, six hours in there," Fuller said.

"Sure," Jawer said.

They quickly made their way back to the shuttle, which was fairly crowded. Nevertheless, to Fuller, it seemed like home. They quickly repressurized and Fuller was glad to have his helmet off again.

While the others gave the survivors water and emergency rations, Fuller told Quatrocchi what they needed to do. Fuller turned on the shuttle's tractor beam, which grabbed the command and propulsion module of the Klingon ship while Quatrocchi began to slowly accelerate. They had to do it slowly, taking precious minutes, because it was a lot of mass for the shuttle to be pulling, and because too fast an acceleration could easily overload the relatively low-powered tractor beam.

"What are you doing?" Christine asked.

"We're towing the ship on a course into populated

Klingon space. They will be picked up in a few weeks, or a few months," Fuller said.

Nearly twenty minutes later, they were close enough to light speed for Fuller to release the ship. He shut off the tractor beam and Quatrocchi veered away. For a few seconds, Fuller watched the cargo ship as it coasted away behind them. Free of its burden and pointed toward the *Enterprise,* the shuttle quickly accelerated to top speed.

"You could have just left them," Christine said. "You'd have gotten no argument from me."

"That's not what we do." But Fuller was uncomfortable for a long moment. He had strongly considered doing just that.

"You're a real humanitarian," the man said, speaking for the first time.

Fuller didn't know what he meant, but he understood the tone and ignored the comment. They still had nearly two hours to go before he could even signal the *Enterprise.* Fuller tested his equipment and saw that the scanners were back online. They must have overloaded during the battle and then reset themselves when they finally cooled down.

Even though they were still in Klingon space, Fuller found himself relaxing by degrees. The mission had succeeded. And incredibly, they had not lost a single hostage or officer. That was a hell of a lot more than luck; it was practically a miracle.

Chapter Sixteen

U.S.S. ENTERPRISE
FEDERATION-KLINGON BORDER

"Captain, I have the shuttle," Uhura said.

"Put them on audio," Kirk said.

A moment later, Michael Fuller's voice came through the system, and Kirk felt a wave of relief. "*Galileo to Enterprise.*"

"*Enterprise,* Kirk here. It's good to hear your voice, Michael. What's your status?"

"*We have recovered four hostages. No casualties for the hostages or the team.*"

For a moment, Kirk thought he had heard that incorrectly. *No casualties.* No simulation he had run in his own head, or that Spock had run on the ship's computer, had predicted that as even a possibility.

Kirk felt a smile spread across his face. "Any injuries?"

"The hostages are pretty banged up, but everyone is stable. You can tell sickbay there is one patient with two badly broken arms who will need immediate attention."

"Mister Fuller, I look forward to your complete report."

"Yes, sir. We are prepared to rendezvous in fifteen minutes."

"We'll be ready for you. Kirk out." The captain was on his feet immediately, giving Uhura his instructions, then quickly headed out the door.

He arrived at the shuttlebay a few moments before Scott and Spock, and the three of them headed for the control room together. He told the two men what he knew, and Scott immediately cleared the shuttlebay and started depressurizing it.

Just a few minutes later, Scott announced, "I have them on sensors. Ten minutes until arrival."

The time passed slowly, but finally Kirk could see the shuttle through the open bay doors. It entered the bay a short time later, and Kirk could see that it was intact, though a single black line on one side of the hull showed that it had come under weapons fire. The only other sign of the mission was the leftover mounts on the top of the hull that had held the photon torpedo and the probe.

As the shuttle glided into the bay, Scott studied it with a careful eye and then closed the bay doors. The wait for repressurization seemed endless, but finally the light on the control board turned green. Kirk opened the

Kevin Ryan

door from the control room and made his way down the ladder to the deck.

Before his feet touched the floor, McCoy and his team were racing toward the shuttle with four stretchers. Kirk kept out of their way and watched them help four bedraggled, but alive, civilians out of the shuttle and onto the stretchers. One of them, the only man, was unconscious. The others were able to move under their own power, but McCoy put them on the stretchers anyway.

After less than two minutes, the doctors, nurses, and new patients were all headed to sickbay, and Kirk approached the shuttle as Fuller and the others stepped outside. They were in standard uniforms and looked as if they were reporting for duty on a normal day.

Kirk didn't hide his pleasure. Stepping forward, he shook Fuller's hand and said, "Well done, all of you." Though at attention, the squad looked pleased. "I look forward to hearing your story. If no one needs anything, let's adjourn to the briefing room."

On the way out, Kirk hit the intercom and said, "Mister Sulu. Best speed to system 7348."

The briefing was an amazing thirty minutes. Even Spock raised his eyebrow a few times, which—for him—was quite a display. Kirk made a few notes on his data padd for his formal report and for the commendation recommendations he would need to prepare. It was a pleasant business. He had seen missions go terribly wrong and take the lives of good people. It was rare when things went the other way.

"Why don't you all get some rest. I'm going to need you when we get to the system," Kirk said.

The officers filed out and Kirk called sickbay.

"I'm busy down here, Jim. It will be a few hours before I'll want them talking to anyone. And you can use that time to get some rest yourself, Captain."

"Kirk out." He stood up and headed for his quarters. It was time to finally take his doctor's advice.

Chapter Seventeen

**ORION-BUILT MINING FACILITY
SYSTEM 7348
FEDERATION SPACE**

KAREL AND HIS TEAM beamed down into a clan pit. It seemed to be right out of Klingon history texts, or the re-creations he had seen as a child. In the days before Kahless and the many years of wars that had divided and finally unified Qo'noS, the clan had been the central social and political unit of Klingon society.

The meeting pit built around a bonfire had been a prominent feature of clan life, though this one was much larger than the ones he had seen. It also had modern lights standing around its perimeter. And he noted flying weapon platforms that hovered nearby and seemed to be standing guard over the pit. Immediately, he recognized the technology as Orion. His brother's final message to him described fighting against cowardly Orions who turned those vehicles on the native Klingons and then the Starfleet security teams.

The people piloting them now wore armored suits so he could not make them out, but he assumed they were natives. The question was, why have the weapons at the ready? Reports said the natives lived together peacefully. And the natives thought they were greeting a friendly force of their brothers from space.

The people in front of him were definitely Klingon. They wore cloth and leather and, again, looked as if they had stepped out of a museum display. There were more than thirty of them.

Duras was finishing an embrace with one of the natives. The councillor turned to Karel and said, "This is Gurn, the great leader of our proud brothers." To Gurn, Duras said, "This is Karel, the trusted first officer of our ship's captain."

"I greet you in the name of our people, who share your noble Klingon blood." Gurn seemed sincere enough, and Kell had spoken of these people's honor and courage in battle. However, something in the familiarity between Gurn and Duras made Karel uncomfortable.

"Come. We shall talk, and then we shall feast," Gurn said.

Karel and his people took seats next to Duras's force. Karel leaned in to Gash and whispered, "Remain ready, and watch carefully. My blood is calling out a warning."

Gash nodded and turned to keep his single eye on the center of the pit. The large Klingon had been Karel's commanding officer in the port weapons room. Karel had taken the warrior's eye in a dispute and had won the

Klingon's respect. Demoted from weapons officer, Gash had been made *QaS DevwI'*, in command of the ship's troops. Though he had been a nearly incompetent weapons officer, he was a powerful and aggressive fighter who led his warriors well. He was also one of the few Klingons that Karel trusted nearly completely, which was rare in these times.

In the center of the clan pit, Gurn took a moment to prepare himself. Karel could see that the man was about to make a speech. For a moment, Karel's blood screamed out a fresh warning as he saw another point of resemblance between Gurn and Duras.

"Brothers, we welcome you in the spirit of friendship and shared blood. As you know, our world was nearly destroyed by the green-skins, who wanted to steal our dilithium. We fought them and saved ourselves from destruction by their machines. However, we have learned that there are still great dangers to our planet and our people. We have learned that the Earthers who came here claiming friendship had hired the Orions to do their bidding. They wished to take our wealth, the crystals from our ground, and use them to fuel their treacherous war against our Klingon brethren."

It was a lie. Karel's brother had told him that he had spoken with a Klingon in the mines during his mission. It had been Kell and the crew of the *Enterprise* who had prevented the world's destruction. Karel was not surprised to see that Duras was party to such falsehood, but Kell had told him the Klingons on this world were honorable.

Looking at Gurn, Karel saw that at least one of them was not. And, unfortunately, he was in a position of great power with his people. *This will not end well,* Karel realized.

"Our brothers have offered us much. I have been speaking to one of the great Klingon leaders for weeks now. Councillor Duras has offered his friendship, his protection, and his great wisdom. He has also offered us trade so that all of our people may enjoy the wealth of this planet's crystals. Until recently, access to the Orion machines and weaponry was limited by the narrow vision of some of us. Soon, we shall all enjoy the power and the security that we and the Klingons can achieve together. And we shall be able to help our brothers in blood defeat a dangerous foe, the Federation, which threatens them and tried to destroy us all."

There were cheers from the crowd. Gurn seemed popular, and, more important, he was offering his people a number of things they wanted. They had seen that technology was power. Stolen Orion technology had helped them defeat the Orions and save themselves. The tale he told of treacherous humans who had nearly destroyed them obviously played on their fears. The only problem with his story was that Karel knew it to be false. Looking at Gurn's face when he spoke, Karel thought that the man did as well, or at least suspected as much. However, the cheers he was now basking in represented another kind of power, a power that Gurn clearly enjoyed.

Duras made a short speech of his own, promising victory over the Earthers and wealth and security for the planet's people. He also promised them an honored place as a partner in the Klingon Empire.

More cheers. More lies. More power.

Then Gurn said, "Now, we shall make our first exchange. Councillor Duras has brought engineers and technicians to help us bring our mine to full power. We will soon speed up the safe removal of these dilithium crystals and begin building our future. In return, it will be my pleasure to present him with our first shipment of crystals."

Duras turned to Karel and invited, "Join us and see the beginning of the end for the Federation."

Karel stood, gathered his Klingons, and left the meeting pit. Duras had been scheming for some time to get the crystals this planet had to offer. That much was obvious, and Karel had long suspected it. Yet, he could not help feeling that something else was at work here.

Deception was Duras's nature, but how deep did his treachery go? And would all of his deceptions be in the interest of the empire? Karel could not answer those questions now. All he could do was watch Duras carefully and prepare himself for when those truths eventually revealed themselves.

Kirk woke suddenly in his quarters. His internal chronometer told him they were still at least two hours away from the system. That was just enough time to take care of the things he needed to do and prepare for arrival at 7348. Of course, not knowing what to expect when the *Enterprise* got there made it impossible to truly prepare, but, then again, that described many if not all of the ship's missions.

His first stop was to the bridge. Spock immediately got out of the command chair and headed to the science station. "Time to planet, Mister Spock?" Kirk asked.

"One hour, fifty-eight minutes, twelve seconds. Ship's

sensors confirm a Klingon heavy cruiser in orbit around the second planet. No other signs of activity on the world."

"Uhura, hail the Klingon vessel," Kirk said.

"Hailing now. . . . The Klingons are responding."

"On-screen," Kirk ordered. The image of a Klingon Kirk recognized immediately filled the screen.

"My dear Captain Kirk," Koloth said.

"My dear Captain Koloth," Kirk replied.

"It was my understanding that the Enterprise *would be waiting for us in this system."*

"Rest assured, Captain, the *Enterprise* will be joining you shortly."

"As our sensors have confirmed. I hope your ship did not encounter any trouble. Perhaps you will require assistance when you arrive?"

"I thank you for your concern, but the *Enterprise* is more than equal to any task it encounters. That said, I want to put you on notice now. You are in Federation space with the permission of the Federation president himself. The parameters of your diplomatic mission to the second planet in this system are very clear. Any deviation from those parameters will be considered an act of war."

Koloth smiled at that. *"As much as I would enjoy an open conflict with you and your ship, Kirk, I assure you that my orders are also very clear. I was to deliver the* diplomatic *team to the planet, which I have done."* Koloth spoke the word *diplomatic* as if it were a curse. However, something else was in the Klingon's voice: sincerity. A hunch told Kirk that what the Klingon captain had just told him was the absolute truth. But he felt

167

that something else was going on here, something that Koloth wasn't saying.

Interesting.

"I look forward to seeing you shortly. *Enterprise* out," Kirk said. "Mister Spock, you have the bridge. I'll be in sickbay."

Kirk got up from his chair and met McCoy in his office a few minutes later. "How are the patients, Bones?"

"The young man had two badly broken arms. However, I was able to reset them without surgery. Otherwise they're suffering from minor injuries. They came in malnourished and dehydrated, but we've loaded them with food, water, and vitamins."

"There's a *but* in there, Doctor."

McCoy raised an eyebrow. "Physically, except for the broken bones, they'll be fine and ready for release from sickbay tomorrow. These kids have been through hell, Jim. Their bodies will recover quickly, but psychologically . . . well, that is going to take some time."

"Were they tortured?"

"Not formally, no, but they were locked up in a small, cold, dark space without adequate food and water for days, while they waited to be handed over to the Klingon military for interrogation. I can make them comfortable, but there are things here I can't fix, not in a few days anyway."

Kirk nodded. He had seen people in similar situations before. Hostages, refugees, and their like. The galaxy seemed to produce too damned many of them.

"You did the right thing, Jim. I know I wasn't convinced when we diverted the ship for the rescue, but if we hadn't arrived when we did, they would have faced much worse than they did, and then they would've died."

"Thanks, Bones. Our team did the impossible. I'm sorry that I can't get your patients off the ship before we reach the system. There will be some danger, but we can't afford any delay to make a rendezvous with a transport."

McCoy nodded. "When we do, we need to book a space for Lieutenant Parrish."

"She's leaving the *Enterprise*?"

"Yes, she came to speak to me. She's gonna have her baby. And her best chance of success would be on Earth."

"Understood. I'll alert Command. In the meantime, I'll try to keep your patients and the rest of the ship out of any unnecessary danger." Kirk got up.

McCoy stopped him before he exited sickbay. "They're not up to very many questions, not a full debriefing anyway."

Kirk nodded. That was fine with him. He had plenty to worry about in the short term. Giotto could debrief them later. Stepping through the sickbay door, Kirk was surprised to see Ensign Jawer in a chair next to one of the beds. Lying in the bed was a pretty, dark-haired young woman.

Jawer stood immediately. "Captain."

"Ensign."

"I'll leave you—"

"No," the young woman said quickly, fear in her voice. "Please stay," she said to Jawer. Then she turned her attention to Kirk and asked, "Can he stay?"

Kirk smiled. "Of course." Then he looked at the others: two other young women and one man who had

Kevin Ryan

braces on each arm. They already looked much better than they had coming out of the shuttle, except for their eyes, which still held too much of the lost look he had seen earlier. "I'm Captain James T. Kirk. Doctor McCoy tells me that you are all going to be fine."

"If we survive your next piece of aggression," the man in the arm braces murmured under his breath.

"Excuse me?" Kirk asked.

"Is it true that you are taking the ship into battle? Against Klingons?" he asked accusingly.

Kirk took a deep breath. He had dealt with the Anti-Federation League before. Most recently, there had been a mission in which the *Enterprise* had saved nearly sixty Anti-Federation League colonists, at the cost of too many members of his crew. Of course, in that case, the colonists had been grateful.

"The *Enterprise* is going to monitor a Klingon *diplomatic* mission in Federation space," Kirk said.

"Since it is a diplomatic mission, will the *Enterprise* be carrying its usual arsenal of deadly weapons?"

"The sort of weapons used to rescue you? Yes, it will. And as a point of fact, the Klingons are less likely to attack if they believe the *Enterprise* poses a credible threat."

"Typical Starfleet double-talk."

"Alan, please shut up," the dark-haired woman said. "Captain, please don't mind him. Alan forgets his manners when people risk their lives to save his."

Kirk approached her bed and she smiled. "I'm Christine Alvarez. I want to thank you for what you and your crew have done for us." Suddenly, she seemed near tears. "We thought we were going to die . . . and then, we were afraid they were going to keep us alive only to . . ."

Kirk put a hand on her shoulder, but she shook off the fear herself. "I appreciate what you've done. *We* appreciate it," she said, shooting the man with the broken arms a look. He didn't respond, and given the way she was looking at him, Kirk judged that wise.

"But, Captain, I have to ask. Will we be in any danger from the Klingons?" she said.

"This is purely a diplomatic mission, arranged by the Federation president himself, but I won't lie to you, there is some danger. The situation with the Klingon Empire is dire, but you are on a starship and we'll do our best to keep you safe."

She nodded as if she understood both what he had said and what he had left unsaid.

"In the meantime, as soon as Doctor McCoy releases you, you will be escorted to your temporary quarters."

"Thank you, Captain," she said, and the thanks were echoed by the others except for the man, who simply scowled.

The Orion mine was a short walk from the meeting pit, which was not surprising to Karel. Obviously, the natives thought that the mine, its technology, and its mineral wealth were a source of great power. However, it had also almost destroyed them. Now, it was leading them into a partnership with Duras, a Klingon who never showed his true face—if he even had one.

From the outside, the facility looked innocuous enough. It was three or four levels high, built in a generic industrial style. But this was a deep-core mine, which meant that the reactor and most of the important equipment would be underground. The doors were guarded by natives armed with Orion pistols. Again, Karel wondered what they were defending themselves against. Gurn seemed to trust Duras completely.

Gurn took them a few levels down and showed them the heavy equipment, the control rooms, and finally the reactor. Interestingly, Gurn seemed to know almost nothing about the equipment his people had inherited, and the natives tending the machines looked unsure of themselves. Yet, somehow, they had kept the power on, and even—according to Gurn—restarted the warp reactor.

Duras looked on politely and assigned technicians to work with the natives at each station. As they moved through the complex, Karel saw that Duras was impatient and seemed eager to move on.

They reached the mine's central shaft, where there was a short fence and a seemingly bottomless abyss. "And finally, let me show you our storage facility, which I think will be of particular interest," Gurn said.

Duras nodded and Gurn showed them onto a flying platform that Karel recognized as an ore hauler. With his technicians dispersed throughout the mine, Duras's party was down to five, the same number as in Karel's group and Gurn's. Three groups of five—the number in ancient Klingon hunting and war parties. Yet, there the similarity between the three groups ended. Karel felt uncomfortable around Duras and his Klingons, and Gurn made him feel the same way.

All fifteen Klingons fit easily in the ore hauler. One of Gurn's people took the controls. He seemed nervous and didn't inspire confidence. Yet he managed to get them down several levels in one piece. It was a short walk to a large open chamber where about a dozen cargo containers stood waiting.

"Let this be the first of many exchanges between our two peoples," Gurn said as he strode up to the first container and flung its lid open dramatically.

The box was completely empty.

No, not completely empty. A note was written on the underside of the lid. It mentioned Gurn by name and had a suggestion for the Klingon that was creative in its way but clearly biologically impossible.

Karel and his Klingons laughed out loud, while Duras said indignantly, "What is this?"

"Check the others," Gurn ordered his people, and they immediately began tearing open containers. They were all empty, except for the notes they held, which all carried messages for Gurn and interesting uses of language.

"Gurn, what is going on here? You gave me assurances," Duras said, menace in his voice.

"The dissenting clan we spoke of, this is their work. Adon is their leader," Gurn said, nearly choking in his fury. Looking at Duras's displeasure, he said, "We will destroy them immediately and get you your crystals."

"No more of this incompetence. Show us where they are and *we* will do it," Duras said.

"No," Gurn said, surprising Duras. "This is *our* world and *our* fight."

Karel smiled. Gurn obviously had *some* pride.

Duras nodded, keeping his anger in check. "Then we shall accompany you to observe and provide assistance if you need it." His voice was back to its overpolite tones.

A few moments later they were back on the surface, and Gurn sent messengers off to collect his people. It took several minutes and tried Duras's patience. Obviously, some of the natives had a limited mastery of the Orion weapons and technology. They still did not use communicators, instead relying on direct contact. Yet here Gurn was, trying to lead them into the middle of a brewing interstellar conflict.

Finally, Gurn had a dozen armed Klingons and four of the Orion weapons platforms, and the group moved out. For the natives, that must have represented an overwhelming force. He doubted that this Adon would be able to stand against it. That was a shame. Karel had already decided he liked him.

The combined group marched to the outskirts of a small village, and Karel had the feeling that he was stepping into his own people's past. "Destroy them, kill every last one of them!" Gurn said.

"Wait!" Karel said reflexively.

"Is there a problem, First Officer Karel?" Duras said, putting an emphasis on his rank.

"This is not a very honorable fight."

"This is *our* fight," Gurn said to Karel. Then he turned to his soldiers and the pilots hovering nearby. "Leave no one standing."

Karel's blood boiled at the thought of the uneven massacre to come. Apparently, even Gurn's men were unsure. They hesitated and looked at their leader. "Do it now!" Gurn screamed, and two of the weapons platforms moved forward, trained their energy weapons on one of the simple, wood dwellings, and fired. The home went up in a burst of flame and exploding wood.

There should have been screams, movement from the destroyed home or one of the others nearby. But there was only silence. The platforms moved forward again and struck another home. Another explosion and more silence. Karel realized that the village was empty.

When they'd arrived, no one was about, and Karel had assumed that the natives were hiding in their homes. Now he realized the entire clan had disappeared. The ground fighters moved forward and started checking the houses. Each was empty. Karel smiled and realized that he would like to meet this Adon.

Duras was furious. "You promised me the crystals!" he said, both anger and a warning in his voice.

Gurn's bravado disappeared. "We will find these crystals. And we can double our efforts in the mine—"

"We are about to fight a war. We need them now!" Then Duras stopped to collect himself. He smiled and forced a pleasant expression on his face. Karel thought it made him look even more menacing. "We shall do this together. The first step in our new partnership."

Chapter Eighteen

SYSTEM 7348
FEDERATION SPACE

FULLER ENTERED SICKBAY with the rest of the squad, except for Jawer, who was already there, sitting at the bedside of the young woman named Cyndy. The ensign looked embarrassed and stood up to greet them.

"Hello, Mister Fuller," Christine said.

Fuller nodded. "Just came by to see how you were all making out."

Suddenly, the man with braces on his arms—Alan—was on his feet. "We're all fine, thanks to your *rescue.*"

"Alan, don't," Christine said.

He ignored her and took a step toward Fuller. "You killed them, you know."

The rest of sickbay drew a collective breath.

"Excuse me?" Fuller said.

"Tomas and Ronald, *you* killed them."

"If you are referring to the two deceased members of your group, the fact is that the Klingons killed them. According to your own story, they killed Tomas in the initial attack on your ship and Ronald later."

"You created this situation," Alan said, contempt in his voice. "Your Starfleet with your weapons, your tools of Federation expansionism. You chew up and spit out new systems, pillaging them and leaving them dead husks."

Fuller knew better than to get into an argument with an irrational, angry civilian, but he could not resist saying, "Odd that you should say that when each system that joins the Federation enjoys unprecedented trade, peace, and prosperity. Stubborn facts, I'm afraid." He turned to the others. "I'm glad you are all doing well, but we have duties."

"More murder," Alan said, and Fuller felt the hair on the back of his neck stand up.

Fuller decided to let it go and turned away, but Parmet stepped forward. "As a matter of fact, this man has saved more lives than you will ever infect with your stupidity, and his son just a few months ago led a mission to rescue fifty-nine of your Anti-Federation friends," Parmet said, his face reddening.

"So your son is a murderer too," Alan said to Fuller.

Something threatened to tear loose inside Fuller, and for a moment it took every bit of control he had to keep him from hitting the man in the face.

Alan went on, "It's a family business. You take your weapons into space, seek out new races to subjugate, and then call yourselves heroes for killing them when they finally stand up to you. Did you teach your son how to kill, Mister Fuller, or was he a natural?"

Something snapped inside Fuller. He knew the man in front of him wasn't worth it, but he felt his fist balling itself on its own. He raised his hands, and the only thing that stopped him was that someone else acted first. Another fist came flying through the air and caught Alan right on the chin.

The strong blow sent the man backward into the bed. Fuller turned to see that it had been Parmet, who was nearly choking on his own fury and still had his hand raised as if ready to strike again. Fuller said, "Enough." And Parmet froze where he was, his chest heaving, staring daggers at Alan, who was looking up at them dumbly.

When the man could finally speak, he pointed to Parmet. "He tried to kill me. This man tried to kill me."

Fuller shook his head. "That's impossible, if he had tried to kill you, you would be dead now."

"What's going on here?" a voice asked from behind them. It was Doctor McCoy, who was looking at them with a raised eyebrow.

"Doctor, I want to report that this officer assaulted me," Alan said, pointing to Parmet. Then he shifted to Fuller. "And *he* was harassing me."

"I find that very hard to believe," McCoy said.

"But he hit me!" Alan said, his voice a high-pitched whine.

"Well, that's just plain unlikely." Something in McCoy's tone told Fuller that McCoy had seen the whole exchange or enough of it.

"You're not going to do anything?" Alan said, frank disbelief in his voice.

"On the contrary, I'm going to release you immediately. Two security officers will be here in a moment to escort you to your quarters, where you will stay. My medical advice would be to be extremely polite to your escorts. Once there, you can file whatever complaints you wish."

For the first time since they'd arrived, Alan was speechless. A moment later, he was whisked away by two guards. "Mister Fuller, I'm afraid that visiting hours are now over," McCoy said.

"Understood, Doctor." Then Fuller turned his attention to Jawer. "You're on duty as of now, Ensign."

Jawer nodded and said a quiet good-bye to the young woman in the bed, and the squad left sickbay.

"Next time, I'm not going to rescue him unless he apologizes for his behavior *and* says please," Jawer said. There was a burst of laughter from the squad, and Fuller was surprised to see that some of it came from his own mouth. Glancing over at Parmet, Fuller saw that one of the squad wasn't laughing. His face was red and the naked fury was still there in his eyes.

"Get me the Klingons on-screen," Kirk said. A moment later, the Klingon battle cruiser appeared on the main viewscreen. He stood, his body reflexively reacting to the threat the warship posed.

"The Klingons are holding position," Spock said. "Sensors show no power to their weapons, though their shields are at full strength."

Kirk nodded. That was fair enough. The *Enterprise*'s own shields were at full power as well. "Why not? They're on a *diplomatic* mission. Uhura, send out hails on all frequencies used on our last visit here."

"Aye, Captain," Uhura's hands worked the controls. The last time they were here, the local leader, Gorath—whose people had a large hand in defeating the Orions—had asked for his people to be left alone. He had seen what involvement in the larger galactic community had nearly brought to his planet and wanted no more to do with it. Kirk couldn't blame him, but the galactic community had come to them in the form of the Klingons. And for whatever reason, Gorath had apparently agreed to talk to them.

"No response to hails in the mining complex or in any of the portable transmitter-receivers," Uhura said.

Kirk was not surprised. The planet had stopped talking to Starfleet some time ago. Kirk was prepared for this. "Lieutenant, hail the communicator we gave to Gorath himself." The captain had given that device to the Klingon leader personally—a final fail-safe method of communication.

A few seconds passed. And then a few more. Finally Uhura said, "No response."

That did surprise Kirk. He and his crew had earned Gorath's respect, but something strange was going on here. Kirk knew he needed to get to the bottom of it, and fast. The Klingons had already been here for too long, with too many opportunities for mischief. "Lieutenant, send a message to all receivers in the mining complex. Tell them to prepare for our immediate arrival."

"I have a response, audio only," Uhura said.

Kirk nodded to her. "This is Captain James T. Kirk of the *U.S.S. Enterprise*. I wish to speak with Gorath."

"This is clan leader Gurn." Kirk recognized the telltale sound of the translator at work.

"Is Gorath available?"

"I lead my people, you may speak to me."

"I ask again, is Gorath available?"

"Captain, what do you want?"

"We wish to meet with your people to continue discussing your relationship with the Federation. We are also here to monitor the visit by the Klingon diplomatic team. We have reason to believe you may be in some danger."

There was a laugh on the other end. *"We are in no danger. The Klingons come to us in friendship."* Something was definitely going on here. And whatever it was, this Gurn was part of it.

"We also come in friendship. We would like to meet with you to discuss the future of your planet." For now, at least, Gurn was apparently the one Kirk would have to deal with—at least until he could reach Gorath.

"We can decide our own future. We have no need or desire to meet with you. Please leave this system at once." Gurn paused. *"Will you respect our wishes? My Klingon advisers have made it clear that you represent a threat to my people. They have told us the truth about the Federation's involvement in the Orion mine. I'm telling you for the last time, Captain. Leave this system immediately."* Then there was a click as the connection was broken.

Kirk looked over at Spock, who said, "An interesting development. Clearly, the local leader is in league with the Klingons."

Kirk had been afraid of just this kind of situation when he had decided to effect the rescue that had delayed their arrival. Now they were not welcome. Well, Kirk had been instructed to use diplomacy, to approach the situation delicately to try to diffuse any tension in the system while the diplomats kept working on the larger situation with the Klingon Empire. If possible, he was to make sure that the first shots of a war with the empire were not fired in this system. On the other hand, he was under orders to make sure that the Klingons did not get their hands on the dilithium under the planet's surface.

"Our options would appear to be limited," Spock said.

"Not completely," Kirk said. "We're going to beam down and talk to them in person. Mister Spock, our landing site will be Gorath's village. Feed coordinates to the transporter room and to the helm. Mister Sulu, take us out of range of the Klingon vessel's weapons, but keep us in transporter range of the landing site."

"Aye, sir." Almost immediately, Sulu started adjusting orbit to make that possible.

Hitting a button on his command chair, the captain said, "Kirk to Giotto. Are your security teams ready?"

"Yes, sir," Giotto answered.

"Have them meet me in the transporter room." Getting up, Kirk turned to his first officer. "You have the conn."

Kirk found the security teams waiting for him in the transporter room. Fuller and his team were assembled, as were Greenberger and his team. Lieutenant Parrish was there as well. Of course, she had been on the first mission to the planet and had fought well against the Orions. Earlier she had briefed both teams on the mine and the area. Now she was there to see her old squad off.

She hadn't done that before the rescue mission, but Kirk understood why. Now the team had been tested together and would not be distracted by their attachment to their former leader.

He looked over the men and women waiting to beam down and wondered what he was sending them into. *I should be going with them,* he thought. It was tempting, but clearly impossible with a Klingon cruiser a few thousand kilometers away.

Fuller was more than up to this command. If Kirk had had any doubts about him before, they had disappeared during the rescue mission. If force was required, Fuller could handle himself as well as any officer Kirk had ever known. And if finesse was required, Fuller could manage that as well.

Kirk briefed them quickly on what he knew and laid out the two most important mission parameters. "First, you are to establish a Federation presence on the planet. Whatever is going on there, let the Klingons know we won't tolerate any mischief in our backyard. Second, find out what has happened there in the last few weeks. Has there been a transfer of power among the natives? Find Gorath if you can and find out if the Klingons are behind whatever changes have happened."

Fuller's team stepped onto the transporter pads.

Kirk added, "Good luck, Michael. Good luck to you all."

"Thank you, Captain. If you would give the word . . . ," Fuller said.

"Energize," Kirk said. A few moments later, Greenberger's team had also dematerialized, leaving Kirk and Parrish to consider the empty pads. They left the transporter room together in silence. In the corridor, Kirk said, "Doctor McCoy told me that you have made your decision."

"Yes, Captain, and I want to thank you for helping me do that."

"Me?"

"Yes, sir. Something you said about not sacrificing who we are even when it serves the greater good."

Kirk remembered saying something like that in the meeting before the rescue mission. For a moment, he was uncomfortable with the responsibility there. The decision to go ahead with the rescue was sound, but only time would tell what the cost of that decision would be on the surface of this planet and to the Federation.

Kirk stopped in front of the turbolift door.

"I didn't mean to make you uncomfortable," she said, obviously reading something on his face. "But it did help me figure out who I was and what I was willing to sacrifice. I believe that Jon Anderson meant something and that our baby means something. I just wanted to thank you."

"Good luck to you, Lieutenant," Kirk said as he entered the turbolift.

Fuller was immediately alert as he materialized in the center of the village. He saw immediately that no one was in view. The silence also told him that no one was around—or that whoever was there was hiding.

Drawing his phaser, Fuller scanned the site as the second team materialized nearby. He recognized the ground. The captain had briefed him, as had Lieutenant Parrish. And the computer had extensive images from the report Commander Giotto had filed—the report that proved conclusively that the Klingons were behind the Orion mine.

He had also read the reports of how small teams armed only with hand phasers and with the help of some locals had fought off the Orion flying weapons platforms. Later, there had also been heavy ground fighting with both phasers and blades in an intense battle in and around the mine itself.

Brave people had died here, both Federation and native, though surprisingly few considering what they had accomplished. Nevertheless, the Klingon Empire seemed to have moved in and Starfleet was no longer welcome. Well, this mission would allow Fuller and his people to have something to say about that.

The mission.

His mission.

They were two different things, not necessarily contradictory, but not necessarily complementary either. He had failed to finish a job with the Klingons twenty-five years before, and too many had died because of it. *Sam* had died because of it.

And these are the Klingons who killed Sam. It was the D'k Tahg *that attacked Starbase 42,* a voice in his head supplied. That voice had been fairly quiet lately. It had even been still during the rescue mission, which was the first time since Sam's death that he had been face-to-face with Klingons.

He had felt a black rage when he had seen them, but they were civilians and his training had held. The old habits were hard to break. He had let the Klingons live, but until the moment he had done it, he had not known if he could. However, the time would soon come when he would have to break those habits and forget that training.

Revenge was part of it, certainly. But the much more important part was that he knew things about the enemy that Starfleet and the Federation were too blinded by their own principles to see. The Klingons gave no quarter because it was in their nature. And unless they met a force of equal power and resolve, the cancer they represented would take over the galaxy one world at a time, smashing the Federation and destroying everything that good people had built—that too many had given their lives to protect.

Fuller had failed at the Battle of Donatu V because of his weakness and lack of resolve. He would not fail again. It would likely cost him his life, but pieces of him had been dying for years, and the last part worth anything had died when he'd received a message of condolence from his son's captain.

It amazed him that those around him couldn't see what was missing in him, but their blindness allowed him to pursue the last course left to him, his final purpose. A mission. The only one that mattered. The only one of his career that would make a difference.

"Sir, I show multiple targets converging on this location," Parmet said, his tricorder out and scanning.

"Everyone move! Find cover!" Fuller said, but before they could take even three steps, Fuller saw four small platforms hurtling toward them. "Phasers ready." He aimed with his own even though the weapons were out of range. A quick mental calculation told him that they had zero chance of dispersing in time.

"Form a circle," he said, knowing that their chances in that formation were only slightly better. Each of the two squads had two phaser rifles. They were the only weapons that could penetrate the Orion weapons' shields without a constant bombardment, but even they would take a little time.

More time than he guessed they were going to have.

"Hold fire until my mark," Fuller said. There was a chance the Klingons on the platforms weren't hostile. That was their only chance of walking away from this encounter. The pilots of each platform were wearing flight suits, which made it impossible to determine if they were natives or Klingon warriors, but the slight unsteadiness of the flying suggested to Fuller that they were natives without much flight experience.

That might help, he realized. The weapons were getting closer. "Ready rifles," Fuller said. He could see Mc-Calmon and Quatrocchi raise their weapons and take aim. The phaser rifles had almost the same range as the Orion weapons so that would be another point in their favor.

The first blast came from the platform farthest out, striking the ground five meters ahead of them. It threw up a fair amount of dirt and left an immediate crater. "Fire all weapons," Fuller shouted.

Fuller aimed and fired his phaser as the thirteen people around him did the same. Some of the phasers hit their mark, making the platforms glow as their shields dissipated the energy.

Kevin Ryan

More fire came in now and Fuller realized that the
platforms were now within range, but the deadly bolts
still missed. The attackers were simply bad shots. Still,
it would only take two or three direct hits on the group
to kill them all.

Fuller realized that their chances had gone from
about zero to 10 or 15 percent. He cursed himself for
letting his team get surrounded in an area with no cover
to protect them from the weapons they now faced.

Both his personal mission and the mission for the
ship were about to end, and he would have accomplished nothing. "First time we get hit, survivors disperse immediately!" he shouted.

And then the game changed. Fuller saw a new
weapons platform streaking across the sky, heading for
the others. This one was piloted by a man in native
clothing, not a flight suit. The new platform's weapons
came alive and, at a considerable distance, made a series
of direct hits on one of the platforms firing on Fuller's
team. The Orion vehicle exploded in a brilliant display.

Immediately, Fuller's attention was caught by another
new platform coming in at high speed, weapons blazing.
This one was also piloted by a native without a flight
suit, this time a woman. It scored another series of hits
and the other vehicle firing on Fuller's team exploded.

The final two attackers came about and tried to engage the new craft, but their piloting was clumsy. The
people in suits got off a few shots, but none even came
close to hitting the natives. More important, they turned
to show their backs to the security team.

No one on the ground needed to be told what to do.
They all took aim at the platforms' exhaust areas, the

188

most vulnerable sections of their shields. With the combination of phaser II and phaser rifle fire, the barrage took only a few seconds to overwhelm the shields and turn the weapons platforms into balls of flame.

"Hold fire," Fuller said, and the phasers went quiet.

In a quick series of maneuvers, the new pilots turned and approached them. "Phasers down," Fuller said, lowering his own weapon.

Fuller had studied the reports and expected to see Gorath on one of the platforms, but this Klingon was too young—a teenager—and the young woman on the other platform was no older.

"Do you speak English?" Fuller said when they were hovering nearby.

"I do. Are you Starfleet?" the young man said.

"Yes, I am looking for Gorath."

"You are not Captain Kirk?"

"No, but he sent me to speak with Gorath."

"Gorath is dead. I am his son. Come with us. This place will not be safe for long." The native, who looked like a Klingon, turned his platform and pointed it away from the village.

"Let's move," Fuller said.

Chapter Nineteen

U.S.S. ENTERPRISE
SYSTEM 7348

"Captain Koloth," Kirk said. "My landing party has come under fire."

"I am sorry to hear that, Captain," Koloth said. *"I hope they died well."*

"Actually, they are all well, though there were some losses on the other side. The question is, did your vessel have anything to do with the incident?"

"Captain Kirk, if I strike you or your ship a blow, you will not have to wonder if it comes from my hand."

"Be that as it may, someone using heavy weapons attacked my landing party."

"Captain, I would welcome the opportunity to test my ship and crew against yours. And we both know that that time may come soon. However, for the moment, I am here only to serve the diplomatic team."

"Then you won't mind if I talk to them?"

"Not at all, I will have my communications officer transmit to you the frequency for Duras now."

Then Koloth's face disappeared from the main viewscreen, replaced by space and the planet below.

"Receiving transmission now." After a moment, Uhura added, "I have the communicator frequency."

"Jim," Doctor McCoy said. "There may be trouble in paradise. Sounds like Koloth is having trouble with his diplomat."

"I think you may be right, Bones," Kirk said.

"Captain, Starfleet records indicate that there is a Duras on the Klingon High Council," Spock said.

"A *councillor* sent to begin talks with an undeveloped planet? To begin a process that might take years?" Kirk said.

"The logic is not immediately apparent," Spock said.

"No, it isn't." It truly didn't make any sense to Kirk. Neither did Koloth's insistence that he knew nothing about the attack on the landing party—which, to his surprise, Kirk found that he believed. "There's only one way to find out what's going on here. Let's ask the councillor. Uhura, open a channel."

"I have a signal," Uhura said.

"Who is this? What do you want?" a translated Klingon voice said.

"This is Captain James T. Kirk of the Federation starship *Enterprise*."

"Captain . . . ," the councillor said, and seemed to be at a loss for words.

"I thought it was time you and I talked. I propose that we meet face-to-face."

"Impossible, I am deep into talks with the natives here. Talks that the Enterprise is here to monitor, not interfere with."

"And I was prepared to do just that, until my landing party was attacked."

"You were warned by the local authorities not to beam down."

"I'm afraid that the Federation does not recognize Gurn as the leader of this world."

"The Klingon Empire does, and Gurn has our support."

"Councillor, did your team have anything to do with the attack on my people?" Kirk said, putting steel into his voice. There was silence on the other end for a moment. "Do I need to repeat the question, Councillor?"

"No, we had nothing to do with the attack, but I cannot protect your people if you will not respect the will of the native population here."

"I will deal with the natives in my own way. But you need to understand that if I see any sign that you are assisting in another attack, or using the ship to scan for so much as a Starfleet communicator on the surface, I will consider that a hostile act and will react accordingly. Do we understand each other?"

"Captain, I am here in a diplomatic capacity. I seek only to have productive talks with the local, Klingon population."

"Then you and I will not have a problem. Kirk out."

About twenty minutes after their rescue from the native Klingons, Fuller and his team had followed the flying platforms to a rocky hill. After a few minutes of climbing, they found themselves on a small plateau facing about 150 more of the indigenous people—men, women, and children.

Klingons, Fuller thought in wonder. No, not Klingons, not like the ones who killed Sam. According to Captain Kirk and the other reports from the previous incident on this planet, the natives were normally peaceful, honorable people. And their entire world had nearly been another victim of the Klingon Empire.

Yet they had proven to be warriors at heart. And from what he had seen, the other tribes were more like the Klingons he knew. The young native landed his platform and stepped to the ground.

"Who is in charge here?" Fuller said. All eyes turned to the young man who had just stepped off his vehicle.

"Adon, son of Gorath, is our clan leader," an older adult said, pointing to the young man.

"What has happened here?" Fuller said.

"Gurn, one of the other clan leaders, is working with a Klingon leader named Duras, who promised him power, weapons, and other machines in return for the dilithium crystals. Gurn murdered my father for standing against him and has turned the clans against us. They now control the green-skins' mine. They also have most of the weapons, and now the help of Duras and his people."

That sounded like the Klingons Fuller knew—betraying their own people for equipment to make war on and kill others. Gurn was getting into bed with the devil, a devil who had tried to destroy every one of his people for some rocks. Clearly, Duras and Gurn—and the people that followed them—deserved one another. But what of Adon and these people?

"We mean to put a stop to this alliance. Captain Kirk aided my father before. Would he help us now?" Adon asked.

"Does Duras have the crystals he came for?" Fuller asked.

Adon smiled. "No, we removed them from the mine. They are safe."

That changed things. If Duras and the Klingons already had the crystals, the *Enterprise* would have no choice but to stop the ship from leaving the system, and the *Enterprise* would deal out Fuller's revenge for him. But since the Klingons didn't yet have what they came for, things were different. With the crystals out of the equation, Fuller would have been content to let the Klingons kill each other, but that decision was not his to make—at least not yet.

"I have to talk to my captain," Fuller said.

"You cannot find fourteen Starfleet officers?" Duras shouted.

"No, Councillor," the technician replied.

"They do carry communicators, don't they?"

"Yes, but our passive scanning capability is limited, and there is some interference from the local hills. This installation was built with mining in mind only," the Klingon replied.

"Then scan from space! What of the *D'k Tahg*?" Duras demanded. If Koloth scanned for the Starfleet Earthers, Kirk might react violently, and then the *D'k*

Tahg would fire the first shots of this war even earlier than Duras had expected.

"The ship does not respond to my signal," the technician replied.

"Use satellites, then!"

"Councillor, there are none . . . this installation was designed to operate in secret."

Duras knew that. He had issued the orders that had funded and built it—through Orion subsidiaries—himself. He felt things slipping away from him. He should have had the crystals by now. Every moment he stayed on this world increased the risk to his mission.

Gurn stepped forward. "My people will find Gorath's people. We will destroy them and any Earther who stands with them."

"You incompetent fool!" Duras shouted at Gurn. "Your job, and your only job right now, is to stay out of our way. Do not test me further."

Gurn cringed and took a step away from Duras, who turned his attention back to the technician. "And the reactor?" Duras asked.

"We will have it up to full power in one hour."

Finally, some good news. At least part of the plan was on schedule. Now it was time to put the rest of it into motion. He lifted his communicator and said, "Duras to Koloth." And waited. And waited.

"Duras to Koloth," he repeated.

There was a delay and Koloth's voice came on the line. *"What do you want?"*

"I need you to scan for the Starfleet people on the surface. I need their position immediately."

After a long delay, Koloth said, *"Our scanners don't pick up anything. Are you sure they are on the surface?"*

Duras felt his rage deepen. Koloth was lying to him, toying with him, thwarting him. He grunted once and broke the line. He noticed Koloth's *targ* Karel looking at him with clear pleasure on his face. This was intolerable! He was a member of the High Council! On urgent business for the empire!

Duras forced down his rage. They would all pay soon enough, Koloth, Karel, and any who would follow them. Then Starfleet, then . . . Well, before the day was out, Duras would win a number of great victories, and he *needed* the victories. The failure of the mine had cost him on the council, as had the failure of the infiltrator program. He had placed dozens of agents, *betleH 'etlh*, throughout Starfleet, but they had been found out too early to do any good. Another costly failure.

But today his fortunes would change. Through force of will, he calmed himself and walked over to Gurn. "Fear not, victory will be ours by the end of the day." Then he turned to his technician. "Come with me. I need to send a secure message."

"I am sorry to hear about your father," Kirk said into the intercom.

"His murderer will pay, Captain," Adon said through the comm system.

Kirk would have preferred to have this conversation face-to-face. But under the circumstances, Kirk could not leave the ship and Adon would not leave the planet.

"My father was right, Captain. The arrival of the Orions and their machines has brought us nothing but grief.

First, it nearly destroyed us, now it has set my people against one another for the first time in our history."

"We will help you however we can."

"Thank you, Kirk. You may help us immediately by seeing that Gurn has nothing of value to trade. Can you use your transporter to remove the crystals from the surface?"

"Yes. And we can offer—"

"I ask for nothing above what you have already offered. Remove the crystals and we shall see how strong the alliance between Gurn and Duras remains."

"If you can show Mister Fuller where they are, we can retrieve them."

This was a good, if surprising, development, Kirk realized. The most immediate danger was that the Klingons would get their hands on the crystals to fuel their war effort. The dilithium would help the Federation now, as long as the *Enterprise* was able to deliver it safely to Starfleet Command.

There was still danger. In the long term, more crystals could be extracted from the mine. But the war would likely begin before that. The border would be closed and the Klingons would have to fight for every system.

A few minutes later, Fuller called with the coordinates. "Mister Spock?"

"Scanners show twelve cargo containers near Fuller's position. Sending coordinates to the helm and transporter room now," Spock said.

"Mister Sulu, very low orbit. Put as much of the planet between us and the Klingon ship as you can. Mister Spock, let me know if the Klingons so much as vent plasma."

A moment later, Sulu reported ready. They had a reasonable safety margin. By putting themselves at the extreme range of the transporters, they were safely out of the range of Klingon weapons.

"Lower shields, begin transport," Kirk said.

Less than two minutes later, Scott reported that the containers were on board. "Shields up. Well done," Kirk said.

This mission was far from over, though. There were too many unanswered questions for one. And second, Kirk had a large ball in his stomach telling him that the Klingons were planning something.

Koloth smiled when Councillor Duras broke the communication. If Duras was interested in starting an honest fight with the Earthers, Koloth would be pleased to deliver the first blow. The *D'k Tahg* was ready to pay Starfleet back for the indignity of the failure of the assault on Starbase 42.

Of course, Duras had other concerns. The empire had lost the dilithium crystals on the other planet that the starbase had been protecting. Now, Duras wanted the crystals on the planet below. The empire's leaders had to think on a high strategic level. A wise warrior knew when to choose his moment to begin open battle. However, for a coward that moment would never come.

And Duras, Koloth was convinced, was a bloodless coward. There was also more going on there than Duras's precious rocks. At this point, it would not be crystals that won the coming war for the empire, it would be the strength of their blood. Yet, Duras was still conniving and scheming for stones.

First, Duras had tried to convince Karel to turn against his commander to help the councillor take the ship. Now, he was plotting with some spineless representatives on the planet below. And still, the *Enterprise* waited just a few thousand kilometers away, taunting Koloth and the whole empire with its arrogant existence.

Soon, matters would come to their culmination. Eventually, Duras would have to stop cowering in the dark and reveal his plans. Then Koloth could take matters into his own hands. The tale that Karel had told Koloth about the dishonorable mission that had taken his brother's life had revealed what Koloth had suspected for too long: the empire was rotting from within.

Seeing Duras in action had further convinced Koloth that there were basic problems with their leaders. The High Council had made much of the stain on Klingon honor left by the inconclusive Battle of Donatu V, but there were worse things a warrior could face than a tie in battle. There was the loss of honor he brought upon himself.

Yes, there was much wrong with the empire, and Koloth would have preferred his people enter war with the Federation with both their strength and their honor intact. However, no warrior chose all the terms of every battle he fought. Perhaps the coming war would purify the empire, burn away the pettiness and dishonor that had taken hold. Perhaps his people's better natures would emerge, their honor made whole by a battle well fought and won.

These truly were dangerous times for the empire, yet Koloth found that he was untroubled. He felt a wave of optimism, like the euphoria he had felt after a particularly sweet victory.

But there has been no victory here, a voice in his mind shouted.

That was true, but the feeling persisted nevertheless. He felt his body and mind begin to relax, as it did after a good meal and a few glasses of bloodwine.

Bloodwine . . .

Something is wrong. Koloth stood, or tried to. He found his legs wouldn't respond to his commands.

I've been poisoned, he thought, felled by the weapon of a cowardly assassin who would strike without showing his face. Koloth opened his mouth and found that he couldn't speak. His eyes still worked, and with them he could see the ship's pilot struggling in his seat, also apparently immobile.

Then Koloth understood. *Gas.*

He realized an odd, faint smell was in the air. Duras had brought a great deal of cargo, full of classified equipment that was shielded from sensors. First, Duras tried to incite a mutiny on his ship. Then, failing that, the councillor had had his soldiers gas Koloth and his crew.

The ship would now be Duras's. *This is intolerable!* his mind screamed. Koloth cursed his failure to see this coming. He had given the councillor too much rope, even after he knew that Duras was plotting against him. Of course, taking on a member of the High Council was suicide, but it still offered a more honorable death than being gassed like an elderly pet *targ.*

Koloth's eyes grew heavy. He fought to keep them open, to keep the darkness at bay. There were still things he could do, actions he could take. If only his traitorous body would respond . . .

The world around him went dark. As a final insult, he heard footsteps behind him. The bloodless cowards who served Duras had entered his bridge. In a moment, the ship would be theirs.

Koloth screamed his outrage in his mind. Then the darkness finally came and even that silent scream was ended.

Chapter Twenty

STARFLEET COMMAND
EARTH

LIEUTENANT WEST WAS ON HIS FEET before he was halfway through reading the intelligence report. He only read a few more lines before he stopped and turned for the door. Lieutenant Lei was outside his office door when he reached it. From the look on her face, she had read the same report.

"Come with me," he said, already sprinting down the corridor. Lei followed and they reached Admiral Solow's office a few seconds later. The admiral's yeoman waved them in, and Solow was standing when they arrived.

"You've read the report," Solow said, making it a statement, not a question.

"Yes, sir," West said. "We don't have much time."

"I'm afraid it may already be too late."

"Sir, the *Yorktown* is nearby. Perhaps—"

"If we send a starship blazing in, they'll just kill Fox and the team sooner," Solow said.

"Sir, with all due respect, that might be the best thing," Lei said.

"The best?" Solow said, unable to hide his surprise.

"A quick death is much better than what they will get if the Klingon diplomats carry out their orders," Lei said.

West thought about it for a moment. "Lei is right. If they are interrogated, they will die . . . very slowly."

"This is insane. What is happening to this galaxy?" Solow said, clear frustration in his voice. "They are diplomats, *unarmed* diplomats."

West knew how the admiral felt. As a diplomat, Fox was of limited intelligence value. He knew little about Starfleet and the Federation's military readiness—at least little that the Klingon intelligence network didn't already know. Whatever Fox and his people did know, they would tell a skilled Klingon interrogator in hours.

And the interrogation would last for days beyond that.

"Sir, there is one thing you should know: they are not completely unarmed," West said.

"What?" the admiral asked. West told Solow about his gift to Fox before the negotiations. He had sent a small number of old-style laser pistols, of the kind that Starfleet had used so successfully against the Klingons in the Battle of Donatu V. They had been meant to send a message of strength to the Klingon negotiating team. But West had seen that they were fully charged and operational so they would have more than purely symbolic value.

"Perhaps we could send a message to Fox. He may choose to fight . . . or to see to it that he and his team are not taken alive," West said.

Solow winced in pain. "Is that all we can offer our people now? Suicide? Because all of their other options are so much worse!"

West had no response for that.

Ambassador Fox stared at the message in silence. For a moment, he considered keeping the information to himself, but he decided that his staff deserved to know the truth. They had struggled too hard for anything less and had even watched one of their own die in service of the ideals they shared. Now, in all likelihood, they would join Fronde in his sacrifice.

Fox assembled them in the common room that connected their individual quarters. "I have just received a communication from Starfleet. They have intercepted and decoded a transmission from the Klingon High Council to Ambassador Morg. He and his team are to wait for final word from command, then they will apprehend us and keep us in custody for transfer to the Klingon Defense Force. Once that transfer is complete, we are to be interrogated."

There was frank disbelief on the four faces in front of him. "But our diplomatic status . . ."

"Means nothing to the Klingons. We've known for some time that these negotiations were a fraud. Despite all of your efforts and despite Fronde's courage, the Federation is facing war, and we are facing . . ." Fox didn't

finish. There were words he had already used: *custody* . . .
transfer . . . *interrogation*. But those terms were thin eu-
phemisms for what they were really facing: slow torture
and an unimaginably painful death.

To their credit, his team took the news with surprising calm. After a long silence Helen Fitzpatrick, his new
chief of staff, asked, "Is there any chance of rescue?
Will Starfleet . . ."

Fox nodded. "Starfleet has informed me that they are
working on a plan, but I won't lie to you, the chances of
help arriving in time are small. We will likely be alone
in this. We knew we might face this situation, and I have
given the matter considerable thought. We do have some
options; one of them is to fight."

Stepping over to the computer terminal, he picked
one of the laser pistols that Lieutenant West had sent
with them. Originally, Fox had been offended at the
man's presumption and arrogance when he had placed
laser weapons and ceremonial swords on a *diplomatic*
shuttle. However, Fox had later seen that the Klingons
did respect the weapons, and they respected the team
more because they carried them.

"I know that some of you are opposed to violence—"

"I will fight," Fitzpatrick said, standing up. There
was a chorus of agreement from the others.

Fox nodded. "Then I suggest we wear the weapons at
all times. Further, we should always stay together. And
for now, we should continue the negotiations. That may
buy us some time."

There were nods, and for the hundredth time since
these negotiations had begun, he saw their belief in him
and what they were doing. They would follow him even

in this, even when his failure was so plain, even after he had led them on a path to death or something even worse.

"We're with you, sir," Fitzpatrick said.

Fox nodded, not trusting his voice. After a moment, he composed himself. "There is one more thing. If we are prepared to fight, we will be facing trained Klingon warriors—whatever diplomatic cloaks they wear. We need to be prepared for the possibility that we will lose. In that case, I strongly suggest that you not let the Klingons take you alive."

"We understand. We'll be ready, Ambassador," Fitzpatrick said with firm resolve in her voice. He saw the same resolve on all their faces. They were all good people, talented and brave, and they had placed their faith in him and a series of ideals that they all shared. Now they would likely pay for that faith with their lives.

Chapter Twenty-one

SYSTEM 7348
FEDERATION SPACE

WHEN FULLER CLOSED his communicator, Adon said, "Your captain said you would help us."

That had been Kirk's instruction to Fuller. "We will do whatever we can. What are your plans?"

"A sickness has affected my people. Gurn makes pacts with our enemies and puts himself and his desire for power over the lives of all of us." There was pain in the young man's face, and something else: determination. By the way his people were looking at him, they looked as if they were ready to follow him anywhere.

There was no shortage of courage here, but courage alone was not always enough to win the day. "Gurn and his people outnumber you by a considerable margin.

They also control the mine and have many weapons at their disposal. And Gurn also has help. So I ask you again, what are your plans?"

"I plan to defeat Gurn, put a stop to this partnership with our enemies, and kill the man who murdered my father," Adon said with perfect seriousness.

For a moment, Fuller felt ashamed that he would have been so quick to let these Klingons and the ones on the ship kill each other. He found that he understood this young man well. Now he thought that perhaps he had more in common with Adon than he had with the members of his own squad. There was also something almost familiar about this young man—a set in his face, a seriousness of purpose and a determination that he had seen in his own son.

Earth had a saying, one that the Klingons shared in an altered form: "The enemy of my enemy is my friend." Well, Fuller didn't think he would ever call a Klingon friend, but they could share an enemy. The man that had killed Adon's father was working with the Klingons who had killed Fuller's son.

"What is your plan?" Fuller asked again.

"My plan is victory . . . though I am still working on some of the details."

There it was, that determination again. And not just in this young man's face, but in the faces of the men and women around him. They would fight for him and for their world. They might lose—Fuller had seen too many determined people die young to pretend otherwise—but they would fight as long as they had breath.

And, as it turned out, so would Fuller.

* * *

"First Officer Karel," Duras said, approaching him. "Koloth has commanded you back to the ship."

Karel was immediately on his guard. Koloth's orders had been clear: keep an eye on Duras and his people. Why bring him back to the ship now?

"There has been trouble with the Earther vessel. There is a danger to the *D'k Tahg*," Duras said, as if reading Karel's doubts.

Karel studied the councillor's face, looking for deceit. The problem was, he doubted he had ever seen anything else in Duras's features. The councillor shrugged and said, "Contact your captain."

Karel intended to do just that: the only problem was his communicator would not penetrate the mine. There was new interference coming from somewhere. He would have to go outside to make that call. Turning to Gash, he said, "Assemble your men, we are returning to the surface."

He was tempted to leave a few warriors here to watch Duras, but his blood was calling out a warning. There was danger everywhere; they would be better off if they stayed together.

The trip to the surface was faster than the trip down since they were able to use the lifts that Duras's technicians had repaired. *At least they are good for something,* Karel thought.

On the ground level, they walked quickly through the complex, and Karel could not shake the feeling that Duras was up to something beneath the ground, something dishonorable—a plot that required darkness to plan and execute. He quickened his pace, and as soon as he was out of the mine, he reached for his communicator.

"Karel to Koloth."

"First Officer Karel, this is the D'k Tahg." Karel was immediately aware that something was wrong. He didn't recognize the voice.

"Who is this? Give me Captain Koloth!" On instinct, Karel turned to Gash. "We need to get inside. Now!" But before he could move two steps, he felt the transporter beam take him.

He expected his next sight to be the *D'k Tahg's* transporter room, but a moment later he and his warriors were standing in a field. They were obviously still on the planet, but the terrain was different here. Gone was the rocky forest, which had been replaced by grassy plains. Those plains were empty for as far as the eye . . .

No, not empty. There were bodies a few meters away. *Klingon* bodies. A lot of Klingon bodies. As he approached, a quick count told him that about a hundred lifeless warriors were lying on the ground: the entire crew—or at least the part that was still loyal to Captain Koloth.

That meant Duras and his people had taken control of the ship. Karel saw his captain lying in the grass and felt a howl of rage building in his throat. He gave it voice and vowed that Duras would pay for this outrage.

Doctor McCoy entered the bridge. Kirk could see the scowl on the doctor's face. Kirk guessed what was bothering him.

"How are your patients, Bones?"

"Physically they're fine, but I would like to throw one of them in the brig."

The doctor had told Kirk about the incident in sickbay, the altercation with security personnel. "I thought you confined him to quarters?"

"I did, but he keeps leaving and harassing the crew. Security has been calling me every five minutes," McCoy said. "Between that and filing complaints with Starfleet and Federation authorities, he's kept himself quite busy."

"I'll have Giotto put a guard on his quarters and keep him inside—it'll be almost as good as the brig."

"But not nearly as satisfying. In his latest complaint to Command, he claimed that he was treated better by the Klingons."

Kirk gave Giotto the order himself. The crew was tense, on standing yellow alert, with a constant threat of a Klingon warship nearby. The last thing they needed was an unbalanced civilian making mischief. Even if the man caused no physical trouble, he would keep crew members from focusing on their jobs.

"Captain, the Klingons are activating transporters," Spock said.

"What are they moving?"

"Personnel." After a moment the Vulcan added, "Interesting, they are transporting several members of the crew at a time to the planet's surface."

"How many?" Kirk asked.

"Thirty so far and they are continuing."

"They could be troops. If the Klingons are readying for an assault on the landing party—"

"Unlikely, Captain. The crew is being transported to another continent, more than two thousand kilometers away from the inhabited part of the planet. In fact, there are no natives in this area."

"What?"

"Transport complete. One hundred and seven members of the crew are now at that location. Now the transporters are being reactivated. They are sending heavy equipment down to the area around the mine."

Kirk had heard enough. "Lieutenant Uhura, get me Captain Koloth. Let's find out what kind of heavy equipment the Klingons need for their diplomatic mission. And maybe we'll find out what's going on here."

"No response to hails," Uhura said.

That wasn't good. Kirk was immediately on his feet. "Get me Councillor Duras."

"I have him on the surface," Uhura said.

A moment later, the councillor's voice came from the intercom: *"Captain Kirk."*

"Councillor, I am concerned about the recent transporter activity. If you are moving heavy weapons to the planet, understand that I will deal very strongly with any threat to the landing party."

"Captain, I am under no obligation to reveal to you the nature of our dealings or our trade with the natives of the planet. However, in the interests of peaceful cooperation, I will tell you we are providing spare parts and upgraded communications and mining equipment."

Kirk knew when he was being lied to. It was time to bring this confrontation out in the open. "Councillor, in the interests of *peaceful cooperation,* I will inform you of our ongoing negotiations with the *legitimate* planetary authorities. They have generously given us their complete supply of dilithium crystals." Kirk paused, letting that sink in.

Finally, the councillor said, *"Really, Captain?"*

"Councillor Duras, I tire of these games. We both

know that you came here to acquire the crystals, since the Klingon Empire failed to get them previously from their Orion agents who built the mine. You also failed to take the crystals from Starbase 42. You just failed again. If you want any of the planet's dilithium, you had better be prepared for a long stay. Our estimates show that it will be months before the mine produces any significant number of new crystals."

When Duras replied, his voice was smooth. *"Captain, as you know, the Klingon Empire denies any involvement in the Orion operation here. And the incident at Starbase 42 was the result of a rogue operation by one of our commanders. As for the dilithium currently in your possession, you misunderstand the Klingon Empire's clearly stated position. We are here to talk to the native Klingons on this world. We do not seek their mineral wealth, we merely desire an opportunity to develop ties with a race of brothers. Frankly, I find your suspicion and insinuation insulting."*

There was a click as the councillor broke the line.

"Fascinating," Spock said.

"Jim, he sounds like a man who thinks he's still holding a few good cards," McCoy said.

"My thinking exactly, Bones, but which ones?"

There was no answer, but Kirk had not expected one. Whatever was going on here, Kirk was sure of one thing: the situation had just become even more dangerous.

Karel was surprised to see that his captain and the others were unconscious but alive. He called to the ship and was not surprised when there was no response. Duras had obviously taken the ship and had gotten Koloth and all those loyal to him out of the way. The only remaining questions were why he had done it and where had he put them. The hand scanners could find no sign of the mine. They could be anywhere on the planet. And wherever they were, he was sure it was far from the mine. Duras would take no chances now.

Karel ordered Gash and his men to check on each of the crew, to see if all were alive. For the moment, they were out of options. No, Karel had one thing he could do; it just wasn't an appealing option. Pulling out his communicator, he said, "Karel to Duras."

A moment later, Duras came on the line. *"Yes, First Officer Karel?"* His voice was even, pleasant actually.

"What are you doing, Councillor Duras?"

"What am I doing? I am striking a blow for the empire, something you are too weak and bloodless to understand."

"You have taken action against the captain and crew of a Klingon battle cruiser, not the enemies of the empire."

"I do what I must to serve the empire. I offered you the D'k Tahg, *but you refused me, choosing loyalty to your pathetic captain rather than the greater interests of the Klingon people. I presume Koloth is still unconscious, lying on the ground at your feet—while I am about to set into motion the most glorious chapter of the history of the Klingon Empire."*

"By attacking in darkness, by using gas and transporters to betray your people?" Karel snapped.

"By achieving victory. You made your choice, now you will die with your captain."

So Duras did intend to kill them, but why hadn't he

214

already? Karel realized that he knew: Duras wanted to gloat first, to revel in his victory as he enjoyed Koloth's and Karel's defeat. Such would be their penalty for standing against him.

"I will kill you," Karel said.

"You are now an ocean away from the mine and you have no weapons or vehicles that can reach us, but by all means bluster away, Karel. While you do, I am going to destroy this world. But fear not, you will make a contribution to my victory. My report will show that the Earthers destroyed the planet, killing all of our Klingon brothers, and, unfortunately, Captain Koloth, you, and the rest of your pathetic crew. However, we will avenge you and destroy the Enterprise *in your names. The war begins here, the result of a cowardly attack by Earthers on a defenseless Klingon people. The entire empire will rise up in fury and crush the Federation for its treachery. You will be remembered as heroes, which is more than you deserve, but one of the sacrifices I am prepared to make."*

"You would kill an entire world of people of Klingon blood, in service of a lie?"

"This is war. No victory is won without sacrifice. Great leaders understand that, while lesser Klingons like you and Koloth die helpless as the battle rages around you."

The empire had built the mine and then tried to destroy the world to hide their involvement. Now, Duras was going to finish the job to launch a dishonorable war. A moment of insight told Karel something even more important.

"You built the mine. The orders came from the High Council."

Kevin Ryan

There was silence on the other end for a moment. *"Yes, I did. The failure of that operation cost me quite a bit with the council as well. This operation will change all that however."*

The councillor spoke for a few more seconds, but Karel wasn't listening. His mind was stuck on one essential piece of information: *Duras authorized the operation to build the mine.*

According to the information he had gained from the informant on Qo'noS, the same member of the High Council that had built the mine had instituted the infiltrator program that had swallowed his brother.

"You know quite a bit for such a pathetic servant of mediocrity. Well, you soon will take that knowledge to the River of Blood with you."

A bellow of rage escaped from Karel's throat. When it subsided, he realized that Duras had broken the line. There was noise behind him. Captain Koloth was on his feet and some of the others were starting to stir.

He could see rage on his captain's face. "First Officer Karel, report!" Koloth demanded.

Chapter Twenty-two

SYSTEM 7348
FEDERATION SPACE

"*MICHAEL, I'M PARTICULARLY CONCERNED about the heavy equipment that they're moving in,*" the captain's voice said through Fuller's communicator. "*Duras is planning something, but it seems to have nothing to do with dilithium, at least for the moment.*"

"I can think of one way to upset his plans, whatever they are. Adon is planning an assault on the mining facility," Fuller said.

"*I see.*"

Interesting. Fuller had just told the captain that a race that was completely preindustrial less than a year ago was planning to attack a much larger force with modern weapons and the help of the Klingon Empire—and Kirk simply accepted that without question or comment. Of course, Fuller had read the reports. He knew about the captain's feelings about these people in general, and Adon's father in particular.

"Have they asked you for help?" Kirk said.

"They have, Captain, and under the circumstances I am inclined to give it."

"I authorize you to take whatever action you deem necessary to protect Adon's clan and the interests of the Federation. What do you need?"

"We could use some more phaser rifles, one for each of us."

"Done. We'll monitor the situation from space." Fuller noticed that the captain had stopped short of promising help from the ship's weapons if it came to it, and Fuller understood why. Something strange was going on aboard the Klingon warship. Dissent? Mutiny? Whatever it was, it had put half of the crew an ocean away.

There was an excellent chance that the *Enterprise* would be too busy to intervene directly when things started on the surface. That meant that Fuller would have to assume that the landing party would be operating on its own.

"Kirk out."

Fuller closed his communicator and turned to the landing party. It was time to tell his people what they were up against.

"Are you mad?" Koloth said to Karel, shouting. Most of the crew were on their feet by now and looking over at their captain and first officer.

"It is the one thing that Duras doesn't expect, the one response he cannot plan for," Karel said.

218

"But the Earthers . . ."

"Captain, we have no weapons that can reach Duras, no method of stopping him from destroying us and our brothers. He left us with our uniforms, our hand weapons, and our communicators—and only one of those things can help us now."

"But the Earthers are our enemies."

"I would say that Duras, who threatens us all and insults the honor of the empire, is our enemy. We are not at war with the Earthers at the moment. When we are, I will leave not one of them standing. Until then, the enemy of my enemy—"

"Is still my enemy but may be useful," Koloth said, finishing the phrase.

Karel lowered his voice. "I have told you my brother's story. This Kirk is an honorable man. He risked his own life and the lives of his crew to protect this world from Duras's greed and treachery once before. Kirk earned my brother's loyalty, and we have nothing to lose by seeking a temporary alliance with him now."

Koloth silently considered Karel for a moment. The captain was weighing his suggestion and Karel could see that it was not because of its merits as a plan but because as unpleasant as it was, it was their only option—at least the only one that had even a chance of stopping Duras.

Yet Karel could see the resistance in his commander and understood it. Klingons were raised on tales of Earthers' treachery and cowardice. Officers in the Klingon Defense Force were schooled on similar stories about Starfleet. Kirk held a special place in many of those stories.

Karel's brother Kell had proven the falsehood of those tales, and Karel had told Koloth his brother's story. However, a single wild report from his first officer might not be enough to combat all the information fed to Koloth in his lifetime and career.

"Better for a warrior to die with his pride intact," he said.

"And better still to take victory with honor," Karel said.

"Then know this: if I humble myself before this Earther and we do not taste victory, you will be immediately demoted from first officer to a junior *trainee* weapons officer."

Karel smiled at that. If they did not taste victory— and soon—they would never live to return to the ship. On that level, the risk to Karel's career was small. "Fair terms, Captain,"

The last batch of phaser rifles came down and Fuller distributed them. He had offered Adon and his people phasers, but they had politely refused. They were more comfortable with the particle-beam pistols they had recovered from the Orion mine. Fuller understood. It was better to go into a fight with weapons you knew well. And from what Fuller had seen as Adon and his people took practice shots, they knew their weapons very well indeed.

He also saw them practicing with swords he clearly recognized as *mek'leths*—a small variation on the *bat'leth* that he had seen used to such deadly effect at the Battle of Donatu V. Quite a few of the people seemed skilled with the weapons, moving like masters of a refined martial art. From what Fuller understood, the weapons were for hunting and sport. Until recently, there had been no fighting among clans in this planet's history for as far back as it could be measured.

Until the Klingons came, he thought.

Fuller had to remind himself that these natives *were* Klingons, at least biologically. Perhaps they represented what Klingons could have become or should have remained had they not spent centuries perfecting methods of killing one another and then exported those methods to the stars.

Now Klingons were nothing more than a disease infecting the galaxy, devouring everything in their path— even these innocent people who represented whatever Klingons had that passed for a better nature. Well, whatever the empire's plans were today, Fuller would do his best to keep them from being successful. In this endeavor, at least, he had the help of two full squads of Starfleet officers and an unlikely group of natives.

When that job was done, Fuller hoped he would have an opportunity to do even more. He would take the kind of action that was necessary when dealing with species like the Klingons, but that the Federation too often refused to take out of principle. Well, survival was the only principle Fuller respected now. His job was to help ensure the Federation survived. He had seen too many people—Sam included—give their lives to protect it.

Fuller would do what he had to do now to see that those sacrifices were not in vain, and that would mean getting his hands dirty. He was determined to do whatever it took.

"Fuller," a voice called from behind him, and Fuller turned to see Andrews approach him.

Kevin Ryan

"Sam . . ." It was impossible; Sam Andrews had given his life twenty-five years ago so that Fuller could have a chance to return home to see his son born. He had named his son after Sam Andrews. . . .

"Fuller, are you okay?" Greenberger asked. Andrews disappeared and in his place stood Section Chief Greenberger. The man was thinner than Andrews, without even a hint of resemblance between them. How in heaven's name had Fuller seen Andrews in him? He knew the answer to that, and he knew it wasn't good. It didn't say much for his long-term mental health prospects.

Of course, Fuller had ceased worrying about his long-term prospects years ago. Whatever good he accomplished, he would have to do in the short term. Still, he willed himself to keep it together. He owed that much to the men and women who were still depending on him to see them through this mission.

"I'm fine. Let's take our inventory," he said.

He and Greenberger walked through the assembled Starfleet and native people. Adon had two weapons platforms, and Fuller had seen Adon and the young woman in action—they were expert pilots. The natives also had an ore hauler, which Adon had stolen from the mine on the day he had taken the dilithium. Adon's people wanted nothing to do with the hauler because it was slow and lumbering. To Fuller, it seemed like a good armored vehicle that would provide cover and a mobile defensive position. And Quatrocchi would be able to fly it.

They had fourteen security people, each with a phaser II pistol and a phaser rifle, which for the moment were slung over their backs. They also had forty native men and women, half of whom were armed with Orion pistols

222

and all of whom carried the Klingon swords. Adon had offered blades to the security officers, and Fuller had left the decision up to the individuals. All of them had accepted except for Parmet and, of course, Fuller himself. He had held and used an authentic *bat'leth* years ago and had not picked up another Klingon-built weapon voluntarily since.

Adon stood in front of his people and addressed them in their language. Fuller noted that some traditions crossed almost all cultures, though it was jarring to hear Klingon spoken by this young man he had come to respect.

Fuller took his position in the ore hauler with his squad. Greenberger and the others were in front of them below and would make up the ground forces. Fuller began, "You all know why we are here. Our mission is clear: stop the Klingons from getting a foothold in Federation space. For the moment, they are in league with certain native elements and have control of the dilithium mine. But the dilithium they came for is safely on board the *Enterprise*. It's going to be up to us to see to it that this is a total loss for the empire today. We're going to take the mine and make sure it is never used against the Federation. Now, it won't be easy. We'll be attacking a fortified position and facing greater numbers who will be very well armed. On the other hand, I have seen for myself what you are capable of. And we do have some help." Fuller gestured to the natives assembled around Adon. "It has been an honor and a privilege to serve with you on the *Enterprise*. We've lost good people to the Klingons, and yet it seems like we are barely in the beginning of what may come. Well, today, we can have something to say

223

about how things will end. The empire understands one thing: force. Up until now they have been a race of conquerors who have moved virtually unchecked through their portion of the galaxy. Starfleet and the Federation have different beliefs, we live by different principles, but we also understand force. And today I say we teach the Klingons about that force. They have fought humans before and have not won a single major battle against us. I think it's time for another lesson."

There were nods of approval from the officers around Fuller. They had the look of people ready to do their jobs. He looked over at Adon. The young man boarded his platform as the young woman next to him did the same. Fuller nodded and Quatrocchi started powering up the hauler. In less than a minute, they were in the air.

Fuller opened his communicator and hit a button programmed by Ensign Jawer. A channel opened immediately to Adon. "We're ready," Fuller said.

"So are we," the young man replied.

"Then let's move out," Fuller called out as Adon did the same to his people. The group started moving. They might have looked like a motley group of officers and primitively dressed hunters, but as a strike force they were in pretty good shape. They had fast attack craft, an armored vehicle, and dedicated, highly motivated ground forces.

Fuller was beginning to think they might actually have a chance.

Kirk listened with surprise to Koloth's story. Of course, he was immediately wary of a trick. He had suspected dissension on board the Klingon warship, but a dispute of this nature with a member of the High Council? "What are you proposing, Captain?" Kirk asked.

"I propose that you use your transporters to move myself and my crew to Councillor Duras's position. We will handle the situation from there." Koloth's voice was pained, which Kirk understood. If his story was true, Kirk guessed that it had taken quite a bit for him to ask the *Enterprise* for help. Klingon pride would have made that request difficult indeed. Even given the life-and-death nature of the situation, Kirk guessed that the decision to do it had been a near thing for Koloth.

"Provided that you are successful, what would happen next?" Kirk asked.

"Next?"

"What are your orders regarding the planet below?"

"I see. My orders were to deliver Duras for his diplomatic mission. Pending completion of that mission— either with success or failure—I have standing orders to return to the empire. I intend to follow those orders." After a moment, Koloth added, *"I do not forget my debts, or my honor, Captain. Though I do not fear war with the Federation, or battle with you, I do not intend to begin either. And I will not allow thousands of my brothers to die in service of a lie."*

Much of what Koloth said made sense. If Duras was in command of the mission and Koloth was in command of the ship, there was bound to be conflict between them, particularly if the mission was the murder of thousands of Klingons.

And yet, the Klingons had lured the *U.S.S. Endeav-*

our into a trap at Donatu V. Even if Koloth was telling the truth, this diplomatic mission to the system was a cover to destroy a world and plunge the galaxy into war. Was Koloth's request yet another deceit?

"One moment, Captain," Kirk said. Then he motioned to Uhura, who suspended the transmission. "Thoughts?"

"Koloth's story does fit all the facts," Spock said.

"Could they sabotage the ship through the transporters somehow, Scotty?" Kirk asked.

"Not likely, and I can take extra precautions," the chief engineer answered.

"They would be able to give the landing party some help, *if* he's telling the truth," McCoy said.

That was it, the only question that mattered. Klingons had killed Sam Fuller and other members of Kirk's crew on Starbase 42. Could he trust Koloth and his people to help Sam's father now? Kirk had all the information he would have, and he was out of time for this decision. As with most of the important calls he'd made in the center seat, he would have to trust his gut.

"Mister Scott, ready the transporter," Kirk said. "Lieutenant Uhura." He heard the click of an open line. "Captain Koloth, prepare your people for transport."

"Captain, the Klingon vessel is powering its weapons," Spock said calmly.

"Red alert!" Kirk said, immediately on his feet. "Shields on maximum. Full power to phasers and arm photon torpedoes. Lieutenant Uhura, inform Captain Koloth that his request will have to wait."

"The Klingon vessel is breaking orbit," Spock said.

The sound of the red-alert klaxon filled the bridge

now. "Battle stations. Mister Sulu, get us out of orbit. Give us some maneuvering room."

Well, it looked as if Koloth had been telling the truth after all. However, at the moment, there was nothing Kirk could do about it.

Chapter Twenty-three

KRAETIAN SPACE STATION
NEAR THE FEDERATION-KLINGON BORDER

"AMBASSADOR, I AM RECEIVING a message from the Kraetian administrator. He says our *relief team* will arrive shortly via high-speed shuttle," Fitzpatrick said.

Could it be Starfleet . . . ?

"Acknowledge the message. Ask where and when we can meet them," Fox said.

Fitzpatrick nodded. "We're not expecting a relief team. Sir, what's going on?"

Fox assembled the others and said, "I think Starfleet is mounting a rescue. We can't be sure because the last message from President Wescott included a code that said our communications may have been compromised. We have to assume that this is a rescue attempt. This will likely be our only chance. Carry only what you must. We'll leave all the equipment behind." Fox didn't have to tell his people to take their weapons. They wore their laser pistols at all times, even while they slept—which for the last few nights they had done all together in the common room.

Fox felt the dim flickers of hope begin to swell. He forced them down. Whatever happened today would not be easy.

"Will the Klingons let us leave?" Fitzpatrick asked, saying what was on all their minds.

"Not voluntarily, but we can trust Starfleet to have a plan. And we are not without resources ourselves," Fox said. There it was: hope, on all of their faces. Well, they had had precious little of that lately and had lived with a death mark over their heads as they continued the farce of the negotiations.

"Twenty minutes until the shuttle docks," Fitzpatrick said. A moment later she added, "I have the Klingon ambassador."

Fox felt his own hopes fall a bit. No matter how good Starfleet's plan, if the ship never got to the station, their one chance was over before it could begin. *"Ambassador Fox, what is the meaning of this?"* Ambassador Morg said as soon as his face appeared on the viewer.

"Ambassador, I do not know what you mean," Fox said.

"A Starfleet vessel is approaching this station right now."

"Yes, they are bringing supplies and additional staff," Fox said evenly.

"Why wasn't I notified?" the Klingon demanded.

"Because the Federation is not in the habit of asking

permission for routine exchanges from its negotiating partners."

"Is this a trick, Fox?" Morg asked, his eyes narrowing in suspicion.

"We have been nothing but forthright throughout this entire negotiation, Ambassador. I am insulted that you would suggest otherwise. Why, I wonder, are you so suspicious? Is there something that *you* are keeping from *me?"* Fox asked pointedly.

The comment struck home, Fox could see. The Klingon ambassador had been lying to him from the start and was lying now. Klingons could sometimes be deceitful, but there were strong cultural taboos against it in large segments of the society. "You have nothing to fear from us," Fox said.

Anger flashed on the Klingon's face. He considered humans—Earthers as he called them—inferior. To suggest that he was afraid of them was an insult. Now, for Morg to take action against the shuttle would be an admission that he had something to fear. Fox realized there was one more thing he could do.

"Ambassador, I must admit that my superiors are not happy with my progress in these negotiations. As a matter of fact, they have found some of the concessions you have won to be troubling. I'm afraid that my team and I are to be replaced by more senior and more experienced negotiators who are more conversant with the current state of affairs in the Federation Council."

Fox had just offered Morg an even more valuable prize than his own team. The only question was, would the Klingon ambassador take the bait?

After a moment, the Klingon smiled. *"I'm surprised*

it did not happen sooner. Your leaders are not as foolish as I thought. How soon can I meet with you and your replacement?"

"I'll have to check with the new ambassador, but I would assume that he'll want to see you as soon as he has settled in." As soon as Fox finished speaking, he closed the channel.

After twelve straight hours at the negotiating table, Fox and his people had been tired. Now, he felt like a first-year diplomatic aide on his first assignment.

"Let's begin shutdown procedure," Fox said. Quickly, he and his team purged the computer system, taking the tapes that held the little data they needed. He set the timer on the computer so that it would destroy itself and all of its code keys in one hour.

"I'm getting a message from the shuttle," Fitzpatrick announced.

The face of a man that Fox didn't recognize appeared on the screen. *"Ambassador Fox, it is good to see you."*

"And you too," Fox said.

"Please wait in your quarters. I would like to meet with you immediately. Ambassador Fenig out."

"Ambassador Fenig?" one of Fox's aides said.

"Apparently he's new to the diplomatic service," Fox said drily. His group smiled at that. Then for an excruciating few minutes, Fox and his team waited for an alarm to sound—some sign that they had been found out—that their small flicker of hope had been dashed. However, the alarms didn't come. Instead, a few minutes later there was a buzz at the door.

Fox stepped in front of the door himself and hit the button to open it. Standing in the doorway was a human

231

male, perhaps forty years old, wearing formal civilian clothes. Fox recognized the man immediately from his transmission. "Ambassador Fenig," he said, shaking the man's hand.

"Ambassador Fox." Then Fenig turned to his Kraith escorts and said, "Thank you." The Kraith knew when they were being dismissed, and Fenig stepped into the room.

"Is there any chance we are being watched or listened to in here?" Fenig asked, keeping a pleasant smile on his face.

"No," Ambassador Fox said. Diplomats might not be warriors, but they were not fools either. "We have taken standard precautions."

"Then we can talk freely." Fenig's eyes narrowed and he seemed suddenly more alert. "I'm *Lieutenant* Fenig. I'm here to take you home."

Fox felt a catch in his throat. "Thank you."

"Don't thank me yet—wait until you're safe. I have a pilot standing by in a diplomatic shuttle. I need you to all come with me immediately."

"We're ready," Fox said.

He looked at the man's hip. Fenig was wearing a laser pistol. "We couldn't risk phasers. My team and I are carrying the same ceremonial weapons that you brought along. We can't do anything to arouse suspicion. For that reason, we couldn't arm the shuttle, since the Klingons know we don't usually arm diplomatic craft. We need to move quickly and get away clean. I don't think we can trust the Kraith either; so once we're outside, don't discuss what we're doing."

Fox nodded. "Their interest in hosting these talks is

purely financial. I have no doubt that if the Klingons paid them for other assistance, they would offer it."

"Our thinking exactly," Fenig said.

"How are you going to keep the Klingons from firing on the shuttle after we launch?"

"We're docked on opposite sides of the station. They will have to release their ship to pursue. And we'll try to hold them up a bit. Now, we really must be going." Fenig stepped out into the corridor.

Fox and the others followed and walked calmly through the halls. It was evening as the station reckoned time, and most of the people there were eating or in one of the bars. Though few people were around, Fox would have preferred to have the corridors empty. They passed Kraith and a few other races that Fox recognized.

"I'm anxious to have you meet the Klingon ambassador," Fox said.

"What?" Fenig said.

"Ambassador Morg is anxious to meet you as well."

Fenig understood. "Of course. I am . . . curious about your progress."

If the Kraith or the Klingons were listening in, Fox was determined to give them something to hear. "The Klingons appear to be in a strong position," Fox said.

"Yes, they are very . . . strong."

Fox had no doubt that Fenig was a capable Starfleet officer, but he was a poor liar. Yet his performance was probably good enough to fool the Klingons.

When they were about halfway to the docking port, two more humans in civilian business clothes appeared. They were younger than Fenig, and Fox could tell the lieutenant knew them.

"Your aides, Mister Fenig?" Fox asked.

"Yes." Fenig made quick introductions. Fox could tell the man was impatient, but Fox had the feeling they were being watched closely.

Leaning in, he whispered to Fenig, "We should linger for a moment."

Fenig looked at him and nodded. Fox made small talk with the aides, and his people did the same. The rhythms of professional interaction in the diplomatic world were different from those in Starfleet. Fox understood that the people who had been sent to retrieve them were probably from Starfleet security, not intelligence. That made sense given the speed with which the mission had had to be put together.

It would be up to Fox to make sure that everyone behaved normally. Finally he said, "I'm looking forward to seeing that communications equipment on board the shuttle."

"Of course," Fenig said, and the group started moving again.

"We sent that *message* you requested," one of Fenig's "aides" said to him.

Two Kraith approached from the other direction. One was male and the other was female. They had their race's distinctive reddish coloring and deep-set eyes. Fox realized that he recognized the two people. They worked for the station's administrator.

"Ambassador Fenig," the male called out. He smiled as he approached. "The station administrator asked us to find you. Do you have a moment for her?"

"I'm really very busy. Perhaps later," Fenig said.

"Really, it will only take a moment. The administrator has something important she wishes to share with you," the female said.

Fox spoke twelve languages fluently and was a particularly astute student of humanoid and alien body language. He scanned the faces of the two Kraith and made his determination in an instant.

"Sir," he said, to get Fenig's attention. The lieutenant turned to him, and Fox said clearly and forcefully, "They're lying."

Before the recognition fully registered on Fenig's face, his laser was in his hand. Without a moment's hesitation, the officer aimed and fired the weapon at the male in a single, smooth motion. A fraction of a second later, he aimed and fired at the female. The two aliens hit the floor one after the other.

"Maybe they didn't have time to sound an alarm," one of Fenig's "aides" said.

As if on cue, a klaxon started to sound. "All bets are off, run!" Fenig shouted. Together the nine people dashed down the corridor. The Starfleet officers had their lasers out and were aiming them forward.

"Shoot at anyone you see," Fenig said. A moment later, a Kraith appeared and Fenig and the other two officers fired nearly simultaneously. The being went down.

"There," Fenig said, pointing at the intersection ahead. Fox knew they were approaching the outer rim of the station. Their docking port was just a few hundred meters away now.

A moment later, there was a flash of movement ahead of them. For an instant, Fox saw someone lean into the corridor from behind cover, and then a flash of green energy passed inches from Fox's left ear.

"Disruptors!" Fenig called out. Immediately Fenig and one of the others started firing continuously on each side of the corridor, preventing any Klingons hiding there from getting off another shot. One of the security officers grabbed Fox and Fitzpatrick and pushed them to one corridor wall, while the other officer pushed Fox's other three aides against the opposite wall.

Slowly, the group inched forward. When they were less than twenty meters from the intersection, they came to a stop. They were in trouble, Fox realized. As long as the Klingons were around those corners, they couldn't reach the ship. And while they could keep the Klingons at bay, it was just a matter of time before reinforcements arrived. If anyone got behind them, they would be stuck out in the open with enemies on both sides.

"We can't wait. We'll have to rush them," Fenig said. It made sense, Fox realized. The Starfleet officers had to move them forward to take the fight to the Klingons. If all four security people raced around the corners, there was a fair chance that one or two of them would survive to get Fox's team to the ship. At least some of these officers were about to die for them, Fox realized.

"On my mark," Fenig said.

"Wait, Lieutenant. I have an idea," Fox said.

"What is it?" Fenig said, urgency in his voice.

"Diplomacy. Let me try something." Fox drew his ceremonial Civil War sword—another gift from Lieutenant West—and clanked it against the deck. "How many are there?"

Fenig checked his tricorder. "Two."

"Klingon warriors. I am Ambassador Fox. You know me. I carry a blade and challenge you to combat if you have the courage," he called out.

"I can't allow this," Fenig said to Fox.

"Trust me, Lieutenant. This is my area." Then Fox called out to the Klingons again. "Face me with blades now unless you are afraid to face an *Earther* in combat."

There was silence, and then a Klingon said. "No tricks, Earther."

"No tricks."

Two Klingons appeared from around each of the two corners. They had their disruptors holstered and were holding their *bat'leths* in the air.

"Ambassador . . . ," Fenig said, his voice nervous.

Fox felt completely confident. He knew what he had to do and would not hesitate.

"Lieutenant, shoot them now," Fox said evenly.

As soon as the words left his mouth, twin laser beams lashed out and struck each Klingon full in the chest, the heavy stun setting sending them flying backward to the floor. Fox took a moment's satisfaction at the stunned surprise on the security team.

"Your diplomacy is pretty effective," Fenig said.

"Years of study and training to master the subtleties," Fox replied, returning the man's smile. Then the group was on the move, rounding the corner to the right and racing toward the docking bay. A human in civilian clothes was waiting to greet them—most likely their pilot, Fox guessed.

"Lieutenant," the man called out.

Fenig checked his tricorder and said, "Brace yourselves." Fox saw the security people grab hold of the

237

wall and did the same. A moment later, the deck shook under his feet. Then he felt an outward pressure, like centrifugal force, pushing him against the outer wall.

"The Kraith just had a malfunction in their thruster system. We need to disembark before the rotational speed of the station gets too high," Fenig said.

A moment later, two humans came running down the corridor, firing behind them as they ran. "They're with us . . . our *malfunction* team. Okay, everybody inside," Fenig said, pushing Fox's aides through the docking port and into the shuttle. Fox insisted on going last. By the time he was inside, he saw the five security people right behind him. Fenig hit the docking port hatch and said, "Get us out of here."

As Fox tried to find a seat, he saw the planet speed past a shuttle window. The station must be rotating quickly now, he realized. A moment later he heard a click and the shuttle shot away from the structure, and he could see they were in open space.

As Fox took his seat, he could see they were in a standard diplomatic shuttle. That meant there was little in the way of shielding. "The station is armed. They can fire at us."

"They can try. If they do, they'll have a pretty serious weapons malfunction," Fenig said.

"Warp speed now," the pilot said, and Fox saw the stars suddenly streak past the front windows.

"The Klingons won't give up. They will try to pursue," Fox said. And unlike Federation diplomatic shuttles, Klingon diplomatic ships were heavily armed.

"Well, they will no doubt try," Fenig said. "Unfortunately for them, they will find that the magnetic clamps holding their vessel to the station have also *malfunctioned*. They won't be able to release them without significant trouble, and by then the rotational force will probably have torn the ship free. I'm afraid they'll be facing a considerable repair bill either way."

"Federation space in fifteen minutes. No sign of pursuit," the pilot announced.

Fox turned to his people and smiled. Then he turned back to Fenig. "All of your people made it out?"

"Yes, we were lucky today," Fenig said.

When the pilot announced they had made it to Federation space, Fox felt the last bit of weight lift from his chest. They were safe. That reminded him of something.

"Lieutenant Fenig, is it time to thank you yet?" Fox asked.

"Sure. It's as good a time as any. But I think we owe you some thanks as well. We wouldn't have all come through this in one piece without your interesting use of *diplomacy*."

Fox smiled.

Chapter Twenty-four

U.S.S. ENTERPRISE
SYSTEM 7348

THE *ENTERPRISE* HAD BARELY cleared orbit when Spock announced, "Klingon vessel is preparing to fire disruptors."

"Evasive action," Kirk said.

Kirk didn't feel a weapons hit. A moment later, Spock said, "Glancing blow on port shields, no damage." That made sense, they had to be at the extreme range of the battle cruiser's weapons.

If Koloth was on the planet, who was in command of the ship?

"Give us some more room, Mister Sulu. Full impulse perpendicular to the orbital plane," Kirk said.

"Incoming message," Uhura said.

"Audio only," Kirk replied.

"Cowardly Earthers, you may run, but it will not save you," a Klingon voice said.

A taunt, in the middle of battle? Who was this commander? Kirk wondered. "Klingon vessel, you are in violation of Federation space. Your hostility will not be tolerated." Kirk kept an eye on Sulu, who turned and nodded.

"Is this the great coward, James T. Kirk? It will be my pleasure to rid the galaxy of you and your treachery."

"Cease fire or prepare to be destroyed."

The Klingon laughed. *"You show me your back as you retreat and yet you make threats?"*

"Cut audio, Lieutenant Uhura. Mister Spock?"

"Klingon vessel is at extreme weapons range, still in pursuit. Wait, I'm showing—Klingon vessel has launched two torpedoes."

"Rear view," Kirk said. Instantly, the viewscreen showed the Klingon vessel in the distance and twin glowing torpedoes heading away from the ship and quickly approaching the *Enterprise*.

"We are at extreme range for torpedoes. Detonation in ten, nine, eight, seven, six, five, four, three, two, one," Spock said.

There was a flash as the torpedoes exploded a short distance outside the ship's shields.

"No damage," Spock said.

"I have the Klingons," Uhura said.

"Surrender now and you will die quickly," the Klingon voice said, then cut the line.

More taunts? It was absurd, but it did show Kirk two things. First, the Klingon commander was not very experienced. And second, the reports Kirk had seen from Starfleet intelligence were correct: despite the empire's recent setbacks, Klingon command did not think much of humans, particularly in battle. Well, Kirk would be happy to give this commander something new to think about.

"Mister Sulu, prepare to come about on my mark. I'll want a full barrage of torpedoes."

"Aye, sir," Sulu said.

Karel's blood burned. He had found his brother's killer. In moments, he would be in battle with Duras, who had dishonored Karel's brother and taken his captain's ship to bring further dishonor on the Klingon Empire. Duras had to die, and when it happened, it would be by Karel's hand.

As first officer, he would be in the first group to transport over with Koloth. He and the captain would be the first to join the battle. Karel waited impatiently.

And waited.

Finally, Koloth's communicator beeped. The captain answered the device, and Karel could see from his commander's face that the news was not good.

"The *D'k Tahg* has attacked the *Enterprise*. There will be no transport until the battle is done. And even then . . ." Koloth put the communicator away.

Only if our ship is defeated by the Enterprise, Karel finished silently. He growled in frustration. If Duras and the *D'k Tahg* won, he would die, helplessly, on the planet with the native Klingons. If the humans won, they might have no ship to go back to. And if the battle took too long, the planet might be destroyed in the meantime and Karel would never take his revenge.

Karel found that the thought of his own death didn't bother him in the least. But the thought that Duras might live to see another day, that was intolerable!

A howl of rage gathered in Karel's chest, making its way to his throat and filling the air around them.

Koloth waited until he was finished and said, "We will not stand here and do nothing." Calling to a nearby officer, he said, "What direction is the mine?"

The Klingon checked his scanner and pointed across the field. "We're going!" Koloth called out.

"Captain, it is two thousand kilometers away," Karel found himself saying.

"Yes," Koloth replied evenly.

"And there is an ocean."

"Then we had better get started," Koloth said, perfect seriousness in his voice and face.

"You heard the captain, move out!" Karel said. As a group, the remaining loyal crew of the *D'k Tahg* started their trek.

As he walked, Karel felt his rage turn from frustration to a fine, pointed instrument. He was glad to have a task, and he saw the wisdom of Koloth's orders. Even if they died, it would be *doing* something. Not waiting like *trigaks* for the slaughter.

The *Enterprise* was in battle. To Fuller, that meant he and the others would be on their own. In some ways, that made things easier. There were things that Fuller had to do that Captain Kirk would never allow, *could* never allow.

Simply having a thought like that at almost any other point in his career would have disturbed Fuller. But Sam's death had changed a lot of things for him. It had also freed him to do the things he knew were necessary without worrying about his own future.

Fuller's squad was on the ore hauler with him. He briefed them quickly, then Adon and Greenberger by communicator. "We have to assume that Duras has already set a warp-core breach." That was the method the Klingons had tried to use last time. The *Enterprise* had barely prevented the breach, which would have ejected the warp core deep into the crust of the planet and torn it to pieces.

"No, sir. He won't be able to eject the warp core, at least not easily," Jawer interrupted. The ensign had been on the previous mission to the planet and had had a direct hand in preventing the warp-core explosion. "The warp core needed some attention and we didn't have much time, but before we left, we built in some safety protocols on Captain Kirk's orders. It would take some time for the Klingons to work around them. However, if they wanted to be sure this time, they would probably use a kinetic explosive, set deeper in the shaft. That would also take them some time, but much less."

Fuller nodded. "The plan remains the same: we are going to take this mine, and it looks like we have good reason to hurry." The combined Starfleet/native force moved closer. Fuller scanned his squad—they were alert and focused.

"We're with you, sir," Ensign Parmet said. There was determination in the young man's eyes. Determination . . . and something else—respect, admiration. When they had first met, Parmet had surprised him with his knowledge of

Fuller's career. Like others who'd seen his record, Parmet had made a common mistake. He had thought successful missions were the result of Fuller's doing instead of what they really were: the result of sacrifices made by better men and women.

Parmet had called Fuller a hero. Well, Fuller had known plenty of heroes, and they all had one thing in common: they were dead and their names were on a large wall at Starfleet Command. One of those names was Samuel Fuller.

The earnestness on Parmet's face pained him. Whatever happened to this young man in the next few hours, that look and the feeling behind it would not survive the day.

The native's young leader favored a frontal assault and Fuller agreed. However, for the plan to work, the Klingons would have to come out and face them. A short time later, Fuller could see the entrance to the mine through the trees. Soon, the entire group was massed at the end of the tree line. Only two hundred meters remained between them and the mine. There was no one to meet them. With any luck that would change in a few moments.

From his position in the hauler, Fuller nodded to Adon, who was nearby on an Orion weapons platform. Immediately, the young man raced forward, as the young woman who had been introduced as Bethe followed. They darted toward the entrance, and a moment later, automated guns started firing on the platforms. The two natives put their craft through a series of impressive maneuvers to dodge the constant fire from the ground-based disruptors.

Fuller saw the disruptors make a series of hits on the

two weapons platforms' shields. They were holding, but it was only a matter of time before they would be overwhelmed.

"Fire!" Fuller called out as he aimed and fired his own phaser rifle at the nearest automated disruptor. As he did, the thirteen other officers did the same. In the *Enterprise*'s first mission to this planet, the Starfleet team had taken out similar guns. The eight new automated guns replaced the weapons that had been placed there by the Orions. Fuller could see that they were powerful disruptors and that each had its own shield.

Duras had no doubt placed them there because he didn't want to fight. And he didn't need to fight to achieve his goals. He was simply waiting for the *D'k Tahg* to destroy the *Enterprise* and then carry out his plan to destroy the planet. Well, Fuller thought that James Kirk might give the councillor a surprise in space. It was now time to give the Klingons a surprise on the ground.

The guns didn't last long under sustained phaser rifle fire. They each went with a satisfying explosion. It was a start. "Move forward slowly," Fuller ordered. Quatrocchi glided the hauler toward the entrance, and Fuller took some preliminary shots at the doors to the mine. There was no response.

They could barrel in and start tearing apart the entrance and the ground floor of the mine, but Adon wanted to try to preserve as much of the facility as possible. Fuller's orders were to cooperate with the natives, and he would try to do that for now. Later, he would likely have to abandon all of his orders, but that time wasn't yet. And while they could make their assault through the ground level of the mine, it would be costly.

The advantage would be with the defenders, as it usually was. And here, the attackers would be forced through the bottleneck of the ground-floor administrative officers and the few ways down into the mine itself. They would be susceptible to booby traps and Klingon warriors picking them off from covered positions.

The Klingons didn't even have to win the engagement, just hold up the assault until they could ensure the destruction of the mine.

"Sir, I have something," Ensign Jawer said, his tricorder out and scanning. "I'm showing a power sink below the level of the warp reactor. They are definitely shunting power down into the main shaft of the mine."

"In English, please," Fuller said.

"The most likely reason to do that would be to feed a kinetic explosive device."

"How long do we have?"

"No way to tell from here. There's too much interference at that depth. It could be five minutes or five hours before the weapon is charged," Jawer said.

Fuller didn't like the sound of that. He could feel time slipping away from them. The squad looked at him, waiting for word, for some sign that he knew what to do. "It's time for a slight change of strategy." Pulling out his communicator, he hit the frequency that the *Enterprise* had sent him. "Fuller to Councillor Duras."

After a brief pause, Duras replied, *"Who is this?"*

"I am the Earther who waits for you outside."

"What do you want?"

"I want nothing. I demand that you meet my challenge and face us in open battle."

"You cowardly Earthers are not worth the time of my warriors."

"Warriors? *Warriors* that huddle in the dark and hide like frightened children, with their cowardly master?"

"You will die for that insult, Earther."

"By whose hand, you bloodless *targ?* To strike me, you will have to come out of your hole."

There was a howl of rage, then Duras said, *"You will die soon enough."* Then there was a click as Duras cut the line.

"Interesting . . . strategy, Chief," McCalmon said.

"Klingons have a hard time resisting open challenges. If he faces us outside, we're in a better position. If he ignores the challenge and keeps his people inside, they'll start to question his leadership," Fuller said.

For the moment, they could do nothing but wait. Adon and the other pilot buzzed around the entrance, firing off the occasional shot. The wait was short, however, and Jawer announced he was reading Klingon life signs massing near the doors.

"Wait until they're out in the open," Fuller said. In this case he didn't have any problem with shooting first, or with firing at enemies as they came out of a door. However, he needed as many of them to come outside as possible. The more they faced out here, the fewer they would have to face inside.

After a tense wait of perhaps two minutes, the large doors burst open and Klingons raced out. *There's something wrong,* his mind screamed as he watched the armed Klingons come out, shooting disruptors at the

Starfleet officers and their native allies. Then he saw what it was: they weren't dressed like Klingons, they were dressed like natives.

Ten, twenty, thirty . . . they raced out, firing forward as they took positions along the front of the building. These weren't the people he had come to fight. Finally, about sixty Klingons were outside, and Fuller could see that only a few more were inside. "Prepare to fire on my mark!" Fuller said, then his communicator beeped. "Fuller here."

"This is Adon. Tell your people to wait. There is something I wish to try."

"We don't have much time."

"I won't need much time."

"Stay back, Bethe, and watch very carefully. I may need your assistance," Adon said.

"What are you going to do?" she asked.

"Just do as I ask," Adon said, bracing himself for an argument.

To his surprise, she said, "I will be ready." Her craft hovered in position near the front of the line of fighters waiting by the tree line.

Seeing that, Adon took his craft slowly and directly to the entrance of the mine. A number of shots hit his shield, but they were not serious—more like warnings than mortal blows.

When he was perhaps twenty paces from the mine, the fire stopped completely. He could see the faces of people he recognized looking at him. He saw the conflict there. He set down his craft and raised his hands, though he did not turn off the platform's invisible protective shield. "Is Gurn among you?" he called out.

He heard, "no," from several of the fighters who would be his enemies. "Is this the leadership he offers you? Who leads you in this battle? Who has the courage to come out and speak with me?"

After long seconds, one stepped forward, pointing a weapon at Adon that he did not recognize. It was Mureth, one of the leaders of the other clans. "I lead."

"Would you kill the son of Gorath?" Adon said.

Something passed over the clan leader's face, but his voice was firm. "I would kill my enemies, or those who ally with them."

"As would any of our people worth their blood. But would you speak with me first to hear what I have to say?"

"With your weapons and the weapons of the Starfleet pointed at me?" Mureth said.

"You point weapons as well."

"But you are the one who wishes to speak."

Adon saw that he had few choices, and fewer that were any good. He decided quickly and hit the button to turn off the defensive shield. "I shall come to you with open hands." He stepped off the small craft, looking at the surprise on Mureth's face. "Would you speak with me with open hands as well?"

Adon took careful steps toward the clan leader. Watching Mureth's eyes, Adon saw that he might just have made the last decision of his life. Then he could see that Mureth had made his own decision and lowered his weapon.

"Do not strike at him!" Mureth called out. Then the

clan leader took a series of careful steps of his own toward Adon.

When they were face-to-face, Adon said, "You hunted with my father, faced him in the games. Would you kill his son now?"

"I would rather you go home."

"If I did, all would end soon. The Klingons would see this world destroyed."

"Gurn has told us that the humans would see it destroyed." Mureth replied.

"You believe a clansman who would lead you into battle from the rear? You followed Gorath into battle against the green-skins. Where was Gorath then?"

"He was first into battle," Mureth said, the pain clear on his face now. "But there were things he could not know. Your father was a great warrior, but we need new kinds of strength now. Gurn has brought us a promise of protection, of machines from the Klingons so we may never again feel the threat of the green-skins and those like them. Gorath was a great man, but he was a fool to think we could keep the stars above us away forever."

"Even if that were so, do you think he was a liar?" Adon said.

"No," Mureth replied immediately.

"Would you call his son liar?"

"No."

"Gurn killed my father, Mureth."

"You know this?"

"I saw it in his eyes. And if you would doubt me, let me ask you, have you seen the wound on Gurn's face? Do you think it was made by an animal, or a blade?"

Adon saw more doubt in Mureth's eyes. "My father called you friend. Would he ever have set our people against each other as Gurn has done?"

"These are different times," Mureth said, uncertainty now clear in his voice.

"Yes, but the call of our shared blood is the same. Gurn asks you to believe the Klingons' words, but where were the Klingons when the green-skins tried to tear our world to stone and sand? The humans fought *with* us, fought with you and my father. I am satisfied they speak the truth. And I have spoken many times to the green-skins' computers, which tell of their Klingon masters. Mureth, understand that I will fight you if I must, because the Klingons are not here for their crystals, but to finish the work of destroying our world. Would you stand with them in this fight, or with us?"

After long consideration, Mureth said, "These are times which test us in new ways. I do not have the wisdom to see the truth here, but I will not strike the son of Gorath today. Let me speak to my people."

Fuller watched the scene in front of him in wonder. The two native Klingons were talking—*not* trying to kill one another. He couldn't hear what they were saying, but it was clear that something was passing between them. As they spoke, the young woman in the other platform buzzed back and forth, nervously keeping watch on Adon.

The one called Mureth went to talk to his people, and Adon slowly walked back to his platform and took to the air. A moment later, he was in front of Fuller's team. The young woman on the other platform and a small group of others approached him.

"They will not fight us," Adon called out to the officers and natives around them. "Some of Mureth's people will lay down their arms and go home. Some will join our fight. Welcome them."

Fuller was stunned. This young man had earned his respect before, but this . . . this was impossible. He had won a victory without firing a shot. In fact, this was better than a victory. Adon had just increased their numbers.

A group of the fighters who had been firing at them a few moments ago were now walking off together, leaving the area. Another group, which had to be at least half the total, were headed toward the tree line. They were greeted by the natives there and quickly took places at their sides. All of the assembled natives were now looking up at Adon as if he were not a young boy just out of adolescence but a person they would die for.

The clan leader who had met with Adon took position nearby. A device on his side beeped once—a Klingon communicator. The man answered it and handed the device to Adon, who barked at it in Klingon. That done, he turned to Fuller and said, "Gurn is disappointed at this turn of events." From the sound of the screaming on the other end of the communicator, *disappointed* was an understatement.

Fuller said to his squad, "Our odds have just improved, but we are a long way from done. It looks like we have to do this the hard way. When we move out, we concentrate fire on the doors. When we get inside, we do it one level at a time."

There were nods all around, but before he could tell them to move out, he saw movement on the far side of the mine complex. A quick scan told him there was also movement on the other side.

He saw flying platforms, quite a few of them, and realized that Duras may have been a coward, but he was far from a fool. He would not engage his warriors in a ground fight where they would be more or less evenly matched against other fighters. The platforms came, and kept coming.

The hard way, he thought. Then he realized that that didn't begin to cover it.

"Disperse and take cover, don't give them big targets," Fuller said. He realized that the approaching craft didn't look like vehicles in attack formations, they looked like a swarm.

Chapter Twenty-five

"ONE HUNDRED THOUSAND KILOMETERS above the orbital plane," Spock announced. A moment later he added, "Two more disruptor blasts on rear shields. Given the extreme range, they had negligible effect."

Kirk knew he could keep this fight going indefinitely. However, the people on the planet didn't have much time. Unless Kirk ended this quickly, those people would die no matter what the outcome of this battle between the two ships.

"Prepare to bring us about to face them on my mark . . . now." Kirk scanned the viewscreen for the Klingon vessel but it was still too far in front of them. "Full speed toward the Klingons. Take us close, Mister

Sulu, and ready photon torpedoes." A moment later, he saw a blip on the screen as the Klingons approached. "Fire as soon as they're in range."

Kirk could see the forward view of the Klingon battle cruiser, and then Sulu said, "Torpedoes away."

Two torpedoes streaked toward the Klingon ship as it barreled toward the *Enterprise*. "Evasive action," Kirk said, and he immediately felt the pull to port as the inertial dampeners struggled to compensate for the high-speed maneuvers.

"Klingons firing disruptors," Spock said. "Clean miss, but I am showing that both our torpedoes have made direct hits on the Klingon vessel. Klingon forward shields down at least thirty percent."

That was something. The Klingon commander may have been inexperienced, but Kirk did not want to risk the same maneuver again. The Klingons would be ready a second time.

"Elliptical course, Mister Sulu. Toward the orbital plane," Kirk said.

As Sulu executed the maneuver, Spock announced, "Klingons pursuing at high speed. Collision course."

"Bring us about to face them. Ready photon torpedoes." The captain watched the viewscreen carefully. As soon as the Klingon ship appeared, he said, "Fire torpedoes." As soon as the torpedoes were away, he said, "Give us some room and ready phasers."

"Klingons altering trajectory. Torpedo hits on their shields. Klingons maintaining collision course," Spock said.

Kirk doubted the Klingons would actually risk a collision, but getting close would allow them to do a lot of damage in a short time. Yet Kirk knew he could not afford to draw this engagement out.

"Fire phasers as soon as they're in range. Maintain fire as long as you can and ready evasive maneuvers on my mark," Kirk said.

The captain could feel the Klingon ship barreling toward them, and the few seconds seemed to stretch out. Finally Spock announced, "Klingons in range."

"Fire phasers!" Kirk said.

Instantly, twin blue beams lanced out toward the Klingon vessel, colliding brilliantly with the Klingon's shields. Almost immediately, green disruptor bolts lashed out from the Klingon warship, and Kirk felt the deck beneath him shudder as the deadly disruptor energy hit the *Enterprise*.

"Fire photon torpedoes," Kirk said.

The torpedoes were away and Kirk watched the Klingon ship come closer, its shields flaring brilliantly as the torpedoes struck a moment later. Then the viewscreen turned white as the *Enterprise*'s own shields struggled to repel the Klingon weapons fire.

"Evasive action now," Kirk called out. He felt the ship shudder once, either from the maneuver or the disruptor fire.

"Incoming torpedo—" Spock said, and before the words were fully out, Kirk felt the *Enterprise* lurch violently and, for a moment, the bridge went dark. The lights snapped back on and Kirk could smell overloaded circuitry.

The ship had been hurt, and Kirk could hear the damage reports starting to come into Uhura's station, but Kirk had to see how much danger remained. "The Klingons?" he asked.

"Heavy damage. I'm showing no power to impulse or warp drives. And no power to weapons. They are decelerating on thrusters only," Spock said.

That was it. The Klingons were out of the fight.

"Damage report?" Kirk asked.

"Forward shield inoperative, port shields at fifteen percent. Phaser control room reporting that one phaser bank is out. I'm showing a small hull breach with decompression in port cargo hold. All other systems functioning," Spock said.

It was over. They had won, but Kirk took no satisfaction in the victory. The *Enterprise* had undergone extensive refits and modifications recently to make weapons and shields more effective against Klingon warships. And Kirk had been facing an inexperienced commander. Nevertheless, the Klingons had hurt them. What would have happened if it had been Koloth at the helm of the *D'k Tahg*?

What if the same scenario played out across the Federation? Evenly matched vessels pummeling each other. In those circumstances, even the cost of victory would be high. And then there would be defeats. Inevitably, there would be setbacks and battles lost.

How many lives?

"I'm getting casualty reports now," Uhura said. "Twenty-two injuries. All minor."

Kirk felt McCoy's hand on his shoulder for a moment, and then the doctor was gone, headed for sickbay.

Hitting a button on his command chair, Kirk said, "Mister Scott, repair time?"

"You'll have shields back at a hundred percent within the hour. Phasers in less. I'll have to take a look at the hull damage to make an estimate there."

"Keep me posted. Kirk out. Mister Spock, are the Klingons disabled?"

"Yes, Captain. I am also showing multiple hull breaches and heavy casualties. They will not be a threat for several hours at least."

Kirk did not want to underestimate the Klingons. They were notoriously good at field repairs—a necessary skill considering how often they took their ships into battle—but a few hours were all he needed.

"Mister Sulu, get us back to the planet, best speed," Kirk said.

Fuller counted twenty Klingon weapons platforms, ten coming from each side of the mine. Adon and his people had only two, and even if they were superior pilots, they would not stand for long against ten to one odds.

"Fire at will!" Fuller shouted to his people. His squad took aim on the platforms from the hauler as Greenberger's squad dispersed on the ground and did the same. "Keep us moving and keep us in the air as long as you can," Fuller said to Quatrocchi.

"Aye, sir," the ensign said. The hauler was built to go up and down carrying heavy loads so it was sluggish, but they needed to keep fire off the people on the ground for as long as possible.

Adon and Bethe were doing the same, darting in and out of the mass of Klingon craft. The two native pilots were good, and if they were lucky, that might buy them a few extra minutes, but in the end Fuller could see that the outcome of this engagement would be inevitable.

Fuller was aware of the Klingon attack craft strafing the ground, hitting at least a few of the natives there. Each blow created a small crater. No, they wouldn't last long. Fuller also noted that these platforms were firing green disruptor bolts, not the red Orion particle beams. Unfortunately, this meant they were even more deadly.

"Chief, look," Parmet called out. Five of the Klingon craft were headed for the platform at the side.

"Turn us to face them," Fuller said to Quatrocchi. It would give the vehicles a smaller target. Fuller took aim and fired his phaser rifle as the squad did the same. Green disruptor bolts tore at the air around them as the craft turned slowly.

They took a hit on the right side and the hauler shuddered violently. Though the chest-high rim of the craft provided them with limited cover, the vehicle had no shields. One or two more direct hits and they would be grounded, or in pieces.

The Klingon platforms were coming in a classic flying *V* formation. Fuller took aim at the craft in the center and immediately the others did the same. In just a few seconds, the platform exploded brilliantly and the other four broke off the assault.

"Target the one on the far right," Fuller said, firing his own rifle. A few moments later, that platform exploded. "Quatrocchi, get us around to the back of the mine. We won't last long out here, so we're going to make a direct assault on the mine from the main shaft. Watch out for weapons platforms, everyone."

Scanning the ground, Fuller saw that this battle was going badly. He counted at least a dozen dead on the ground and saw that at least three of them were wearing Starfleet uniforms.

"Damn," he said as the ore hauler moved with agonizing slowness.

"Chief," Jawer called out, pointing behind them.

A single Klingon craft was approaching. Fuller fired without hesitating and saw at least three beams strike the platform, which fired a single bolt and veered off. The disruptor energy hit them directly in the back, and Fuller felt the craft lurch violently. He was thrown toward the rear and hit the rim of the hauler hard with his chest.

"Chief," he heard Quatrocchi say. And then he realized they were falling. Turning, he saw that Quatrocchi was fighting with the controls. They were going down, and all Fuller could do was hold on. He thought about their altitude at the time they were hit and did a quick mental calculation about their chances of survival—not good.

Before that thought was fully formed, however, he felt the craft slow—not much but distinctly. Then there was a loud crash as he was slammed to the deck. Even as he realized that he was alive, he was climbing to his feet. Scanning the squad, he saw that they were all moving. Quatrocchi got up first and said, "Sorry, sir. I was only able to get the power back up for a second."

"If we're alive, it counts as a good landing," Fuller said, scanning the group. There were cuts and bruises, but everyone was in one piece, though Parmet was still on the ground.

"Son?" Fuller asked. He watched Parmet get up and saw that the young man was shaken and had a cut near his hairline.

Parmet shook it off and looked at Fuller. "Ready to go, sir."

Fuller saw that a Klingon craft was bearing down on them. "Get out of here, now!" he said, jumping over the side. "Get away from the hauler!" He broke into a run. Only seconds later, he heard a loud explosion and felt the warm blast hit his back. He kept to his feet and waited for the shock wave to pass before he turned around.

Spinning about, he saw that everyone was accounted for as a mushroom cloud rose over the crater where the ore hauler had been just a few moments before. "Disperse and pick your targets," Fuller shouted.

The squad spread out, though Fuller noticed that Parmet had stayed close to him. He could use that, he realized, and said, "Parmet, cover me!" Pulling out his communicator, he said, "Fuller to Adon." When the young native answered, he said, "We can't beat them out here with that many vehicles. Can you get inside from the back with your craft and open the door?"

"Yes," Adon said.

Fuller signed off and started shooting with his phaser rifle. He took cover behind a tree, but that offered him nothing but concealment. He had seen the Klingon disruptors tear through the largest trees in the area.

Watching the sky, he saw that at least a few of the Klingon craft were missing. Then he saw the two platforms carrying the natives streak through the battle and head for the rear of the mine. Almost immediately, one of the Klingon craft started trailing them. There was a flash of disruptor fire and one of the vehicles started going down. It could have been Adon, or the young woman—Fuller couldn't tell. A moment later, Fuller saw the remaining native pilot double back for the downed craft, and then Fuller lost sight of them both.

A blast tore a crater a few meters behind Fuller and he spun and fired. The air was still full with attacking Klingons, and they no longer had the two defending platforms in the air. Even if Adon made it, Fuller knew that they would never hold out long enough for the young native to get through the mine and open the door.

Fuller weighed the odds. They were poor and getting worse.

Adon saw the flash as Bethe got hit. Her craft didn't explode immediately, but it did drop toward the surface. Immediately, he swung his platform around and scanned for her. He saw her craft on the ground, surprisingly intact, but Bethe was gone. . . .

There she was, running away from the vehicle, which exploded when she was perhaps thirty paces from it. Turning again, Adon prepared to dive down to retrieve her, then his craft shook under his feet. A flash told him the invisible shield was gone. He headed for the ground. Without the protective shield, a single shot would destroy the platform.

A moment later, he saw a green bolt race by him on his right and pulled the craft to the left. That movement saved his life, he was sure, because when the next bolt struck his vehicle, it hit the extreme right side. The platform shuddered and started tilting badly to the right.

Whatever kept it in the air had been damaged, at least on that side.

Adon had to struggle to hold on as the craft was now almost completely on its side. Slowing his speed, he tried to lower the platform without flipping it. A series of green bolts flew all around him, and Adon decided he'd had enough. He jumped from the craft and landed hard on the ground. Hitting at an angle, he rolled to a stop and quickly found his feet again.

Remembering Bethe, he raced away, looking back when he judged it safe. His platform was still in the air, slowly spinning in place. Two Klingon vehicles approached and slammed it with weapons fire. It exploded brilliantly, and Adon regretted seeing the machine destroyed. His father had raced him with that device. . . .

Adon felt grief and anger rise up inside him. That was one more thing Gurn would pay for.

"Are you done playing?" he heard a voice ask behind him. It was Bethe; she was carrying a *mek'leth* in one hand and a pistol in the other.

"Yes," he said, drawing his own pistol and the sword that had been his father's.

"Do you have a plan?"

"Yes, we attack the mine and I take Gurn's miserable life."

Bethe simply nodded. Adon headed for the rear of the mine at a run with Bethe by his side.

Fuller knew he had little choice but to order a direct assault on the mine. It would be tricky under ideal circumstances, and these circumstances were far from ideal with the Klingons able to strike them at will from the sky.

That was when he saw the first transporter beams. A few seconds later, six Klingon warriors appeared on the battlefield, and Fuller instantly understood: Captain Kirk had defeated the Klingon battle cruiser and returned to orbit. These were the Klingons from the crew of the Klingon ship that had been stranded by Duras. They had come to join the fight, yet it took every ounce of self-control that Fuller had to keep from shooting them while they stood in the open.

These Klingons were possibly the same ones that had killed his son. Perhaps the only thing that stayed his hand was that there were only six of them. Almost a hundred more waited on another continent. Even as he had that thought, there was another transporter beam and another six Klingons materialized. Before they had fully formed, the first group had their disruptors out and were firing at the Klingons in the air.

The crew of the *D'k Tahg* made no effort to find cover. They simply stood their ground and fired. Fuller watched as a single shot from a hand weapon tore through one of the vehicle's shields and into the pilot, tearing a hole in the Klingon and knocking him off the craft, which spun away, crashing a few hundred yards in the distance.

The other Klingons were having similar success, their weapons making hit after hit on the pilots and craft . . . as if the shields didn't exist. Fuller understood. The shields of the weapons platforms had been calibrated to allow the vehicle's disruptor energy to pass through it. Unfortunately for the Klingon pilots, this door opened both ways and would allow disruptor beams in.

In less than five minutes, with less than thirty Klingons on the ground, the weapons platforms were almost all destroyed. Fuller saw that their own chances had just improved dramatically. Now, the only defenses for the mine would be the Klingons inside loyal to Duras.

That was when the mine doors opened and the Klingon warriors inside began to spill out. They were Duras's last line of defense and he was using them. They had just made Fuller's job even easier.

"Fuller to *Enterprise*."

"*Kirk here.*"

"Good to hear your voice, Captain."

"*You too, Michael. Status?*"

"The Klingons you transported over are helping. They've routed Duras's forces' flying craft and are engaging the forces from the mine."

"*Good, but we have a problem. Sensors show a power surge deep in the mine.*"

"A kinetic explosive?"

"*Yes.*"

"Perhaps Duras will turn it off now that his ride has disappeared."

"*Mister Spock's analysis suggests that it can't be simply turned off. It's been collecting energy from the mine's warp reactor for some time. It probably already has enough to destroy most if not all of the planet.*"

"What can we do, sir?"

"*Blow it up. Mister Scott is preparing a charge. I need you to destroy the device. The energy will still be released, but as heat and radiation so it won't have the seismic effect.*"

"Understood. Will there be time to get the team out?" Fuller asked, his voice perfectly calm.

"There's a timer on the charge, but you'll have to hurry to get it down the shaft and escape."

There was a hum and Fuller saw the shimmer of transporter energy three meters from him. An ordinary duffel bag appeared on the ground. Picking it up and opening the bag's zipper, Fuller saw that it held a photonic charge with a simple timer—though he realized that whatever happened next, he wouldn't be needing the timer.

Fuller saw the possibilities before him. He could complete the objectives of this mission, at least most of them. And here was an opportunity to achieve something even more important, to take the kind of action that the times demanded.

"We'll do it, Captain, but the Klingons can help. Can you have the crew of the *D'k Tahg* draw Duras's forces away from the mine?" Fuller said.

"Yes," Kirk said. *"And, Michael, be careful. You'll be able to find the kinetic device by its power readings, but you have to get up and down on your own. Transporters can't reach that far underground."*

"Understood, Captain." At the moment there were things it was better that Kirk did not know. There would be no need for transporters. For Fuller, this would be a one-way trip. It was the only way to be sure that the job was finished. Fuller found that the thought didn't trouble him at all. "Fuller out."

He collected his squad. Everyone was accounted for, though Greenberger's team had lost three people. Eleven security officers were not nearly enough for an assault on a complex as big as the mine, but Fuller knew they would succeed. He had come too far and the work he had to do was too important to fail now.

*   *   *

Kirk had a bad feeling. They had lost three crewmen already, and he had given a nearly impossible task to eleven more. If that task failed, an entire planet would be destroyed—a planet full of good people, a planet that on a previous mission still more of his crew had sacrificed themselves to protect.

It was all troubling, but they still had a chance, a fairly good one. Kirk realized that something else was bothering him, something he'd heard in Michael Fuller's voice.

He sounded like a man ready to die.

Chapter Twenty-six

ADON WISHED HE STILL HAD his flying platform. Even at a full run, it was taking too long to get to the mine. Before he and Bethe made their way around to the side of the complex, he had seen that the Klingons inside had finally gone out to fight. That meant the humans no longer needed him to open the doors from the inside.

He trusted that his people and their Starfleet allies would prevail. Now his thought was only of Gurn. The clan leader was inside the mine, close. Adon could feel his blood boiling with its call for revenge. That the traitorous coward was walking around while his father lay in the ground was intolerable. Nothing would stand in the way of his vengeance now.

A blast passed over his head and exploded into a tree

269

behind them. Bethe tugged at his arm while she fired back. Her weapon found its target and one of the Klingons from space fell. "Careful," Bethe said, a rebuke in her voice. She was right, Adon would never taste his revenge if he became careless now.

Ducking back, he saw two Klingon guards standing by the small door that he had hoped would lead them inside. Adon whispered instructions to Bethe and raced across the open ground to the mine's main shaft, firing at the guards as he ran. Before they could react, he vaulted over the guardrail and landed on the catwalk that ringed the shaft on this side. Just past the railing on the catwalk was a pit that looked endless and might as well have been.

Ducking his head down, Adon heard disruptor bolts hit the ground in front of his position, while other bolts passed over his head. The cover was good, but it would not last. He heard the guards talking and then their footsteps as they approached, thinking they had Adon cornered. He heard two shots from Bethe's green-skin pistol and knew the guards had stepped into her path. He lifted his head to see them lying on the ground with Bethe standing nearby. She was shaking her head.

"Fools," she said. Adon agreed; it was a wonder they had ever reached the stars. However, Adon had to assume that Duras's men were not the best the Klingons had to offer.

But they *were* the people that Gurn had chosen as his allies.

Together, he and Bethe headed for the area the Klingons had been guarding. As he suspected, it was a small access door. Most of Duras and Gurn's defenses were outside engaging Starfleet and Adon's clan. And most of the soldiers left in the mine would be guarding the main entrances. The maintenance door was perfect.

There would be time enough to defeat all of their foes. For now, Adon needed to move quickly before Gurn ran like the coward he was, which would happen as soon as the clan leader realized that the battle was lost.

Inside, he and Bethe crept along quietly. In the distance, he saw a combined force of perhaps ten Klingons. It was a simple matter to avoid them. "It would take a growing season to search this whole place for Gurn," Bethe said.

She was right, he needed to find the man quickly. "Come, we need someplace quiet," he said to her, and led her to one room he was fairly certain no one would be occupying or watching now. In a few minutes, they were standing inside the computer simulation room where he had spent many hours. The last time he was here, he had been playing games with his friends, while his father was dying in the woods. Forcing down that thought, Adon made sure the door was closed and headed for the main computer terminal.

"Computer," he said.

"What do you want?" it replied in its mechanical voice. It used the dialect of Adon's people's language that the Klingons spoke.

"Where is clan leader Gurn?"

After a brief pause the computer said, *"His last communication was from the warp reactor room."*

Bethe was surprised. "How does it know?"

"The machines built by the green-skins and the

Klingons watch everything. There are listening and viewing devices everywhere. The Orions and the Klingons apparently watched their people constantly." Adon found the idea revolting, but from what he had seen of the Orions and the Klingons, he realized that there were good reasons for watching such people. Once again, Adon wondered how anyone of his people, even Gurn, could stand with such as them.

Before he left, Adon said, "Computer. Turn off all of your listening and watching devices."

"Done," the computer said. The devices could easily be turned back on, but Gurn would not think to do it. If nothing else, it would guarantee that Adon and Bethe reached the warp reactor undisturbed.

There were transport devices, called lifts, that Adon could have used to reach the reactor's level, but he did not want anyone to know he was coming. He and Bethe made their way on foot, taking several minutes to reach the ladders that would take them to the warp reactor. Inside the long shaft, they quickly climbed down to the right level and came out near the reactor.

An invisible shield had operated in the corridor in front of the reactor, but that had been destroyed in the last battle. Adon was pleased to see that the heavy door at the entrance to the reactor was open. *Gurn is leaving himself a way out,* Adon realized.

Well, he had also left Adon a way in.

Adon and Bethe crept forward. When they were less than twenty paces from the door, Adon could see that several of Gurn's clan were watching the door with weapons drawn. Interestingly, no Klingons were around. Adon guessed that the grand alliance between Gurn and

Duras had not lasted long after Gurn had failed to provide the Klingon with the promised crystals.

The reactor was a good place to hide. There was only one way in, and if the door was closed, it would take heavy weapons and much time to break through. Adon considered racing in, weapon firing, but he knew that even if he got inside, there was a good chance that Gurn's people would cut him down before he killed their clan leader.

He could feel Bethe, impatient, behind him. He lifted a hand to silence her and called out, "Gurn, you traitorous coward!"

Immediately, there was a hail of weapons fire. None of it came close to their position.

"Would you face me, the son of the man you murdered?" Adon called out. More weapons fire, this time closer as they tracked the source of his voice. When the weapons went quiet, there was the sound of voices from inside.

Adon and Bethe moved quietly to a new position. "Gurn, where are your allies, the Klingons?"

Silence this time and no weapons.

"They have abandoned you as they are trying to abandon this world. They tried to destroy it once; now they mean to finish the job."

"You lie," Gurn's voice said from his hiding place.

"Ask your Klingon masters, if they will even speak with you now. They wish to destroy this world and blame the humans to start their war."

"The humans tried to destroy us," Gurn said, but the uncertainty was clear in his voice.

"Now they fight and die to defeat the Klingons. The

Kevin Ryan

fate of this planet will be decided soon, but either way you will not live to see the outcome," Adon said. "People of Gurn's clan. Your leader is a murderer who has aided those who even now labor to destroy us all. You will never see whatever he has promised you. You can still aid the fight against the Klingons, however, and seek whatever redemption you can find in the battle."

More voices. Raised this time.

"I seek only to face Gurn. I have no quarrel with the rest of you—at least no quarrel that cannot wait."

"Young Adon, your father was weak," Gurn said, arrogant defiance in his voice. "Our people needed a leader, not a fool trapped in the ways of the past."

The words burned his blood, but Adon kept his voice even. "If my father was weak, surely you are not afraid to accept the challenge of his *young* son. Let us see who is weak and who is strong."

"You think me as great a fool as your father. You would cut me down in an instant."

Adon didn't hesitate. He took his pistol and tossed it toward the door. "I carry only my father's *mek'leth*, the one which gave you the wound on your traitorous face. It still carries some of your blood. I would see it carry even more."

Turning, Adon gave a thin smile to Bethe and stepped out into the open, holding the sword in front of him.

"No," Bethe said. He raised his hand, gesturing for her to stay where she was. To his surprise, she did, but she watched carefully, keeping her pistol ready.

"Would you face me now?" Adon said.

He saw Gurn standing inside the reactor room, looking at him in frank amazement. Nearby, Gurn had ten of

274

his clan. They all carried pistols, but Gurn's was the only one drawn. Gurn considered him for a moment and smiled. "Young Adon. You are as big a fool as your father. You think your challenge means anything to me? Our old ways are finished. We have a new way of doing things, new ways to power."

With that, Gurn lifted his pistol and pointed it at Adon, who saw that he had miscalculated badly. He had been counting on Gurn's arrogance and pride to win the day, but it looked as if his cowardly determination to preserve his pitiful life was his greatest motivator.

"You shall die no better than your father did," Gurn said.

Adon could hear Bethe moving behind him. She did not have a shot at Gurn from her position, but she would soon—not soon enough to save Adon's life, but soon enough to end Gurn's soon after.

But before Gurn could fire, two of his clan grabbed his arms roughly, while a third took his pistol.

"What is this?" Gurn demanded.

"Today, the old ways will live a little longer. You will face the challenge of the son of Gorath," one of Gurn's lieutenants said. The surprised clan leader scanned the faces of his people and saw not a bit of support there.

"Draw your *mek'leth*, Gurn, I will not waste much time with you," Adon said.

Adon enjoyed the moment of fear on Gurn's face. Then, slowly, the man drew his own sword, which—to Adon's knowledge—he had never drawn in battle.

Walking toward the clan leader, Adon raised his weapon. Gurn did the same, but slowly, fearfully. Adon would have preferred to kill the man while he was wearing his look of arrogance, but Adon would kill him now just the same—for if all choices were his to make, his father would still be alive.

When he was nearly in striking distance, Adon prepared himself for his final moment of revenge. But before he could strike, Gurn exploded in movement that was faster than Adon would have thought the man capable of. The clan leader's swinging blade passed inches from Adon's head, and even then only because his body pulled his head back before his mind saw the danger.

Then his sword was up and slashing at Gurn, who parried three blows before a fourth cut across his left hand. He cried out and swung his *mek'leth,* but Adon could see that the fight was nearly over. He sliced into the clan leader's side, then again. Each time the blade found its mark, the man who had killed his father cried out.

Then Adon cut deeply into Gurn's right hand—his sword hand—and Gurn cried out again, dropping his weapon. Gurn looked up at him in stunned surprise, searching for mercy in Adon's eyes—mercy that he would not find if he had three lifetimes to look.

Hesitating not at all, Adon reared back and punched the tip of his father's blade into the chest of the coward who had murdered Gorath. Gurn grunted once, looking into Adon's eyes with a look of surprise. With a sharp movement, Adon twisted the *mek'leth* in the clan leader's chest, and Gurn fell to the floor in a heap.

Though he had lived far too long, his father's killer died quickly, his chest rising only once and then going still. It was done. Adon found that his throat was catching. There was nothing left that he could do for his father. His last task for a great man was finished.

Adon heard Bethe behind him, then felt her touch on his shoulder. The touch changed and Adon could once again feel her impatience. True, he could do nothing more for his father, but he could still do something for his father's people.

Forcing down his grief, Adon saw that Gurn's people were looking to him. One of them stepped forward and said, "I deserve no better. I followed Gurn. I took the side of those who would destroy our people."

Adon shook his head. "Perhaps, but now there is something you can do to save them. There will be time enough for judgment later."

"What would you have us do?" another of Gurn's clan asked.

"Come with me and we will destroy our enemies," Adon said.

The Klingons from the *D'k Tahg* did a good job of drawing Duras's warriors out of the mine. Koloth's men pulled back and the councillor's troops, smelling victory, pursued.

There was no way to know for sure if the way was safe, so Fuller trusted his instincts. When he judged the time right, he said, "Let's move," and brought his people close to the entrance. Hugging the outer wall of the facility, he said, "I need two volunteers."

All the hands of the officers around him went up, but Parmet and Jawer were first. To the others he said, "We're going to dart in front of the entrance. Wait for whoever is inside to fire and then hit them."

There were nods all around, and then he took his two people several meters back and away from the entrance.

"Strap your phaser rifles on. Hand phasers only for now. Fire on the run, but don't worry about hitting anything. We're just showing them that we're serious. Okay, let's move."

He took the lead and raced in front of the mine doors, perhaps fifteen meters from the entrance. The defenders would be at least a few meters inside, which meant they would have a relatively narrow line of sight. Even so, Fuller and his people would be vulnerable to their weapons fire for several seconds. However, given the limited time they had, there was no helping it.

As soon as he had a shot, he fired into the open doors, as the others did behind him. For a moment, he thought the Klingons had left the door completely unguarded, but then he saw the first disruptor bolt—felt the first bolt as it warmed the air above his head. There were more bolts, and then the sound of phaser fire, but Fuller concentrated on moving quickly.

A few long seconds later, they were out of the range of the Klingons' disruptors and heading for the outer wall near the door. As soon as his back was against the wall, Fuller could see that everyone was safe. He also saw that Greenberger was leading the rest of the security team inside. Fuller didn't hesitate, he followed them.

He could see Klingons lying on the ground around them. They still had a way to go, however. The ground floor of the complex was mostly administrative offices. His destination was deeper in the mine, and Fuller had no doubt that there would be surprises waiting for them inside.

They met their first bit of resistance outside the large ramp that led down to the lower levels. There were stairs and access ladders—and lifts for that matter, but they were too dangerous. Defenders could simply wait at the bottom and pick them off when the lift doors opened.

The ramp itself was ten meters across, and Fuller split his forces on either side. Wide supports gave them good cover, but the Klingons on the lower level of the ramp were equally well protected. Each side occasionally traded shots, but it would be nearly impossible to hit anyone under the circumstances.

In this case, the advantage definitely went to the defenders, particularly in the short term. And in this case, the short term was all they had. *Damn,* Fuller thought.

"Sir, if you need volunteers for a direct assault . . ." Parmet offered.

Every instinct screamed against it. A direct assault on the Klingons would be costly. They would be charging an enemy in a fortified position. Even if every member of their party charged at once, there was a better than even chance that they would all be killed before reaching the lower level.

And yet the clock kept ticking, Fuller could feel it. The team was looking to him for answers, for word on what they should do. Fuller knew what that was, but still he resisted. His squad had survived the rescue operation on the Klingon freighter and the heavy fighting today. They were good people, and well trained, but Fuller wouldn't kid himself. They had all been lucky. He had known plenty of good people in his career. Too many of them were now memorialized on a wall at Starfleet Command.

Fuller and his squad had somehow cheated fate up until now, but a price would have to be paid. He could see in his people's eyes that they were willing to pay it. He was mildly surprised that he was upset at what was about to happen. He felt regret for these people's young lives that would likely soon be lost. He had thought that the last of those feelings had been burned out of him when his son had died.

"Sir, what should we do?" a voice inquired. He turned his head to see his son staring him in the face.

"Sam," he said weakly, his throat catching.

"Sir," the voice said, and then Sam disappeared, replaced by the concerned face of Ensign Jawer.

"Are you alright, sir?" Parmet asked, wearing the same look of concern.

"We'll have to charge them. We'll do it in two waves," Fuller said as the people around him nodded.

The first wave would be a total loss, but some of the second wave might get through, might be able to complete the mission—not Fuller's personal mission, but the one the captain had sent them to do.

"I volunteer to lead the first wave," Greenberger offered. Fuller could see that the man knew exactly what he was offering to do.

Before Fuller could take volunteers to join the section chief, there was a new sound below. Turning his head, he heard whoops that he recognized as Klingon war cries and then saw flashes of red, the signature of Orion particle-beam weapons.

Suddenly the disruptor fire on their position stopped and Fuller realized why. "Adon and his people must be at their rear. There's a new plan: we charge together." The team was ready in seconds and Fuller said, "Now," as he headed down the ramp.

He had a hand phaser in each hand and fired on the run as the people around him did the same, forming a line that moved down the ramp together. He saw at least five Klingons on the ground with about twice that number still on their feet. His peripheral vision told him that Adon was close, but he didn't bother looking for the young man.

Instead he concentrated on finding targets. He fired on Klingon after Klingon, watching them fall. The warriors were in a terrible position, with enemies on both sides. It was amazing they were able to fire back at all, but some of them got off a few shots before they fell.

In less than a minute, however, it was all over. The Klingons were all down and the entire team was safe. A moment later, Fuller saw Adon. The young woman was with him and he was surrounded by a number of other natives that he must have picked up along the way.

"Gurn is dead," Adon said. "What now?" The haunted look on the boy's face belonged on a much older man, Fuller thought.

"Duras is still here somewhere," Fuller said.

"We will find him," Adon replied.

That was good. Fuller didn't want Adon nearby for the next part of the mission. The young man had helped them considerably, but there was more to do. Fuller realized that they had cheated fate once more. He knew that was only temporary. A price would have to be paid—and soon—but if things went according to Fuller's plan, he would pay that price alone.

Chapter Twenty-seven

U.S.S. ENTERPRISE
SYSTEM 7348

"Fuller here, Captain."

"Status?" Kirk asked.

"Duras is missing and there are still some pockets of his men in the mine, but we are at the main shaft."

"Mister Spock's revised estimate is that we have thirty-seven minutes until the kinetic explosive goes critical. You should be able to get down in an ore hauler, set the charge, and get back up in fifteen minutes."

"Understood. I'll handle this and send the rest of the team outside for beam out."

"No, Michael, I want at least three of you going down there. There may be some instability as the kinetic device approaches full power. We can't afford any mistakes or any surprises."

"Understood, Captain."

"Michael, good work down there."

"Thank you, sir."

"Now finish the job and I'll speak to you shortly."

"Yes, James—Captain. Fuller out."

Once again, Kirk had a feeling that he couldn't put away. Something was still wrong down there. The team had done well and been lucky so far, but another surprise was coming, Kirk could feel it.

Fuller closed his communicator and explained the captain's instructions, at least most of them, "We have thirty-seven minutes until the kinetic device explodes. I want all of you at the beam-out point in ten minutes. I'll set the charge and then be right behind you."

"I volunteer to go with you, sir," Parmet said as a number of the others stepped forward.

"I can pilot the hauler for you, Chief," Quatrocchi said.

Fuller shook his head. "No, captain's orders. I'll handle this alone. You've all done very well here today. Now it's time to get yourselves back to the ship."

Fuller could see the resistance in their eyes, especially Parmet's. He felt a moment of shame at lying to them and hoped they didn't see it. He also realized that for the first time in his career of more than twenty-five years, he was disobeying a direct order from his captain.

"Now get moving. That's an order. I have work to do," Fuller said.

The squad turned to go as Fuller climbed into an ore hauler. He locked his feet into the floor and studied the controls. They were simple enough. He didn't have to be Quatrocchi to take the craft down a few thousand feet.

Hitting the power, he felt the hauler come to life. He raised it from the ground and piloted it carefully into the abyss.

Karel was ashamed that he shared DNA with Duras's foolish fighters—*warriors* was far too grand a term for them. They had gleefully pursued the crew of the *D'k Tahg* until they'd found themselves surrounded by the native warriors.

Koloth had then turned his force, and Duras's men had fallen in twos and threes. To their credit, they fought to the last man and even inflicted some losses on the natives and the crew of the *D'k Tahg,* but the matter was decided quickly and the end had never been in doubt.

When the battle was done, Karel turned to Koloth and said, "Captain, request permission to begin searching the mine for Councillor Duras."

Koloth looked at Karel. The captain understood that what Karel was really asking for was permission to take his final revenge.

Koloth nodded. "Go."

That made things easier, though Karel knew that he would have had to find a way to take his revenge no matter what the captain had said.

"Take some warriors with you," Koloth added.

Karel nodded and took four Klingons with him, including Gash. He imagined they were like a hunting party, or a war party from the days of his people's past. They reached the mine quickly and entered as a group of humans were leaving. There were ten of them, wearing the uniform of the *Enterprise,* and Karel wondered if any of them had served with his brother. Perhaps some had, possibly even on Kell's second-to-last mission, which had been on this very planet.

He wished he could speak to these humans, but that was impossible. Even if time would allow it, the divide between their two peoples would not. The humans eyed them warily and one of Karel's warriors hissed, *"Earthers."*

"Enough," Karel said, and moved his Klingons along.

Inside the mine he headed for a computer terminal and asked it where Duras was inside the complex. *"Insufficient security clearance."*

That did not surprise Karel. He remembered his brother's final message, which spoke of how the Orion's Klingon masters had escaped the mine the last time.

"He could be anywhere," Gash said.

"I know where he is. Duras is hiding in the deepest hole he could find," Karel said. Then he turned back to the computer and said, "Computer, show me all transporters in the complex."

A moment later, a schematic appeared on the viewscreen showing him two locations. One was on the level just below ground level, and one was many levels below that under the complex itself, buried in the rock. A conduit allowed the transporter signal to reach that depth. It was Duras's hiding place, Karel was sure of it.

"Come with me," Karel said. He led the group one level down and found the transporter. At the controls, he used the transporter's sensors to confirm that six Klingons were waiting in the lower transporter room.

In his arrogance, it had not occurred to Duras that whomever he had left in command of the *D'k Tahg* might lose to the *Enterprise.* He had hidden in his hole, waiting for the battle on the planet and the battle in space to be decided. But his people had lost both engagements. And now there was nowhere for him to go. When the planet tore itself apart, even his deep hole would not protect him.

Using the transporter sensors, Karel identified each of the Klingons by their communicators. "Be ready, Gash," he said, then energized. Five surprised figures appeared on the transporter pad. Gash waited until they had drawn their weapons before he gave the order to fire.

The Klingons fell instantly and Gash had his warriors clear them off the transporter platform. "Duras remains?" Gash asked.

"Yes, but not for long." Karel energized again, and Duras's disruptor appeared on the transporter pad. Now, Duras would have only a blade.

Karel put down his own disruptor and stepped onto a transporter pad. Gash seemed to understand what Karel was doing and took the controls. "They are set. Energize on my command and wait for word from me." Gash nodded. Karel drew his father's *d'k tahg* and said, "Now."

Almost instantly, Karel felt the transporter beam take him. The time had come for him to face the Klingon who had sent his brother down a path of dishonor and death. It was time to enter the killing box.

The transporter deposited him in a large single room. Though it looked like a bunker with sleeping and eating areas for five Klingons, Karel immediately saw it for what it was: a hiding place. A wave of revulsion flowed over Karel—revulsion that a Klingon who would build and use this place would have an important position in the empire and any power over spirits as great as his brother's.

"First Officer Karel," Duras said, surprise on his face. "Is Koloth dead? Have you come to talk? Perhaps you and I can reach an agreement."

Karel watched the lies and treachery forming on the Klingon's face. He thought it a particularly ugly sight. "You offered me a ship; what would you offer now?"

"There are greater opportunities than a single ship. You were loyal to Koloth, and loyalty has its place, but if you help me now, there is no limit to what you can have. A ship? A battle group? A seat on the High Council? In time, anything is possible. But there are forces at work here that you do not understand. I must find a way out of here to complete my work. The empire itself is at stake."

At last, Karel thought, *a piece of the truth.*

Karel eyed the councillor coldly. "I don't want your lies or your favors. Today, I will settle for just killing you."

Duras studied Karel in silence for a moment, then said, "Have I harmed you?"

That made Karel smile. "You had your men try to kill me. You took my ship. And you tried to kill a planet full of my brothers. You have dishonored the whole empire. But it is not for any of these things that I will kill you."

"What is it you want?" Duras asked, his voice high and fearful.

"I want my brother back, you bloodless and treacherous coward." There was no understanding on the councillor's face.

"My brother was Kell of the House of Gorkon. He was *betleH 'etlh,* Blade of the *Bat'leth.* You changed his face, altered his very blood, and sent him on a mission of deceit."

There it was, understanding. "He was *betleH 'etlh*?" Karel nodded. Duras said quickly, "I remember him. He served on the *Enterprise*. His mission was to kill Kirk . . . he failed, obviously. And I saw him on this world, in this mine. Your brother had joined the enemy. He may have been your brother, but he had lost his honor."

"Honor? The word should burn the tongue out of your mouth. My brother took the only honorable path in a course you set him down." Karel saw then that Duras would never understand, not if he lived another hundred years—not that Karel would ever allow such a travesty. There had been enough words, and he had suffered the existence of this coward long enough.

Lifting his father's blade, he advanced on Duras, who was not so big a fool that he couldn't see murder in a warrior's eyes. He reached for his own knife. Karel allowed him to hold it out in front of him, then struck, feinting once to the left and then plunging the knife into the center of Duras's chest.

For a moment, the councillor looked at him in surprise, and Karel said, "You cannot even die with honor." Then he twisted the knife and pushed the dying man to the ground. Kneeling down, he wiped the blood on his blade onto the councillor's tunic and said, "You will never cross the River of Blood, you pathetic slime devil. To Gre'thor with you."

Then Karel got up and turned away from Duras. He headed for the transporter and hit the button on the intercom. "Beam me up." He was glad when the transporter beam took him. He did not want to spend another second in Duras's presence.

Fuller could hear a loud rumbling even over the noisy hum of the ore hauler as it headed down the shaft at high speed. *Tremors,* he thought immediately. The captain had said there might be some instability at the end. That was why he had wanted Fuller to have help for this task, but that was impossible. Fuller could not and would not ask anyone else to do what he had to do. The burden and the responsibility would be his and his alone.

Even at nearly terminal velocity, the trip took minutes, and Fuller could feel the temperature rise as he got closer and closer to the planet's molten core. Checking his tricorder, Fuller confirmed that he was close. He started decelerating and saw the chamber. It was easy to find since it was large and the only one with large equipment inside it. Bringing the hauler to a stop, he jumped to the ground. Then he turned and faced the ore hauler, which hung in the air over the shaft. Taking out his phaser, he took aim at the controls and fired. There was a flash but the hauler was still. It took three shots in the end, but the hauler finally shuddered in space, then dropped like a stone.

Fuller didn't give it another thought; he had known from the beginning that this mission would be a one-way trip. Hell, he had known it as he sat at the computer terminal in his apartment where he had listened to the message of condolence from his son's captain. It was then that he had decided to reenlist.

Fuller surveyed the equipment. The kinetic explosive

device was about ten meters high, less than half that wide. There were control circuits nearby and some sort of cooling mechanism. He knew the physics behind such a device, which turned the unimaginable energies of a warp reaction into pure, kinetic force. The charge in the duffel bag could put a stop to that process, but Fuller would never use it. The device would fulfill its deadly purpose.

Fuller was glad that the landing party would be safely on the ship. However, he found that he was troubled by what would happen to Adon and his people. He did not wish for their deaths. He understood them and saw the potential there. However, he also saw how easily they had been corrupted by the malevolent force of the Klingon Empire.

He had had a chance to stop the spread of their sickness twenty-five years ago and had failed out of his own weakness. He would not fail now. And perhaps killing the crew of the Klingon ship would not do much to change the conflict that would come, but it would accomplish one thing: it would kill the Klingons who had taken his son. These Klingons, at least, would kill no more children.

There would be civilian casualties in this operation, but war always required such sacrifices. Nevertheless, the thought still troubled him, but Fuller wondered if the concern was nothing more than habit—nothing more than training.

A tremor shook the floor and Fuller heard a deep rumbling again. The tremor quickly became a shudder, and soon the ground was pitching around him. Out of reflex, he threw himself to the ground, away from the mine shaft. Stones and earth fell around him, and the shaking was so great that he was tossed from his stomach to his back.

Then there was the pop of an explosion, and Fuller wondered if the tremor had somehow done what the charge in his bag was supposed to do and destroyed the kinetic bomb. The shaking stopped and he saw that the device was intact. The cooling mechanism, however, was in pieces.

Fuller felt a sharp pain in his shoulder, and another in his thigh. A piece of metal was in his leg. He instinctively reached down with his right hand and pulled it out. The wound bled freely.

Femoral artery, his mind supplied with detached professionalism. It was bad. He didn't have long, but on the other hand he didn't need long. He just needed to see this mission through to the end. Working quickly, he tore a piece of cloth from his tunic and made a crude tourniquet. He pulled it as tight as he could and judged that it would slow the bleeding enough to let him last the few minutes that remained.

He crawled over to the kinetic device finally, pulling himself up and resting against it. *You can't let those people die,* a voice in his head said.

Yes, I can, he replied, and he knew it was true. He had long since stopped worrying about his soul. His only concern was to do what was necessary for his son.

His son . . .

You can't . . .

Then Fuller recognized the voice. It was Sam's. It was asking him, was he the kind of man who would kill thousands to seek his own revenge? Whatever he had been in the past, the answer to that question was now yes.

But Sam would never do it, he thought. His son had been a better man than him, from his earliest youth to the end of his too short life.

After bearing Sam's death, he had thought he could bear anything, but he realized that he still feared one thing. He could not stand to shame himself in the eyes of his son—eyes that had always looked on him with an admiration that he had hardly deserved.

What would those eyes think of what he was doing now?

What would his son think of him now?

Almost without conscious thought, Fuller reached around and pulled at the duffel bag he still had slung over his shoulder. His left arm wasn't working well, but he was able to manage with his right. The charge fit into the palm of his hand, and Fuller studied it for a moment. Then he quickly hit the button to start the timer and lifted it to the outside of the kinetic explosive. The magnetic surface of the charge immediately locked on the bomb, and Fuller realized it was done.

The charge would destroy the kinetic device and spare the planet . . . and spare the Klingons who had killed Sam. A final failure to taunt him. Well, it wouldn't taunt him for long.

Fuller felt light-headed and realized that he might not live long enough to see this mission through, after all. The circle of blood on the ground around him was growing. He started to feel a chill and knew what it meant.

Fuller had seen too many of his friends and shipmates die to think he would escape their fate. The thought of his own death had not troubled him for a long time. Since that day twenty-five years ago, he'd known he would eventually join his many fallen shipmates on the wall of Starfleet Command. However, he had always thought that his son might visit that wall and remember him rather than him paying his respects to Sam there.

Now Sam would never make that trip. And there would be no one else to do it, certainly no family. A name among many to be viewed by schoolchildren as they visited Starfleet. Sam had been his only real legacy and now he was gone.

Fuller had not thought in years about the few religious beliefs that he had gotten from his mother and grandparents, but he found himself thinking about them now. Perhaps there was something after death. Perhaps there was a place of forgiveness, a place where fathers who had failed their sons might find them again. A place where people found peace even if in their hearts they knew they didn't deserve it.

In the past he would have found such thoughts silly, but they comforted him now. As a haze fell over his mind, he imagined that he would find his son again and that Sam would welcome him, not because he deserved the welcome, but because Sam was a good man . . . a better man.

The thought was so pleasant that he felt even the pain in his body fading away. Then he found that his doubts were replaced with certainty. He would see Sam again. Soon, he knew he would have to stop fighting and let go . . . of everything.

Long ago, he had locked away all those that he had lost. He could feel that breaking now. They started to come, Andrews, Caruso . . . too many others, and finally Sam. He felt them all, as if they had died the moment before. The tears came, and for the first time in his career he didn't fight them.

And then it started to pass, or to fade.

The world seemed to shrink around him. Breathing.

In.

Out.

His work was done. It was time for him to see his son.

Then a light flared across his vision . . . so the light was real. The stories were real. Well, then, that meant that Sam would be there.

No, a voice inside him said. *Not yet.*

There was movement. Sound. Someone was near.

"Sam," he said as he struggled to open his eyes, tried with all of his strength to open them to see his son. He opened them for a moment, long enough to see a familiar face and a red uniform.

Sam?

Then there were voices, hands on him. He felt himself fading, then he was lifted into the air. Then he was inside . . . but inside what he did not know. Something touched his arm, a prick of pain. Then there was movement, the floor under him was rising.

Something pressed against his shoulder and there was a hiss. *Hypospray,* his mind supplied.

A bit of the darkness lifted, then a bit more. He looked down to see a tube running into his arm, one running into *each* arm. His head cleared a bit more and he saw a face looking down on him. For a moment, he thought it was Sam, but then he realized it was Ensign Parmet.

"We've got you, sir," Parmet said. "You're in a shuttle."

He heard a voice—Quatrocchi's—counting down from ten. He also realized that he could feel strong vibrations in the deck of the small craft. They were moving fast, and judging from the sound of Quatrocchi's voice, it was going to be close.

". . . one, zero," Quatrocchi said.

There was a moment of nothing, just the sound and feeling of the acceleration of the shuttle. Then the blast wave hit them. Fuller knew that even if the charge worked, the energy in the kinetic explosive would still have to be released, thought not as kinetic force.

The shuttle shook violently and Fuller felt Parmet throw himself over Fuller's body. Then the craft steadied and Quatrocchi said, "We've cleared the shaft."

Fuller felt some of his strength returning, enough to lift his head to see his squad all around him. "You all had orders," he whispered.

"Yes, sir, we disobeyed them," Parmet said pleasantly. Then he pulled out his communicator. "Parmet to *Enterprise*. We need emergency transport. Please have a medical team standing by for Lieutenant Fuller."

"Why?" Fuller asked.

Something passed over Parmet's face, something that Fuller didn't understand, and Parmet said, "Sir, I owe everything to you."

Then the transporter took him.

Chapter Twenty-eight

"HE'S COMING AROUND NOW, JIM," McCoy said. "You can talk to him, but not for too long."

"Understood, Bones," Kirk said as they entered the room. Michael Fuller was lying on the bed, just opening his eyes, when Kirk approached.

"Fuller, you're going to be fine. Just take it easy on that shoulder and stay off the leg for a few days," McCoy said, and Fuller nodded. "Now, if you don't have any other creative ways of damaging yourself planned, I have other patients to tend to."

When McCoy left, Kirk asked, "Michael, how are you feeling?"

Fuller pulled himself to a sitting position. "Fine, I'll be back on duty in no time I'm sure, Captain. The mission?"

"Completed. You destroyed the device and no one was injured in the final blast."

"Good."

"Michael, what happened down there? You disobeyed a direct order."

"I'm sorry, Captain. I didn't want to put any of the squad at risk."

"You put the *mission* at risk." For a moment, Kirk could almost not believe that he had said that. He had known Fuller for fifteen years and he would never have thought such a thing was possible.

"My pride . . . I am sorry, sir, and of course, I will accept whatever consequences you think appropriate."

Kirk studied the man's face and was sure of two things. First, something had happened down there. And second, Fuller was not going to tell him what it was. The lieutenant had completed the mission and Starfleet owed him a bit of indulgence—certainly Kirk owed him enough. But he had to make one thing clear.

"Michael, I can't have insubordination on my ship."

"I can promise you that it won't happen again, sir."

Whatever had happened on that planet, Kirk believed Fuller. "Take a few hours to rest and then I'll need your report."

"I'll start right away, Captain."

Kirk left and headed to the bridge. He still had one rather large headache to deal with, though he had an idea about how to do that. Stepping out of the turbolift, he said, "Mister Spock, status of the Klingon vessel?"

"Sensors show no power to drives or weapons. Thirty-two life signs aboard."

Those thirty-two people had mutinied against Captain Koloth, but now they sat on the ship. Kirk couldn't allow the ship to stay in Federation space, nor could he allow Koloth and his crew to remain on the planet. And he certainly couldn't have them on the *Enterprise,* even temporarily—as if they would agree to such a thing.

"Approaching Klingon vessel," Spock said.

"As soon as we are in range, I want a tractor beam on them," Kirk said.

A moment later, Spock said, "Tractor beam engaged."

"Mister Sulu, geostationary orbit, directly over the mine," Kirk said.

"Aye, sir," Sulu said.

"Captain, may I ask what you are planning?" Spock said.

"Mister Spock, this is a problem for the Klingons to settle. Koloth has access to the transporter in the mine. They will have to use it to settle their differences and get the hell out of our space. If they can't get their ship operating, we'll tow them to the border and give them a push."

A short time later, Sulu announced that they were in position.

"Disengage tractor beam," Kirk said. "Mister Sulu, give us some room."

"Aye, sir."

"Lieutenant Uhura, get me Captain Koloth," Kirk said.

Karel would have preferred it if Duras's soldiers—he still could not call them warriors—had fought well, but he found some release in the battle just the same. They had inflicted a few casualties when Karel's force retook the ship, but not many.

At Koloth's suggestion he had taken just thirty-two warriors to defeat the thirty-two surviving traitors, but it had ended quickly. Without their sniveling leader, Duras's Klingons were nothing.

"The entire crew is back on board," Karel announced.

"Repair estimate?" Koloth said.

"Impulse engines are back online now." Koloth raised an eyebrow and Karel said, "We retook engineering first. Work started before the last of the traitors were killed. We should have warp power in four hours."

"Excellent, prepare to break orbit."

Karel understood the captain's impatience. They had won against Duras, but they were sitting nearly defenseless in Federation space. Kirk was an honorable foe. Karel understood that, and so did Koloth now, but the indignity was too great.

Karel wished he had met and spoken to the man who had been his brother's human captain and who had won both Kell's respect and allegiance.

In time, anything was possible, but first both the Federation and the Klingon Empire would have to survive one another. However, at the moment, he was most concerned that the empire survive its own failings. External enemies could be guarded against and fought, but enemies who moved among them? Klingons like Duras? How could a tree fight its own rot?

How could the empire prevail in a war with the Federation with Klingons such as Duras on the High Council itself? Duras was now gone, and Karel's brother's spirit was avenged, but he was not fool enough to think that Duras was the end of the dishonor in their leadership.

The empire would have to change, to adapt or perish.

Karel, son of Gorkon, would do what he could to see

that the empire built from the strength of Kahless's blood would not perish. For now. He would enjoy the knowledge that his brother's killer was dead. And though it had been Karel's own hands that had taken Kell's life, he was now certain that the real murderer had been Duras, who had sought to take honor, then life.

For the first time since he had heard news of his brother's death, the portion of Kell's spirit that resided in Karel's own blood was quiet.

Uncle stepped forward into the clan meeting pit and said, "Your father saved our world and our people from the green-skins. Now you have saved us from their masters, the Klingons. The clans have spoken to one another and we see that we need to speak with a single voice. We would like you to be that voice, Adon, son of Gorath."

"I do not have my father's wisdom or his strength, but I will do what I can. We have all won a great victory today, but the danger is not passed. A great and terrible war will soon rage in the space above our skies. We cannot afford to choose the wrong ally, or no ally at all. Gorath wanted us to have a chance to learn, to eventually join the races in space as equals. I still believe that is what we should do. But we shall do it now with a powerful ally, a Federation which has fought with us twice now and shown their friendship." It was not much of a speech, Adon thought, but the people around him did not seem to notice and cheered his words just the same. He knew he was not his father, but he would do his best to safeguard his father's people.

"Kirk waits," Bethe said. She was at his side, where she had been since the news of his father's death and the arrival of the Klingons. Now, he realized, she was standing even closer. Then he looked in her eyes and saw why.

He smiled to himself that he had not seen it before, though now that he had, he did not think he would be able to look at her and not see the truth of it. Leaning down and without another word, Adon kissed her. She was surprised, but not unhappy, and returned the kiss.

Pulling back, he said, "Let us go meet the human."

Walking back to the landing site, McCoy asked, "You like that boy Adon, don't you, Jim?"

"Yes, he's a lot like his father, but much too young for the job he's been given," Kirk said.

"Seems like his people are happy to have him."

"They're lucky, but I wonder, just what have we brought to these people, Bones?"

"We didn't bring anything to them, the Klingons did. These people are still here because of what we did."

"And now we'll give them more powerful weapons," Kirk said.

"And modern medicine, and a dozen other things. It's their choice, Jim. Maybe they were better off before anyone knew they were there, but the galaxy got in. All we can do is help them now the best we can."

"The Klingons offered them help as well."

"And they didn't mean a word of it. You know that, just like you know there is a difference between us and the people who built that mine. I know you do."

The doctor was right, of course. There was a difference. Kirk believed in what the Federation stood for, in what Starfleet stood for, but he was also a pragmatist—his job demanded it. At the moment, Starfleet was the only thing that stood between the Klingons who'd built the mine and the rest of the galaxy. The problem was that he would not deceive himself; the empire had better captains and crews than the ones the *Enterprise* had faced on the *D'k Tahg* today. At their best, a battle cruiser and a starship were evenly matched. When the war came and the battle was begun, all of their fine ideals would matter little against Klingon weapons.

A single truth kept coming back in Kirk's mind: *We will fight with everything we have . . .*

. . . but we might lose.

Epilogue

LIEUTENANT COMMANDER GIOTTO had come by, and then Fuller's squad had come. However, they had come together and Fuller hadn't had a chance to talk privately with Parmet as he had hoped to do. Well, that could wait. They would be in orbit for at least a few more days. There was work to be done in the mine. Repairs and other assistance.

Starfleet had pressing business for the *Enterprise,* but it would not abandon Adon and his people. And the fact was, the precious dilithium that they had provided would be a real help if it came to war.

When it comes to war, he thought.

He was surprised that it was Parrish who came to get him. "Lieutenant, how are you feeling?"

303

"Fine, and you?" he asked. She was starting to show just slightly under her uniform.

"A little sick, but Doctor McCoy says that's normal. I think he'll feel better when I'm in the hands of an expert."

"When is your transport?"

"Two days. I'll be on Earth by the end of the week." Something passed over her face. "I can't help feeling that I'm running out on the ship."

"Nonsense, we all have our jobs to do. We'll handle things here, but your work is important too. And you're doing something I could never do, Leslie."

It was true. And he knew there was more to it than she had told him. Fuller had heard that there were going to be some complications with her pregnancy. There was even a danger to Parrish, yet she was going through with it. That pleased Fuller somehow. Plenty of people could do what he would do in the next weeks, months, and years, but if the Federation was going to survive, they would need people like Parrish as well.

They left sickbay together and he felt Parrish's eyes on him. "Are you ready for this, sir?"

"I am," he said, and found that he meant it. "I wasn't before, but I am now."

She nodded as if she understood, and Fuller thought that he might want to check on her if he made it back to Earth. To his surprise, he found himself thinking about what he would do when he got back. He would also check in on Sam's mother, Alison, whom he hadn't spoken to in years, excluding the conversation they had had when he'd told her about Sam's death.

There was a reunion of the survivors of Donatu V

every year at a San Francisco bar. Fuller had never gone, but he thought he might like to try it. And there had been that woman in his building's gym. They had shared nothing but polite smiles, but he thought that maybe it was time to move beyond that.

The future was unimaginably far away, but he could feel it out there just the same.

Fuller didn't hesitate when they reached the dining room; he simply stepped through the door. Inside, he got a genuine surprise: more than twenty people were waiting and they were applauding him, looking at him in something of the way Sam had done when he was growing up.

It was not what he had expected. A handful of people had served with Sam and known him well. Parrish, Jawer, Clark, and a few others. A few days ago they had wanted to tell him about their experiences with his son. But Parmet was here, the rest of Fuller's squad, and other people from engineering, the sciences, every department on the ship—and three of the civilians from the *Harmony*.

"I think I stepped into the wrong party," he said.

Ensign Parmet stepped forward. "We all wanted to do something for you."

"But I don't know most of you."

"But we all know you." Parmet stopped for a moment and gathered himself. "When I was ten years old, our colony on Lynwood Four was attacked by Nausicaan raiders. They held us for a week until your team came in." Tears formed on Parmet's face. "My parents fought them and were killed. They were going to kill the children next, and then you . . ."

He didn't need to finish. Fuller remembered Lynwood

IV well. There had been children, he recalled. Had one of them really been Parmet? Was it possible? Suddenly, quite a few things made sense: the ensign's behavior around him, his familiarity with Fuller's career, even his punching the Anti-Federation League man a moment before Fuller did so himself.

Parmet stopped speaking, tears streaming down his face. Fuller felt them welling in his own eyes. He knew better than to fight a battle he could not win and let them come. He put a hand on Parmet's shoulder, then the young man threw his arms around him.

A few seconds later, Parmet stood back. "I owe you my life, sir. And there are more of us."

There had been more: *My grandfather served with you on the* Endeavour . . .

My mother was on the Republic . . .

I grew up on . . .

They all had stories that they needed to tell and Fuller knew he needed to hear. In each tale, he heard something he had long ago given up hope of ever seeing in his career or in his life . . .

A legacy.

About the Author

Kevin Ryan is the author of ten books, including the best-selling *Star Trek: Errand of Vengeance* trilogy. He wrote the *USA Today* bestselling novelization of *Van Helsing,* as well as two books for the *Roswell* series. In addition, Ryan has published a number of comic books and written for television. He lives in New York and can be reached at Kryan1964@aol.com.